ORCASEKAI
Memoirs of a Lost Universe

By S. Amaranthine

http://orcasekai.com

Publisher's Note: This is a work of fiction. Names, characters, places, and incidents are a product of the author's imagination. Locales and public names are sometimes used for atomospheric purposes. Any resemblance to actual people, living or dead, or to businesses, companies, events, institutions, or locales is completely coincidental.

Orcasekai (Memoirs of a Lost Universe) / S. Amaranthine –1st ed.

978-0-9963299-4-2

DEDICATION

To: Anais Fantini of Bikers4Orcas.

I met Anais at SuperPod 5 on San Juan Island in Washington. In our few brief encounters it struck me that she embodied the quintessential aura of human 'cool' activism. It ignited the spark which led to the creation of 'Kei', a motorcycle riding, multiverse-traveling, cetacean-saving hero of this book. Anais is also a fun dance partner!

Bikers4Orcas was founded in the Netherlands by Vincent Lensen in August of 2013 with the intention of bringing awareness to the cruelty of keeping killer whales in captivity. Their goal is to utilize the biker image and the sound of motorcycles to motivate others to ride and speak up for captive orca.

In 2017 Anais Fantini took over as the Global Leader. New ideas are coming together, new people joining, and they are not slowing down. Bikers4Orcas give a voice to Orca all over the world using one voice, their voice, the sound of motorcycles.

After all we have everything in common with Orca: We love to ride hundreds of miles a day, we travel in groups, we are a family, and we love our freedom! Let's ride, for them...for Orca!

And to: Newton

A dog. He was the inspiration for 'En', a time-traveling border collie and the best dog in the multiverse.

ACKNOWLEDGEMENTS

Thank you to beta readers: Angi Brindisi, Gretchen Geraci, Laura Geraci, Gayle Langenbrunner and Karen Muldrow. Your read through and feedback were a tremendous help.

Thank you to my financier, beta reader and beloved husband, David Ellerhorst. Without you, none of this would have come to page.

Thank you to my talented editor, Laura Geraci.

Thanks to Liz Bemis (Spark Creative Partners) for your wonderful cover work.

Thank you, all readers and reviewers, of the Vencello and Cetapiens. Your encouragement and interest kept me going on to book three.

Thank you to the ladies of WAG (Writers Accountability Group), whose friendship and encouragement are so appreciated. Special thank you to Karen Kelly.

INTRODUCTION

Letter to the Future.

Dear Progeny:

The first book was conception, The Vencello. The second was childhood, Cetapiens and now I have finished my third gift to you: Orcasekai. Logically, this is the book about adulthood. I've been an adult for longer than any other phase of my life. I've endeavored to capture its essentials. As I approach older age, I find myself thinking about a future I won't be around in. Daughters, you are here, but I've wasted precious time. Grandchild, you're not here yet. I hope I get to meet you, but if not, here I am in these pages. Daughters and Grandchildren, this is a way to share some time with you, beyond my own, when you are ready.

Grandchildren, I won't wait to know you in your human form and then love you. I'll do it now.

Progeny, you're always with me. Since I was born, my daughters were with me. I carried the 'eggs', in a sort of stasis, and their energy was scattered throughout the Earth and Sun, in the steady process of coming together from every source. Advanced wave zero was their conception. There was a flash at that moment, but I didn't see it with my conscious eye. But it happened. It was real. Since my daughters were born, you were with me. They have carried their 'eggs' and you will come together from those orchestrators of physiology, your energy pulled from sources that have been on their way to you since the beginning of our universe. Perhaps you may even come from another's eggs. I live in a miraculous universe.

Despite that, my life has had very difficult times and I thought about giving up. A few other people in our family did. Please, never give up hope.

There is so much more to this world than just a moment in a lifetime. And I know there can be awful moments that seem to stretch on into eternity and have no end, except to a nothingness, which can sound like a relief. But I know that there is no such thing as nothing. I'm sorry you have ever been taught that word. It's a relic of imperfect language, not a truth.

It's really a shame, in my opinion, that I am conscious of very little of what is going on inside of my body at every moment, the wonderful chemical and cellular processes. I hope you find joy in the subjects I have cherished; human, cetacean and cephalopod anatomy and physiology, physics, astronomy, psychology, wellness, philosophy and many more. All that knowledge is half-lived without that wonderful gift, your own imagination. Have fun with all you learn. Let it take you places, like Cetapiens, that your physical body cannot visit. Make it an awesome place to be. Here is a world you can find me, if you wish to spend some 'time' together. I've created some extra for myself; it's a little trick of recorded language.

Adulthood can include reduced imagination and mind play. When I was a kid, blocks were couches and chairs and dolls had conversations. The sun was happy, and it watched me as I walked home from grade school. I allowed myself to suppress those embellishments in adulthood, almost in shame. Proof that sometimes adulthood is not advancement, it's an impediment. I need my 'child' imagination. I was wrong to neglect that essential mental contribution. It was a complement to a whole being. And my love works with both intact. My love for you is 'real'.

You and I are orca, whale, human, cephalopod, oceans, orbs, complex details and echo song, molecules, and thinking universes. We speak, click, sing and flash together in this trilogy.

I love you so much.

Mom (Grandmother)

TIPS FOR READERS

Orcasekai is the third book of a trilogy. Many characters and explanations of who they are, where they are from, and helpful descriptions of the universes in which they travel are found in either The Vencello (Book One) or Cetapiens (Book Two).

The Vencello introduced the Sponge Universe and Home World characters.

1. **Humans**: Delora and Liam. Alvar is their son. Johnny is Liam's nephew.
2. **Orcas:** Akenehi (Matriarch), Arva'Anati and Seasnàn are her daughters.
3. **Sperm whales:** Brough and Param (known by their own kind as Aware Masters of the Ocean)

Cetapiens introduced additional characters.

4. **Priori:** Various types of multiverse time travelers.
5. **Cephalopod Priori:** Pranaya
6. **Orca Priori:** Grandmother and Amaranth
7. **Orion**: Auden, Jomei, and Monifa
8. **Metavoli-2 and Gemini (G) Products:** Alvar-G, Johnny-G, Arva'Anati-G, Auden-G and Jomei-G

Cetapiens introduced the Vencello Universe, the methods of time travel, the Cetapiens culture as a time travelers haven, the temporal paradox resolutions, etc.

Tips for Readers (Continued)

In Orcasekai universes are characters and have familial relationship:

Sponge (ancestral) gave rise to the Vencello (ancestral) which in turn gave rise to Orcasekai (progeny of the Vencello)

Chapters are 'Memoirs' translated from Multiverse Traveler perspectives (human language, echolocation, cetacean whistles, cephalopod chromatophoric, direct shared experience, etc.).

The trilogy begins with a prologue at the beginning of The Vencello and ends with an epilogue at the end of Orcasekai (Memoirs of a Lost Universe).

The trilogy (especially books 2 and 3) does not lend itself to speed reading. Every sentence counts. It was created to be read, enjoyed, then repeat, getting more out of each iteration.

References and Glossary of Fictional Terms are included at the back of the book.

Orcasekai: Memoirs of a Lost Universe

CHAPTER 1

Universe: Vencello (near its end)

"No, don't kill her. Pleeeeaaase! Stop! She doesn't like it! You're hurting her. No!" Delora didn't know everything, yet. She was only a little girl of eight, but she knew the difference between right and wrong. She was no physical match for a grown male. She pulled at him, punched toward his face. She managed an effective blow.

"Stop your WHINING!" He shifted his focus to Delora. He released his grip on the octopus and it released its on him. He seized his daughter by the arms and shook her hard.

Delora was stunned and under control.

He let her go, took a deep breath, bent his knees and submerged. He looked around for the octopus, but it eluded him. He came up and grabbed her again, "DeLORA!" The strength of his exhalation forced her eyes to blink. He only called her that when he was angry. Dripping wet, he caught his breath, then gave her one last hard shake.

"I hope you DIE!" and she meant it.

"Die. There it is. And what was that, before?" Akenehi was an amazingly quick study. She picked up human language almost as fast as Delora could remember it.

"Hurting?" Delora asked.

"No, the compassion call."

"Oh, Please? Stop?"

"No. Your father's."

"Whining? You mean 'whining'?"

"Yes. That's it"

"That wasn't a compliment Akenehi. He meant to shame me."

"And did he succeed?"

"Almost. But no. Or I wouldn't be here." Delora answered.

"Here, now take mine." And Akenehi offered one of her memories to Delora.

In orca whistles and echo clicks the self-similar scene played out. Minor differences were deep water instead of surf, a baby orca, Akenehi, instead of an eight-year-old human, a porpoise in place of an octopus. Similarities were a plea from the young to spare the prey, an opposition to their own adult caretaker, empathy and anger.

"No, don't kill him. Pleeeeaaase! Stop! He doesn't like it! You're hurting him. No!" Akenehi didn't know everything, yet. She was only a little girl of eight months, but she knew the difference between right and wrong. She was no physical match for her family. She tried to swim around them as they blocked her. She bit at them, rammed into them. She managed an effective blow.

"Pay attention, Akenehi! Listen and echo-locate!" Her aunt and sister positioned her firmly between them and pushed in just enough to force a few air bubbles out of her.

Young Akenehi was immobilized for the time being.

Everyone was turning this way and that, surfacing high for air and breaching to stun. The prey did not escape and was still fighting with all it had left to survive. But it was isolated from its pod and it was injured. It was only a matter of time.

The sea was full of sound.

The prey called to his family. Akenehi had imagined the little porpoise was maybe trying desperately to summon their help or possibly to warn them away for their own safety. Perhaps he was saying goodbye to them. In any case, the sound was heartbreaking.

Her orca pod members seemed so cruel as they vocalized right over his. They coordinated moves, discussed and decided how best to share the small amount of nutrition his body would provide.

Her aunt turned her attention to other songs, in harmony, that were much harder for a young orca to distinguish among the din of life and death struggle. For the first time, Akenehi noticed them. Her family admired their prey and was sad with him that he would not live to swim away with his own pod. They sang respect for Akenehi's distress. None of them had ever ceased to empathize with their prey. But that did not stop the long drawn out process of the hunt, or shorten the suffering of that little porpoise that was trying to escape even as the final chomp that would sever him in two was delivered.

Delora asked, "Why couldn't you hear those harmonics on earlier hunts?"

"Why? Good question."

"Maybe they didn't want you to know they felt bad about what they were doing. Maybe they should have stopped," Delora snipped.

"No, they wanted me to feel bad. Those were vital expressions of the polyphony. They sang of the complexity of what we were. They didn't want to deprive me of the natural orca gift of empathy. We carried it in us always and it was part of what strengthens an orca family."

"Empathy is not just an orca gift, Akenehi," Delora sniffed, insulted.

"What about your father's call? Whining? Young orcas whine all the time. They learn to put it into song. There's no shame in empathy. It's sacred. It seems to me he was trying to forbid an empathy call for his prey."

"Yes, I thought so. But it is my memory, not his. I don't know, he and I never shared thought like you and I can. I can only image what was in his mind. He did try to teach me that when I felt bad about what I was doing, it meant that my conscience was telling me to stop. Maybe I was making him feel bad and he was angry that I might be able to make him stop. It seemed he wanted to kill. But I truly couldn't speak for him."

"What was the next hunt like?"

"Well, he didn't take me out next time."

"Do you think that may have been what diminished your octopus hunting skills?"

"No, he never took me out again. It's ok. I didn't want to go."

"Absolutely not orca," Akenehi sighed.

Delora felt like she had won when she could make Akenehi sigh.

CHAPTER 2

Universe: Vencello (its end)

As he spun, Brough cast his coda through the entire Vencello. He listened as the data came back to him. Out in a distance, a slim beacon of echoes had found Delora, Liam, Alvar and Johnny near the moment where they would time jump to their new home in Orcasekai. He focused a series of detail gleaning clicks in that direction.

As if they might have been alerted to his curiosity, their thoughts only grazed Brough for a moment. Emotionally they had gone silent to the whale again. The human family was focused on Alvar's wellbeing and his ability to endure the transition they were about to make. They were certain that their universe was dying, and they hurried to move on to the next.

Brough couldn't hear them, but he imagined them chattering away in human tradition. Without their thoughts on him, he would have to rely on echo scan. As his intensified stream of data clicks returned to him, Brough marveled at the fine detail of Alvar's physical reconstruction they conveyed. As far as Brough could recognize, every bit of Alvar was 100 percent Sponge authentic yet Vencello viable. He was finally put back together from across space and time. It had not been easy or quick. In every way, it had been wondrous.

His scanning skills still reflected his Aware Master precision and accuracy. Data clicks defined how he perceived. He recalled his first shock of human olfaction and orca song. Brough wondered in audible clicks how the scene he had just scanned would be if he were human, without the refinement of echolocation.

Brough had served as the most massive and bright part of the Vencello. He considered that first unexpected multi-species joining, as his favorite of his life. That was before he had learned to count his 'life' units in terms of Vencello iterations. At that first go, he was fascinated by everything and focused for maximum retention. He learned so much of the multiverse. His Sponge ocean origin shrank as he expanded his multiverse experience. Eventually, he feared, when he conceptualized the multiverse, his home ocean would not even exist for him. So, he dedicated a part of his thoughts to home and pod. Always. He never stopped loving, missing or wanting to save it.

Eventually their first Vencello tenure ended, as all things that have beginnings do. The only detail he had recalled of that first end was that he had floated with others of his pod in a deep sleep and when he awoke, the Vencello was at the beginning for a second time but with a subtle variation.

The Priori, who were aware of the inevitability of universe iterations, traveled in and out of the Vencello throughout all of them, shared the Aware Master's experience and took note. Brough had recognized that there was a difference, because he had retained memory from one iteration to the next. Quickly he had the insight that no two iterations would be the same. Thirty iterations passed as quickly as three. Then, before he knew it, 300. Brough didn't care to keep track anymore.

Johnny's claps caught Brough's attention. At least his ears were still working.

By this end, the Vencello had undergone so many iterations that Brough had difficulty remembering details that defined one from another. Akenehi did not seem to mind the repetition, the new starts and eventual ends that they had experienced, subtle variations on their Sponge themes. But he was done with all the starts and ends. He was ready to rest, once and for all.

He continued his slow, steady coda. The return clicks played lazily, suggesting amusing scenarios, in his ancient mind. He imagined his own Master of the Ocean family within them.

Akenehi was still right there, circling as she always did. As they watched and scanned, the lights of the binary, essences of Delora and Liam went out.

Akenehi sang her last to him. She was next. Until then, it was just the Master of the Ocean and the Orca Matriarch. The steady hum of Priori visitors coming and going was trailing to a few sparkles and chirps. It was so quiet. It put him back in time, into the cold, dark, depth of his ocean home. His own clicks for company and her lilting lullaby, his favorite, easing him to rest. "In the end, we all got what we wished for in the Vencello." It was his favorite. He was ready.

He understood her orca song almost as much as his own data clicks. She was not only a member of the Vencello, she was a part of him. He didn't have to sound his sorrow at their parting. She already knew and shared it.

"Do you smell that?" Brough asked Akenehi.

The orca ceased her lullaby but continued in orca. "Yes, I do. Strange. Very odd. Delora and Liam are gone. How is it we…Cetaceans and cephalopods do not have a sense of smell. There must be a human with us…some Priori visitor with a sense of olfaction. Now that the others are gone, it is very overpowering. I don't like it. Let's insist they leave."

Brough hurriedly scanned and caught a fleeting echo image.

"Priori, time traveler. But, it's not human. It scans more like a small dolphin with limbs like…well, this is new. This has never happened before." Brough was rejuvenated with the novelty of an unanticipated detail.

Akenehi found what Brough was scanning and did her own assessment.

"Ah. Resume your calm. I've encountered a few of those. They are not very intelligent. I doubt it is Priori. That would explain why he's not sharing his thought with us, none to sing of or worth sharing. We have observed that they live in obedience with the land squid, humans. The first time I heard one it was coming from a human boat once and when we swam in for a closer look…"

Brough cut her thoughts off, "I've encountered similar bones on the ocean floor but so rarely and have never scanned one intact. Now that I do, it is familiar. Yes, of course. Akenehi, recall Liam's memory of holiday breakfast."

"Does it scan the same as the flesh he was consuming?" she asked.

"No, the friend, near his feet, waiting to be fed…" Brough recalled the shared memory.

"Yes, very much as I recognize. Orca have seen a rare few on boats. They hear some of our calls that humans do not." Akenehi gave Brough her clearest memory.

The pod had approached a boat to investigate incessant barking and whining. A dog was frantically calling to them. Her brother approached first. He spyhopped and raised his head out so he could view it with one eye and perhaps nudge it with the tip of his jaw. He tried an orca call, a command to silence, and the dog grew more vocal. His only redeeming characteristic was that he had a hearing range well above what humans never responded to.

Brough quickly pushed the memory away as soon as he understood that the dog was difficult to reach with reason as they knew it. He dove deep into his memory of Liam's experience with his dog friend and shared the detail with Akenehi. He sounded much like Liam's own human voice in the recall.

"Excellent sense of smell and hears at higher frequency. Smaller brain than humans. Very beloved by my family. We fed it, almost exclusively."

Then Brough dove deeper through his memory in search of knowledge that Delora had shared in science and history. She had many amusing stories of cooperation and communication between species. Brough had learned about 'dogs' from her but those memories were deep and eluded him. He had not appreciated then how interesting they were. But he did now.

Akenehi read his thoughts as he struggled to retrieve the memory. "I can't imagine why you would care," she sang in amused tone. "Even cephalopods are far more intriguing. The dogs we saw were irritating, even threatening and totally unreasonable. Observe." Expecting little to nothing, Akenehi attempted to think with their visitor.

Waves of smell accompanied by a limited color spectrum visual account and sharp hearing washed over her waking thoughts. There was no song, no echo clicks, but there was someone there. An overwhelming sense of friendship defeated her defenses.

There was more going on with that being than she had estimated.

"This…dog…is part of a family. He doesn't name himself in that way. He doesn't call himself anything at all. He perceives mostly in smell. He had a mother who liked him very much and took good care of him. As with orca and long jaw, she nursed him…" Akenehi took a few precious moments and shared the dog's smell memory of his mother and her warm milk. "And taught her young how to be one of their own. But not for long. His family is human. He prefers human to his own mother." Akenehi collected her thoughts. "Very strange."

Brough caught the same wave. He was fascinated.

When he finally came upon Delora's shared memories and could summarize coherently, he thought it to Akenehi. In Delora's own voice Akenehi heard:

The dog and the human had become two parts of the same 'being'. They had formed an alliance deep in their shared history and it drastically changed both species. Up until then, the population of wild wolf and human were both small enough that the earth was unburdened. Humans had thumb products before, but were it not for the help from wolves, that had been taken from their mothers and bred to be servile, those products would have remained primitive. The human population would have never developed into the planet-killers they became. Because dogs improved the humans hunt so dramatically, the history of the planet changed. The death of the ocean, then the land was no more the fault of thumbs than it was the alliance with dogs.

The dogs remained simple and were inbred to the human's purposes. The larger-brained, thumbed-humans advanced their weaponry, and developed a preference for eating the flesh that the dogs enabled them to kill with amazing efficiency. Eventually, humans learned to confine and breed their own flesh sources. They no longer needed the dogs and the alliance was largely forgotten. Some were badly abused and even eaten themselves. All was not lost for dogs because at their hearts they were so good at being friends. They were the last friends for humans that were too damaged or too mean to have with each other. The dogs were bred to be so docile that they endured whatever the humans subjected them to...

"Hurry." Brough clicked over the memory stream. He expected the catalyst to begin the transition process at any moment and he was no longer ready for it. He was suddenly out of time. He wanted to learn everything he could about this visitor who might share with him a whole new universe of olfactory sensation.

Akenehi was annoyed. "No thumbs meant no humans. Delora and Liam understood that. If this dog qualifies as even part of a human, even if only by a fin..."

"What does it matter now? He's Priori. I've scanned him."

"A multiverse traveling Dog Priori?" Akenehi shared her thought while she whistled to the dog.

"If there is one, there must be many." Brough thought back to her. He focused in on any cognition he might be picking up from the dog. There was a surge in friendly feeling toward Akenehi.

"What are you hearing Akenehi? Other than this dog really likes you, I'm not getting much useful detail from this visitor at all."

"He's here just to be with us. He knows it's the end. He's staying, whatever is coming."

Brough was hopeful that the dog was right, that this was indeed 'the end'.

"Too bad, I'd like to get to know this dog, despite the damage he's helped do to our world."

Brough surveyed memory from the Sponge through as many iterations of Vencello as he could summon. He announced to his orca counterpart, "Now that I scan and compare with prior iterations, I may have simply failed to notice. We've had a blind spot Akenehi. I do believe he has been here all along, with us, in the Vencello. He got pulled in with Delora and Liam. He cannot sever such a bond. It was always part of them. Such an ancient alliance has merged them for all time in all universes. They, dog and human, have become one being. Everywhere a human goes in the multiverse some part of their dog counterpart goes too. Devoted right until the end.

"So why is it here? Delora and Liam are already gone. He should be with them if you are correct. You are long jaw. I am orca." She emphasized the last with her family name call but the undertone was perfectly voiced human. The combination rang in Brough's ears. She hadn't even tried. Then Akenehi got Brough's full drift. "Oh, no. No. Hell No."

As if her protest had created a portal, the resonance of their world was disturbed. Then many things happened at once that snapped Akenehi out of her adamant denial. One, Param's greeting filled the universe. That was a signal that she would soon be at Brough's side. Two, echoes of Akenehi's name and clan signature calls had washed in with the long jaw clicks. While they serenaded her ears, Akenehi realized a split moments chance, chomping Brough's infuriating wave of thought, and escaping the Vencello's confinement, before the disturbance dissipated in waves. No time to waste. She homed in and sang as if her whole clan's survival depended on it.

"This is it. It's time. I'm away," Akenehi announced abruptly. She let out an involuntary orca giggle and she was gone from Brough's perception.

Brough wished to stall her, to include Param in their observance about the dog a while longer.

Without the orca's formidable singing mind, the center of the C-60 universe was as quiet as he had ever known it. He was alone with his own thoughts. Memories carried him as if they had caught him in a powerful deep-water current. They kept him company until Param was at this side. She greeted him with gentle, familiar clicks and then gave him news.

CHAPTER 3

Universe: Vencello (nearer its beginning)

For the umpteenth time, Delora retorted, "Inside."

Liam kept right at her, "Outside."

Akenehi listened intently as she and Brough shared the human meaning that accompanied pronunciation.

"Inside." Delora repeated.

This time, Akenehi sang her first attempt at orca translation right over her.

Delora ignored it and did not wait for Liam to respond either. She sounded it out again. "Inside."

Akenehi perfected her whistle. She tried it again.

The humans ignored her.

Brough approved but he refrained from offering a 'long jaw' click equivalent.

Liam blurted out in quick succession, "Outside, outside."

Akenehi produced her own translation for Liam's thoughts and word.

At that, the humans finally noticed her effort and paused long enough to absorb the lesson in cetacean communication.

Brough recognized the teachable moment and clicked his species translation, as he knew he had their necessary full attention, in alternating streams of soft snaps. The differences were plain if one had the brain to discern them, but virtually identical otherwise.

Akenehi recognized Brough's snaps were the same to her ear as the ones he had sounded for 'conception' and 'death'. She found the fresh insight from Brough's click translations most helpful.

Human language was dull to Akenehi's fine ear. She would remember it easy enough, but the thoughts the humans assigned to those words were puzzling. Echolocating species perceived right through barriers and so thought in terms of density and clarity, changing as echoes moved through flesh, water and sediment. Thinking in terms of thin layer distinctions was foreign to Akenehi.

"I hear that." Akenehi acknowledged Brough's information.

She turned her focus again on the humans. "You have each decided you are correct and the other is wrong. Stop. You are both 'incomplete'."

Liam asked, "So we are neither inside or outside of the molecule, sacred bit, or whatever you sing it as?"

"Observe and listen as I know you can." Akenehi turned her scan on the tiny blob of mass that was the young Metavoli. She whistled straight at it. A sphere formed around the little Metavoli. Liam, Delora and Brough all took note of each change that flowed seamlessly from one to the next.

"A bubble!" Delora and Liam exclaimed in unison.

The Vencello was swept along, for a moment, to share vivid memories she had evoked.

Delora recalled herself as a child with friends, standing small in an untended yard, its grass gone seed, in bare feet, blowing bubbles up to the sun. She exhaled, and her breath caused a little miracle, a translucent sphere shimmied up and popped into droplets as she watched. Liam had similar joys to share, with much larger bubbles, some fluttering 'outside' of a complex machine that had been constructed specifically to produce them.

Akenehi noted the movement and subtle rainbow of colors of the film that defined each one. She recognized the importance of barriers, identifying each sphere and linking simple words of streamlined thoughts, and ended them, as each one popped.

Akenehi shared of her own memories. She was still very young, in need of her mother's milk. She recalled placing her head into huge air bubbles her family blew for her delight. She chased them to the surface and dove quickly to catch the next. Hers were very different from Delora's. Akenehi could tap her fin into them, watch them section into tinier sub-spheres and watch some rejoin. But they never 'popped' to nothing as Delora's had. Rather, the ocean bubbles rose to the surface air in their hurry to be returned from where they were inhaled.

Brough had bubble memories too. Masters of the Ocean released massive underwater air patterns in types and detail too complex for even an orca mind to fathom. But as the Vencello, they got a fascinating glimpse into the uses and fondness the everyday miracle of air and water evoked in him.

Delora brought them back.

She hadn't given the small Metavoli much thought before Akenehi's demonstration. She regarded it as if for the first time. "There!" Delora exclaimed in surprised triumph. "You have placed that...*germ*...*whatever* it is, 'inside' a bubble!"

Akenehi refined her understanding of 'inside' now that she had a sample of Delora's real-time reasoning.

"Now," Akenehi assigned, "Get *them* 'outside' without harming them or breaking the sphere."

"Unless it pops on its own, it's not possible." Delora and Liam agreed after a series of mind experiments.

Brough was fixed on Akenehi. At that moment, he believed she would reveal at last, her part in creating their bond. Up until that lesson, he agreed with Delora. He perceived they were inside a sacred bit.

"You do it." Liam was skeptical that she could. Brough hoped.

Akenehi could not hide her intentions or thoughts from Brough as well as she would have liked. Stealth for an orca is not merely a matter of hunting skill. It was a defining characteristic of her kind. Still, she decided to reveal a few of her finest notes. After all, results such as she had just produced required orca perfection. Even if they wanted to, they would not able to replicate *that*.

As they listened, Akenehi broke into slurs, slides and chords. She produced an acoustic sphere with her voice. It encapsulated the tiny Metavoli that had only just begun to share their molecule. It pinched in some places and bulged in others in response to the music. It morphed from one sphere to a moving orb of eight distinct sections.

"Is that some kind of cephalopod?" Delora was impressed. "Six fat legs, twisting like a vine to the next! It has two heads! One up and one down! Look Liam, I count eight sections!"

Then as she watched, the legs blazed colors but the head remained uniform. Akenehi continued to focus her song and as she did, it completed its morph as the embellishments spread to the entire orb and the sections merged into one sphere again. But this sphere was a completely new color.

Akenehi had demonstrated her burgeoning skill at Acoustic C-60 Sphere Eversion.

Liam wondered if Akenehi had tricked them. The cetaceans did love their games and puzzles.

Delora and Liam didn't get it but Brough was beginning to. The humans expected a sudden size swap where the blob became as large as the bubble. The Bubble, they anticipated, would have 'popped' to a singularity within it. But that hadn't happened. Except for the strange movement and color changes of the orb, all sizes looked the same. The 'germ' was still 'inside'.

Brough suspected however, that without swimming or twitching a fluke, Akenehi had switched the Metavoli to the 'outside' and the Vencello to 'inside'.

The Metavoli was a fast learner too. It only took that one lesson and it knew what to do. They kept it going and it never 'popped'. For the remainder of the Vencello, the Metavoli sang variations of Akenehi's 'inside/outside' song for itself. It pulsed and displayed with cephalopod chromatophores as an ever changing, slow growing, bubble in their midst. The song they had learned from their first Grandmother, Akenehi, and the gift she had bestowed on them, their 'ball', enabled multiverse time travel and so much more.

At least the orca music lesson was not wasted on Brough. Delora and Liam were a different matter. They resumed their chatter and thought little more of it.

Eternity was often passed in such ways in the Vencello.

CHAPTER 4

Universe: Akenehi's Acoustic (Post Vencello)

Akenehi sang herself inside Brough's 'sacred bit' and now at the Vencello's end, she sang herself back out. She expected she would be orca again. As if she could unscramble the omelet into which the C-60 molecule had arranged them. But that had not happened. Like a hologram, when she transitioned the 'portion' she had meticulously calculated, the orca amount, she took parts of the whole with her. She still consisted of Brough, Delora, Liam and everything else too.

Even so, her new, separated being was 'fuzzier'. Now that she had escaped, the hologram idea made so much more sense. She mentally broke one hologram into four unequal parts and made the analogy for her to understand. She accepted for a moment that it was not realistic to expect her thoughts to be as crystal clear as they been during her long tenure as part of the whole Vencello. She hoped the transition effect was temporary and that her brain would hone back to her original form and she would soon think in only orca song again.

Akenehi quickly smothered her despair at the thought that she had transitioned to anything other than her mighty orca form. "Remember your birth, youth, your mother, her mother and clan matriarch, your uncles and all of the others."

Her family name, 'Singers' surfaced in pure orca tones at her beckon, and then many individual name calls followed, and she mentally played them in sequence of their birth.

"Excellent," she thought as a tsunami of hope shook her to near bursting. "Now, follow that line to your daughter, Arva'Anati…" Her daughter's signature call was clear in her mind. The heartbreak of that dreadful capture when humans ripped her from their ocean and held her captive for decades was a painful memory, but the detailed recollection was a success.

Akenehi was satisfied. She had not lost herself as an orca.

But even as she thought that, she was dismayed that she was also 'thinking' in long jaw clicks, cephalopod flashes and human language. She appreciated those dimensions, but she didn't want them. She desired to be 'pure' orca. How else could she be reunited with her clan, as they had been before the Vencello?

Now that she was on the other side of the C-60 sphere, what she found herself in was not as she expected either. She struggled to orient herself and instinctively gave out her distress call, a request for immediate help, alternating with echolocation in tight 'beams' as she twisted and rolled in every possible contortion. She hadn't done that since the Sponge. Her call was heard and answered.

Akenehi's return echoes indicated that a group of four beings had become trapped in her echo band. It was as if they were attached en masse by an arm that had a hold on the tip of her jaw.

Akenehi stopped moving, except for her head, which she twitched in a tight pattern to carefully scan them. They came to rest in front of her, hovering and attentive.

There was a frame of reference for all four that came back in her echoes.

One scanned enigmatic and complex. From her human Vencello, Akenehi was schooled in a variety of land machines. This reminded her of Liam's fevered visions of 'cool motorcycles'. But there was much that was oceanic and organic in her return echoes of this two-wheeled vehicle. At the first echo-returns this came back as a being, alive and sentient. She trusted her first impressions.

This, Akenehi thought slyly, could be a cephalopod under finest cloak. She scanned the perfectly smooth chrome radial arms and found them solidly reflecting all attempts to perceive within. But Akenehi was a skilled hunter. She never forgot a song. This cephalopod, if that's what it was, had characteristics of the 'call' she had used to turn the Metavoli's acoustic spheres 'inside' to 'outside'. Perhaps her early Vencello memory of Delora's calling out 'Cephalopod' during that song was confusing her now.

Nonetheless, she was highly interested in learning more about this living 'machine'.

The second was a dog. She had only just learned that a dog had been with them throughout the entire Vencello. She and Brough had just been cut off from discussing it and now here was one again.

Inside the dog's mouth was a solid scan-impervious object that drew her attention. It was the shape of an Orion, or Deeper as Brough regretted he had once called them. Externally, every detail indicated it had the features of a living female Orion. Akenehi could even estimate her age based on her exterior proportions. She appeared to have just entered adulthood. The object did not scan as a living being however, because her orca scans could not penetrate to detect vital signs.

The dog was certainly holding it tightly. Akenehi admired the dog's teeth. They reminded her of an orca, a hunter. If the tiny whale *was* alive, it wouldn't be for long.

Grasping the dog with one arm and holding onto the machine with the other was the third, a human-shaped female. Her internal makeup was different and softer than Delora's. Akenehi's first thought was that this was a cephalopod in human camouflage, but then at finer scan, she decided that was not the case. She did not recognize her and so continued to scan the next, behind her.

The fourth, nestled snuggly against the female, was a human male. He was unmistakably multiverse adapted, a Gemini product, but unmistakably of Sponge land squid origin. At first scan, she recognized him. This was Liam's nephew, Johnny.

Before she could make an intentional sound toward them, the human-shaped female addressed her.

CHAPTER 5

Universe: Sponge (Cetapiens)

Kei and Johnny were walking back to where they had left L-32, their 'ride'. It was a short wade through an upkept path of new undergrowth in the jungle of Cetapiens.

"This reminds me of a deer trail back home," Johnny mused as he pushed a large leaf out of his face. He let go and it snapped back, brushing a tuft of hair to the top of Kei's head.

"Oi! Didn't your mother teach you anything…" Then Kei caught herself. She admonished herself, 'Don't bring up anything 'mother'. *Idiot.*'

Johnny had not noticed. He was off in his own head again.

Kei reached into her pocket and used its loose cloth as a barrier as she felt the resistance of a whale shape. Yes, the cetacean was right where she put it. She moved her fingers free of the cloth, wrapped her fingers around it and listened.

As if the source were coming from the center of her own head, "Akenehi, orca matriarch of the Vencello, in need of help. First time travel as Orca Priori. She's disoriented. Assist to Orcasekai, final universe omni-extinction threat, suicide watch, final phase imminent." She carefully let go and withdrew her hand, using both to clear branches that Johnny was carelessly letting fly back at her.

The back of Johnny's head alternated between visible and covered by foliage as he pushed through.

"Johnny, are you hearing this?"

"It should be right here." He reached out, holding his arms akimbo as he rotated his torso. He looked like a bird, waving them up down, searching for their ride. In moments, his hand bumped the seat. He arranged branches, in rough weave exposing as much of L-32 as he could, "Here it is!"

Kei gave the engine a pat and helped Johnny clear the seat. "Did you *hear* that?" Kei asked again, louder than necessary. He was stopped right in front of her.

"Hear what? Where's En? He was right behind you, wasn't he?"

En was their new friend, a dog, and, apparently, a skilled time traveler. Johnny assumed the dog was responsible for helping Kei complete an important task, just a few short days ago. One so secret even she didn't know she was doing it. They both assumed the dog was following them back to the motorcycle and they would go on at least one more time travel together.

They both stopped and listened.

Nothing.

"Doyt!" Kei cursed barely over her breath. "Where did that dog *go*?" She knew Johnny had no idea either, so she didn't expect an answer. She cupped her hands around her mouth and whistled without waiting. She started low, slid the tone high loud and smooth, above Johnny's hearing range.

They both waited for the response. There was no rustle that would indicate canine movement from the undergrowth.

"Maybe he went home," Johnny suggested. He sounded more than a little disappointed.

"Noooo! I *really* wanted him to join us, at least for a while." Kei looked like she was going to cry. That was not like her. At all.

Kei opened her travel bag and pulled out a t-shirt. She wrapped her hand thinly with it, careful not to touch her flesh to the whale as she withdrew it from her pocket. Already resigned that En was gone, she changed the subject. "Touch this and tell me if you hear anything."

Johnny looked at her sideways, not knowing what to expect. The ginger manner of her handling it, gave him caution. He slowly reached out.

En got to it first. The dog lunged up out of the underbrush, both feet forward right into Kei. In one smooth move, he grabbed the little whale as it dropped out her hand. She steadied herself against L-32 and Johnny helped her. The t-shirt plopped to the ground. She quickly reached down and grabbed it before En could get that too.

Kei began issuing calm, clear commands right away. "Leave it! Leave. It."

Johnny started toward the dog and Kei motioned him back, using her arm as a barrier. "No, he'll think it's a game," she warned. "Don't move. Don't even look at him."

"I've got a better idea, let's offer a trade. Anything in here we can offer, like a treat?"

"I don't think he'll like what I eat. I didn't think to bring anything for him, what was I thinking."

"Not. But then, neither was I." Johnny held out the t-shirt as if to offer a game of tug-of-war, a distraction. Kei nodded him to stop.

"That's one of my favorites." She was firm.

En hopped up on to L-32's seat, turning in careful balance and managed to not fall off. He sat, positioning his feet skillfully. It kept him from sliding off the tilt. He placed his paws on the handlebars and kept a tight chomp on the whale. He looked out of the corner of eye, ears back, near Kei but not directly at her.

Kei could see the whale's fluke extending just beyond En's left canine. She slowly reached up hoping she could just ease it out of his mouth. En let out a low growl as soon as she made contact.

Kei withdrew her hand. "Okay, okay, okay. You keep it then, for now. Pranaya said you can't hurt it, no matter what you try, so…just don't lose it."

Johnny saw the opportunity. "Well, let's ride out of this jungle. He looks ready and willing to go. He brought us here and it was a winner. Your mission was accomplished, no thanks to you." He nudged her in a tease. "Nothing beats a relaxing Cetapiens vacation, complete with orcas and a session on the mats to put one's mind back together. I'm rested as I'll ever be. What do you say we trust him at least one more time?"

Johnny was already mounted and without getting off, helped Kei settle between him and En. When they were ready, L-32 yielded to En's will, and they were elsewhere and elsetime in the multiverse.

CHAPTER 6

Universe: Akenehi's Acoustic

"Akenehi, of the Singer clan, Orca Matriarch of the Vencello. We are," Kei indicated, using orca body language to indicate each of her party as she named them, "Kei, Johnny, En and L-32." She remained still so the orca could get a good echolocation scan of her.

Kei had managed the tiny whale, a translator, away from En. She grasped it in her hand as she spoke a greeting. The sound of her own voice, as if she had sung its orca equivalent, customized to Akenehi's ability and expectations, played over her own vocals. It was gorgeous.

Whatever universe L-32 had brought them to, it was acoustically rich. The medium that supported them confounded Kei's every sense as she addressed Akenehi, except for her hearing. That wonderful little translator had just exceeded all her expectations. Her fingers tightened around it. She couldn't have let go of it if she had wanted to.

"The call…the one you just made. Right before we…" Kei listened to the musical translation that transformed her stammer into an operatic masterpiece. Kei couldn't help but keep talking, delighting in the effect. "So, this is how I would sound, if I were you…" Kei thought out loud that even mindless rambling was poetry, as Akenehi would have sung it. Kei hadn't expected *this*. Her heart pounded with pleasure.

In her many time travels she had experienced an expansion of her own limited senses. Sometimes she perceived new colors. As a novice, she had been overcome and wept uncontrollably. Part of her training was to suppress the emotional joy at those awakenings. She had mastered sensory strategies, but music was her weakness. She promised herself she would make time to weep later.

Kei gripped a handlebar of her 'ride', L-32. In response, gentle pulses and a warm surge was generated. The tension in her fingers relaxed and the effect continued as it spread noticeably up through her arm. It worked, as usual. Kei regained enough of her composure to continue.

The problem before her was an inexperienced Orca Priori was ready to impulsively blunder into time travel at any instant, unaware of proper markers. That would be disastrous for Akenehi and much else.

Breaking protocol, Kei sprang an attention getter; a greeting from one of Akenehi's daughters, Arva'Anati-G.

"Mother, I, Arva'Anati, of the singer clan, am a Solitary Matriarch no more. I am finally reunited with Clear, my firstborn."

Delivering the message in Akenehi's perfect acoustic universe, enhanced with the translator, the song was unmistakably her daughter's.

It worked. Compelled to remain; Akenehi knew what that meant and that more from her beloved child would follow. Her daughter had suffered in so many ways for years in captivity by thumbs. Arva'Anati had been subjected to the heartbreaks that were most cruel for an orca. The humans had forced several pregnancies. Those beloved little ones that survived birth long enough to be weaned were ripped away from her, never to be returned.

Unable to physically rescue her from the concrete human prison, Akenehi kept her company in sleep-song until Johnny initiated Gemini replication. Like Alvar and Johnny before her, Arva'Anati became two individuals, each G, in full command of their prior life's memory. Although both were subsequently liberated into viable universes, neither mother could ever forget her many beloved little orcas.

As their grandmother, Akenehi suffered as much.

This G had been awakened in the Vencello, and promptly filled that universe with an agitated determination to reunite with every one of her children. With the help of many Orca Priori, who flooded in to answer distress calls, Arva'Anati-G was released, despite Akenehi's reluctance to let her go so soon. The search pod dove right into the multiverse and had never returned.

Now Akenehi knew of her daughter's first triumph.

Kei gave her a moment and then continued as Arva'Anati-G had instructed her, enabled to render the remainder of the message in perfected imitation of the original voice as it was sung to her.

"Beloved matriarch, sing true, dive deep. Find each one of our family and be with them again. A part of us will always be together there, too. Thank you,

mother, for the gift of my life and for letting me go to find my own that I have lost."

In any other universe, Akenehi's earsplitting outburst might have shattered them.

Kei swallowed hard as En recoiled firmly against her. She leaned back further into Johnny and held the dog tight to her. The support of their physical contact helped her continue when the earsplitting resonance had gradually softened to a tickle. "This is your first Priori time travel and it is our honor to serve as your guides."

Kei didn't mention in her recital that she had been present when Arva'Anati reunited with Clear. Yet, Akenehi knew from Kei's imitation. Kei's perfect rendition of familial relationship conveyed it. Only if Kei was as beloved as family would the original singer have sung so.

Akenehi addressed Johnny in those affectionate tones reserved for pod members. She assumed correctly that he had been there too. "I know what *you* have done for cetaceans, long tasks of penance through which you have suffered tedium and self-doubt, the gift your efforts have bestowed on Delora, and then to me. And now this."

Johnny did not take the translator from Kei. He spoke to Akenehi in human and she understood him.

"Akenehi, Orca Matriarch of the Vencello, you know I would do *anything* for you. We are here to help you navigate the multiverse to the first of your progeny that needs you. It's not a simple matter to discern where and when to go. There are unspeakable dangers. One poor dive and..."

"Yes..." Akenehi sang slow and thoughtful. "The multiverse has defenses that put an organic body fighting off disease to shame. One must not fall in the path of *immune system* responses. And *predators...*" Her tones dipped in eerie foreboding, "Against which even universes have no defense or escape."

Johnny was unnerved. "*Molecules, cells, organic beings...*"

"I taught you that song." Akenehi was pulled out of her reverie.

"Yes, I loved it the first time I heard you sing it. It's still my favorite human orca duet....'*universes, multiverse, separated by words, one in music'.*" Johnny paused and expected her to declaim her orca history, family lineage singing of transitions from ocean and back again. He would have loved to hear it in the acoustically perfection of Akenehi's private universe. Not only was it relevant to their next time jump, the sentiment that he usually took away from that number was that

Akenehi did not believe in endings.

She offered him nothing so reassuring. Instead, Akenehi scanned the dog and motorcycle.

Kei nudged him.

Johnny was urged back to purpose. "The next generation of the Vencello is calling. She needs you. She's near the end and all markers are clear and safe."

"Yes. I must go to her," Akenehi agreed.

Johnny closed his eyes, raised his arms, and positioned his hands to clap overhead. The sound of each helped him focus. It usually only took two, but this jump was special. This was *Akenehi*. He took a deep breath.

'Concentrate' Johnny thought out loud. Through tightly closed eyelids he squeezed the muscles over them. His eyebrows moved in as close together as they could and began to ache. He continued to speak, and he felt Kei press in, anticipating yet another unknown, against him. "Set, marker…Orcasekai is dying…a universe, and everything within it, is near its end…if she goes, they all go with her, so many lives, so much within…focus…markers…" He clapped one time. There, in Akenehi's perfect acoustic universe, it sounded like the first crack of crystal, clear and crisp. "FOCUS…*so* sad, so *tired*, Grandmother!" Johnny clapped a second time, to finish the time jump to the sound of shattering crystal.

Akenehi gave them her full attention, observing every nuance as she was pulled along. Seamlessly, they homed into their target, a far distant time of the home Vencello C-60 molecule she had just escaped. However, without Akenehi inside of it, it was no longer the Vencello. It hadn't been for a very long time. It was Orcasekai, Akenehi's own Priori descendant.

Akenehi began a flurry of exchanges with the dying universe, assessing, responding. Her guides could not keep up with her speed to help in anyway as she worked. Akenehi was delivered safe and was already on it.

"Time's up." Johnny gave the signal and Kei acknowledged wordlessly as she revved L-32. The acoustic perfection was lost. The echo was not a pretty one.

Once revved, the certainty of their next jump was fixed. Johnny and Kei looked solemnly at each other. In the split moments they remained, they each silently wished Akenehi luck.

En's ears dropped close to his head and he averted his gaze away from Akenehi and Orcasekai, who buzzed as one and smelled of terrifying death to him. In that moment he cowered, his forehead down to L-32 and closed his eyes.

Orcasekai made a quick, albeit slight improvement and in that moment, she sounded.

Responding to that ultrasonic whistle Kei and Johnny could not hear, En's head jerked up quickly to Orcasekai. His ears perked. They were stiffened only until the natural drooping midway up to their tips but turned them to Akenehi and kept them cupped full toward her. En broke free of Kei's arm, loose about him, sprang off L-32 in one athletic leap and dog paddled, as if through water, straight toward Akenehi.

L-32 would not stop once revved. Before Kei could call En back, she and Johnny were navigated away with her, as her riders, on to her next marker. The dog was left behind with Akenehi and Orcasekai.

CHAPTER 7

Universe: Akenehi's Acoustic and Orcasekai

Kei, Johnny and L-32 were gone. Akenehi didn't have time to wonder how. The dog had responded to the call, obeyed and was settling in near her while she worked on Orcasekai.

The situation before her was grim. Orcasekai gave off indications of prolonged hopelessness. Akenehi feared she had been guided to a time that was too far gone in her progeny's apathy. Suicide sounded imminent.

Akenehi had kept Arva'Anati's spirits up during that long captivity. Admittedly, this was a different situation. Arva'Anati was her *orca* daughter. Orcasekai was so many *countless* generations and even a couple of *universes* removed from that Sponge clan. An entire universe was a congruous expanse of sentience far from the narrow range of an orca, even if Orcasekai was only a C-60 *molecule* universe. Molecules, orcas, universes. Music unified them and blurred the boundaries. The acoustic neuroanatomy she brought through the Vencello and out of it had taught her that. Still, she had much to learn as a Priori.

Despite the ambiguity of accepting a molecule as progeny, a universe and more, she loved all her family, regardless of generation count and the changes that resulted. Orcasekai was as her descendant. That was all she needed to know. She was determined to give her best efforts, recalling what her own grandmother had sang to her, "There is an ocean's difference between crying and crying among a family pod that loves you."

*****

Akenehi heard a familiar call. A perpetual 'Amaranth' washed over the surface resonance of the C-60 molecule. That was not a defining characteristic of the Vencello she had called home, but it was familiar. Akenehi never forgot voice, or an orca name call. She recognized that voice. The singer of that unending 'Amaranth' had visited her in the Vencello long ago, as a child Priori accompanied by her matriarch and grandmother of that name. Then, that voice had called her 'Grandmother', but it was unmistakably the same.

'Amaranth' gave the C-60 molecule a distinctive characteristic, quite different from the Vencello. It defined it as an entirely new universe, the molecular sphere encapsulating worlds and sentient beings within. Orcasekai had inherited the ancient Vencello C-60 molecule, and was keeper of its precious contents: cetacean, human, Priori and others. But they were one, as a mind is with a body. Orcasekai was the mind and the worlds and beings within the C-60 sphere were the body. This body was suffering a long phase of coma as far as the mind of it was concerned. But inside, things were quite awake.

It made sense to Akenehi that she was brought to fix this. She was the matriarch of the Vencello and had kept it going. She knew a thing or two about troubleshooting C-60 harmonics. And she was a specialist in Metavoli cultivation.

What did not make sense to her is why the dog, En, had jumped to her. Orcasekai seemed to be increasingly aware of him and any response at this critical phase was good enough for Akenehi.

CHAPTER 8

Universe: Akenehi's Acoustic and Orcasekai

En whimpered. His utterance echoed an emotional familiarity that drew Akenehi's attention.

She was intrigued. She replied with her pod's inquiry call. *What's the matter?* She never expected him, possessing such a small brain, to answer. She was startled that she got one.

"Music." The answer was sleepy and cryptic. And orca.

Akenehi realized it was Orcasekai who had replied, not En. She was very encouraged. She coaxed, "Explain."

En barked and yapped excitedly.

Orcasekai chattered over his cacophony, and answered as if the dog had made the request.

Akenehi had no problem hearing them both at once. She rather enjoyed the burst of energy shared between the two.

"Any C-60 molecule is a singing life generator." Orcasekai worked in rhythm with the dog and they played off each other. "It sings the music of all universes. For that reason, and many others, it can come up with solutions for life in any one of many compatible universes. Akenehi sang *around* it, and then she was *in* it. Akenehi and Brough and Delora and Liam…"

Orcasekai's song resembled a teasing duet, as if she were explaining to a baby orca. She kept time with the dog's sharp yips, echoing each with strong emphasis on the next note.

En was energized and became even more excited.

Orcasekai continued, "Akenehi helped sing them *all* inside. They became…the Vencello! She kept them there. Until the end and then," her voice trailed, "Akenehi sang *herself* outside."

During the long pause, En became quiet too.

Orcasekai's voice became expressively sad and lost its playful rhythm. "She left Brough behind. He's still *here*. *I'm* still here."

Orcasekai addressed Akenehi. She was fading again. Her voice slowed. "I remember you, Akenehi. You've come back to me. I am not just any C-60 molecule. Cetaceans, humans, others, there was so much inside to work with."

Akenehi realized that when she left the Vencello, a part of Brough had transitioned with her. So, it made sense that a part of her remained behind with him. She switched to echolocation and homed in for an assessment of just how stupid they had become without her.

"Am I singing with Brough or Orcasekai?" She tested for flawed logic by forcing a choice that would have tripped up Delora or Liam, whose language invited such error prone oversimplifications; one *or* the other. She inquired in her best long jaw clicks. If enough of Brough had remained and was answering, she could expect an in-kind response, including a feast of details spewing in a fast streaming echolocation.

"Yes," Orcasekai answered in clicks, whistles and flashes. "And know this, the unsung hero of the dramatic survival story of a thinking molecule, from Vencello to Orcasekai, was not you *or* Brough. It was *our* colony; your own Metavoli. The Metavoli was conceived from Vencello organic material and genetic instructions from you, Brough and the others. You brought it with you from the Sponge to the inside of the C-60 molecule. That 'stuff' that you threw unceremoniously off your living bodies as your spun into multiverse adapted forms, was as trapped as you were. The C-60 molecule didn't waste a thing, including your organic shedding. It all condensed on its own. It *lived!*"

"Priori visitors came to shower your tiny Metavoli baby with gifts. Do you remember them, Akenehi? There were so many at first, those visiting friends from the multiverse, so interested and helpful. If it weren't for Brough, they might not have come. It's a good thing they did."

"Well, enough of their gifts fused viably and replicated in self-determined cycles into a sweet little colony. Not surprisingly, the colony soon began exhibiting predominantly cetacean characteristics. The Vencello was mostly cetacean after all. Delora was afraid, but you knew we were all family, Akenehi, do you remember? Yes, all parts of the Vencello."

"Of course. And..." Akenehi was cut off before she could continue.

Orcasekai buzzed on, "The Metavoli was self-similar in many respects to our ancestral mammalian bodies, made up of specialized cells with interacting functions. But 'cells' of our colony did not always stay fixed together in their body. Often, we wandered away from our colony, from each other, like a slime-mold, in cycles. Individuals could go time travel, but we always came back. We didn't die, and our absence did not kill the colony. Our intelligence and memory improved through the process. Eventually we were stimulated through the O-O to come together again in formation.

"Each formation stimulated reproduction. Like a simple fertilized mammalian egg, it first split from one to two. After some time, each of the two wondered off from the other, and then came back together. Then it split again from two to four. Each of the four went off to time travel and then rejoined when called. They reproduced again, pinching away from each other into eight and so on. The transition from one to two resulted in an individual that was the 'mother', that is the one, and the daughter, which was the two. Rather the mother *becoming* the daughter, that is the mother's essence absorbed and transitioned to a new being, this colony consisted of individual time travelers that remained very different from one generation to the next. A cetacean generation might reproduce a tardigrade/cephalopod/human. They were like cells but much more sophisticated. So, the mother went forward to progeny or backward to ancestors and assisted in their survival.

"Usually, they really loved each other. A liberated individual 16 could meet with an individual 32 and time travel together if they liked. And so, it was. They were as individual related neurons firing on their own, but collectively remaining connected through O-O as a complex brain. Each wanderer had their unique experiences as themselves, sometimes together with their progeny and ancestors. It was a lot to take in.

Cyclical rejoining was necessary. When they came together, each formation was different due to the addition of the newest generation to the whole. It was during that phase that the 'whole' was perceived. They learned about their new varying abilities. When they were off on their own adventures, they were as they had been. They still perceived the others but usually as little more than a cacophonic hum most of the time.

"So, we, the Metavoli colony, were in constant flux, time traveling, coming together, replicating, growing, breaking free of one another again, serving as a chaotic albeit thinking, healing part of the Vencello. We took on a life of our own.

"The result was a time-bending, magnificent Metavoli; a vital organ of the sentient C-60 molecule.

"So," Akenehi interrupted, "Your song, you are honoring your generations, your grandmothers…"

"Yes!" Orcasekai was happy she brought that up. "One of our greatest generations was my own Grandmother. She was a vast, complex multiverse catalyst. This meant she kept Metavoli life going, almost by herself. Unlike enzymes of mammalian cells, she did not bend *molecules* as a sing-function in a long que of many to facilitate it. Time traveling in a delicate weave of her own design, she *linked* certain marked *coordinates* of her own choosing across universes.

"In my case, she orchestrated a chain reaction, ensured the combination of her selections within the salvaged, ancestral Vencello molecule. Her correlatives interacted, tied, and were subsequently fixed within the vacated C-60 shell. The instantaneous capture of those elements within that vessel inhibited replication to the next generation and established my unique adult phase. The chances of a viable transition from precarious youth to stable adulthood were drastically shifted from nil to virtually assured. That is, she worked out a unique universe, under my chosen name, Orcasekai, a combination of elements from preexisting ones.

"Sung another way, she *chewed up* a bunch of ingredients together and *tricked* me into swallowing it." Orcasekai giggled at the memory of her own surprise.

"Well, you might *imagine*, I was so altered by the sudden mish-mash of transplants inside from different universes that I wasn't getting their *signals*. I didn't know *how*. I couldn't hear much at all. I could no longer time travel as Priori either. That was the agonizing, worst possible ramification.

"Instead of joyfully gliding through the multiverse, when and where I so desired, I was stuck to my C-60 ancestral sphere. There was nothing to hear but the echoing buzz of perpetual energy. A hum of monotone laments voiced by talentless sub-atomic particles, fermionesque choirs, that threatened to round eternally. And although it had seemingly already been forever, it was starting again in eternal reiteration, at an unbearably tiresome sub largo tempo. I perceived the sub-molecular *everything* moving through me as a consuming slow cold tar. It taught the cruelty of infinity as no other teacher.

"Grandmother had observed my tardigrade toughness looping our first blue giant. She must have trusted I could survive prolonged stagnation and even freezing. I think she made a real mistake."

The rich textured music of Orcasekai's Priori voice collapsed to flat human language as she concluded with her own prognosis.

"Yes, this…what I have become…a broken universe…was all a mistake. I cannot continue. Not *this*. No more."

Orcasekai fell quiet and Akenehi could not rouse her. Such despair was not uncommon among the sick and lonely, for cetaceans or humans. This suggested orca coma. Akenehi had ancient treatments sung from past generations to administer accordingly. Now that she had heard the quality of Orcasekai's voice, she had a note to start on.

En rested his long jaw between his two extended front legs and exhaled. Even he knew this was going to take a while, but he wasn't leaving either.

Akenehi appreciated him even more.

CHAPTER 9

Universe: Sponge (Cetapiens)

The most comfortable place for a Dog Priori to sleep in all Cetapiens was upon a Templesekai mat. Their favorite way to relax before the snooze was to chew on a new toy.

Pranaya had fallen asleep, among her friends, mid conversation. They had exchanged a tiny object between them all evening. En had been scolded if he drew too near to it. For that reason alone, he wanted it more than anything. All attention, save his, was elsewhere. En perceived his chance. He easily snuck the tiny Orion away from her and held it tightly between his teeth. She had not roused thanks to his stealth. He looked around. None of the other drowsy elders that were sharing the sleep hut for the evening had noticed his actions either. He had sniffed for this chance all evening and now he finally had his prize. He would use these quiet moments to chew, undisturbed. En left her and made his way, quite alone, to the nearest ceremonial hut where his favorite mat lay.

He trotted quietly through the village, soon arriving at the innermost chamber. Had there been any other Dog Priori visiting Cetapiens at that moment, he was sure there would have been a fight for it. But there were none. Since Pranaya was asleep, he could take his time. He easily followed a trail of her distinctive scent, mixed with his own, through the dark that lead him directly to the mat that was most rich with it. It was laid out, right where she had left it just hours ago, away from the wall.

He stood squarely on all fours on it, scratched in place, sniffed and watched intently as a soft glow that resulted from each swipe spread. He made several tight circles, careful to stay on the mat, stopped again to scratch, and observed the effect. When he settled into his spot, he plopped the little whale under his jaw, between his paws, readying it for chewing.

As soon as his prize hit the mat, the room was filled with flourishes of light, orca song, echo clicks, human language and heavy scent. En instinctively grabbed it back in his mouth. The chamber resumed dark except for the mat glow that emanated from under him. When enough time had passed and En was certain no one was going to come in and take his toy away from him, he released it.

At contact, a whistle filled the room. He tilted his head in its direction and held his ears ready for the next. He did not go for the little Orion again. Not yet.

En was the only Priori present at that moment, albeit a dog. The mat was singularly activated by the combined contact of whale and Dog Priori. So, a revelation played out in all multiverse perceptions, including En's dominant sense of smell. He also had ears, eyes and pressure receptors. He heard, saw and felt too. Most of all, he was aware in odors so delicate and strange. In whines and howls, he was overcome by the sensory revelation. He sniffed in no general direction as he inhaled between involuntary spasms of excitement, and took it all in. It was coming from everywhere. He recognized his own scent in the scene, a memory of Orcasekai, as it played out around him. Among subtle others, he got strong whiffs of illness, extreme old age, suffering and death.

In distinctive whistles and clicks, an Orca matriarch called out, "You have been dormant too long. Breathe." I scanned her. It was NOT my Grandmother, Amaranth.

It was Akenehi, much as she had been in her home Sponge universe. Through a cool water dreamscape, I detected an orca heartbeat, skeletal structure, air in her lungs and food along her digestive tract in varying stages of decomposition. In her ancient organic form, gliding beside me, she transferred warmth to me with a gentle bump. That set me into a slow spin during which I detected a dog's presence in the water with us. Akenehi turned to scan my revolution. She continued echolocation from various close positions, practiced a few pure tone whistles and patiently awaited my reaction.

"You're awake again. Your dog, En, is still here."

I managed to protest the disturbance. "Again? Then I'm done already. And, that's not my dog."

En whimpered.

"Good dog. Good En." I wanted to pat his head but couldn't.

Akenehi listed to our exchange. "You sound much better. Breathe."

Through our shared sleep song, I implicitly understood her to mean a vital first was about to occur. I comprehended, in both human and cetacean thought, any 'first' lead eventually to a 'last'. As soon as I took that first breath, it meant I would surely dissipate. Which was welcome enough considering eternity's trap I seemed to be in. But breathing meant I would be fighting it. Dissipation and the release that came with it would not happen soon enough if I did as she wished. Why prolong the inevitable, especially if it was attractive?

I knew detail of every inevitable, slow, molecular hum but could not time travel to escape that collective drain. And if the next transition did not include a cure for Orcasekai adulthood then I would proceed to the next. Ignorance would truly be bliss. Better to be a rock, I thought, than the post Vencello C-60 universe. If I could help it, I would pause only as a universe of petrology, unless, of course, I could regain the ability to time travel.

Akenehi may have been the orca matriarch and acoustic driver of the Vencello universe, but whether I took that first breath was going to be entirely up to me. I wasn't having it.

Warmer, I switched from human to orca vocals. I clicked abrupt and decisive. "No. Better or not, dog or no, I want to get on with the next transition."

Akenehi didn't twitch. She wasn't giving up on me, yet. "Don't you have somewhere better in the multiverse to be?" I asked.

Akenehi said simply, "If En's not yours, I'll send him traveling. I don't know what to do with him. He is here for you."

That helped. I involuntarily took a vital inhalation of sweet air instead. Sleep song or not, I felt every molecule of it teasing lungs to function that, until that moment, I had forgotten I had. Akenehi began an ancient orca healing procedure passed down from matriarch to matriarch.

As the Orion's disclosure had begun to play out, Pranaya woke up and realized that En was gone. So was the little whale. Careful not to awaken her sleeping companions, she stood up and tread lightly to the nearby ritual hut. She knew her Dog Priori friend very well. If En had what he had been so interested in obtaining all evening, he would likely have taken it there and was probably trying at that very moment to consume it. But she knew, he would not be able to; no matter how long or how hard he chewed.

As she entered the inner most chambers she saw the familiar 'mat glow'. A session was going on without tea and without her. She picked up the pace in her last few steps and stopped abruptly in the doorway.

There was En, back hips relaxed, semi-curled up on his mat, his front erect and perched on elbows. His ears perked up and cupped toward her. He stared for her, jaw tense and ready to act, at any sudden response.

She saw in one sweeping glance that the whale was clearly visible in the glow, positioned between his extended two front paws. So, she mused, *the Orion and En together were the source of the vision. This should be different.* Without the aid of tea, it was a session she would not have tried. She took two steps in but did not threaten to take the whale from En, lest he jump off the mat and end the vision. He lowered his head over it to protect it. She stayed where she stood. From there, she selected the mat closest to her and sat down upon it.

CHAPTER 10

Universe: Sponge (Cetapiens) and Orcasekai

The vast array of multiverse perceptions in which the session played was lost to En. As Pranaya settled into her mat, she accessed many others that he could not. For one, she possessed a range of color sensitivity that exceeded even the mantis shrimp from her ancestral Sponge Ocean. She had experienced many privileged visions that a Cephalopod Priori could handle, from delicate and beautiful to brutish and hideous. But En's presence was a factor that was proving different in ways that she could not have imaged. It strained their every combined sense. Further, this vision was coming from a mind that was an entire universe that she herself had once loved as home. These were perspectives of the whole of Orcasekai. None of it presented as the cephalopod realm she had known. Like En, she was overcome. Unlike En, her next thought was to get off the mat and mix up an elixir after all. However, she forced herself to sit right as she was, and let her many brains interpret without the intermediary aid of the Cetapiens jungle. Soon, she recalled her Templesekai training and focused as Orcasekai filled the chamber.

Pranaya, you may understand that I wanted to stay with En, my friendly Priori companion. By his mere presence, I was brought around and tempted to linger. It allowed time for Akenehi to work. She wanted so desperately to save me. Although a part of me was cephalopod, there was plenty of orca too.

Even in our ancestral Sponge ocean, Orca survival depended on their beloved grandmother. Each pod member knew her devotion was as ubiquitously supportive as the very ocean in which they lived.

The mature female orca was a healer. Her vocal physiology, in which the young and all males were deficient to varying degrees, could produce precise songs that were more than just pleasing music or communication. From embryo to fetus in utero, the developing orca was monitored and treated accordingly by the matriarch through echolocation and song. No birth was ever a surprise and only rarely was a birth defect such. Indeed, every baby orca emerged into the ocean well known by each clan member and in turn, already knowing a great deal about them. Before birth, family names, sounds that represented emotions, sleep song and much else were already experienced and learned. Some critical issues could also be evaluated and corrected if necessary before emergence, especially those associated with nursing and breathing instincts.

Seasoned matriarchs possessed highly refined acoustic methods of neural stimulation, including coma prevention. Because the air-breathing cetaceans all lived their entire lives in the water, falling unconscious or comatose was extremely dangerous. Each of those species had methods of dealing with such critical conditions. However, it was the most senior female orca that could best stimulate a brain back into consciousness with her own voice.

Other species achieved a lesser degree, as acoustics were not as central to their culture and neurophysiology. The People of Cetapiens received healing during certain musical rituals, but that was due less to their understanding and more to the guidance of the Priori.

Pranaya, even as you hid away in Cetapiens, you were a musical gift to all. Your fluid grace and respect of every instrument was deeply appreciated. The small Cetapiens human population, that you guided as they composed and performed their music, pleased the orcas of Cetapiens immensely. In turn, the People were happiest when in the combined presence of orcas and songs, thus swept along in a physical expression of that joy which rendered them fit dancers.

Indeed, small graceful moves were an important part of their body language even when they had returned to land. Health was evidenced by keeping excellent time with the rhythms of the surrounding jungle, the ocean and even the breezes, as well as each other. It reinforced their bond. Even when they walked, they preferred physical contact, be it holding hands or frequent gentle bumps. In those ways, calibrating synchronous movement was helped by pressure receptors. Their language, more singing than spoken, kept time with the shared rhythms. Falling out of time too often, too long was a sign of illness. Healing in music and movement was known even to the People of Cetapiens to provide a wide range of essential benefits.

And you, Pranaya, were a central Priori through much of it.

It is no fault of the People that they revered orcas, and not cephalopods. From their boats, the People observed much to adore; the orca's lifelong devotion to family, their undisputed might, patience with the People, beauty, skill in the hunt, love of music, and more. The orcas were their models of perfection.

As much as the People revered orcas, orcas revered their matriarchs even more. She was the difference between life and death. And she loved them all so very much. When their matriarch died, another would have to be well prepared to take her place. If not, they were in grave danger of seriously shortened lifespans, due in part to badly broken hearts.

Akenehi had survived the multiverse transition to the Vencello and more. She was a distant ancestor of my own time-traveling matriarch, Amaranth. Indeed, she had known every single bearing of our kind. I was one of her Priori progeny, albeit countless generations removed from her Sponge dwelling clan. But I was sure she knew little of me other than she brought me a dog when I needed him.

Before I was Orcasekai, I had measured love in a small range of familiarity units. In fact, she did know and love me.

She awakened me with an ancient orca command: survive!

En threw his head back and howled, joining in Akenehi's pulsed volleys of clicks and fine whistles, each harmonized with the O-U-O song, the name 'Amaranth', my grandmother, just so. That music of familial vitality washed over me. Each refrain acted as a heart-wrenching reminder of generations of love and friendly concern as it peaked.

Non-linear memories flashed in a jumble, unexpectedly triggered by the waves of music. Each crashed against a C-60 electron, and at that instant it was if the very energy of those slow orbiting pulses was a secret keeper of all stories. It seemed Akenehi's revival song washed open those volumes that had awaited just the right voice to expose a beginning of the remembering.

With all of that, my resolve to diffuse was substantially weakened. However, neither the promise of a dog, her tutelage nor all the stories with which my electrons could entertain me was enough to entice me to go on. I could not endure the gauntlet of glaciers that was perpetual Orcasekai adulthood. It just was too darn temporally challenged. I had already experienced the freedom of Priori time travel and was therefore painfully aware what its loss meant in comparison. I had not retained the ability that defined a Priori: to time travel the multiverse at will, and that was all I needed to know. My next transition was already beginning by my will, not Akenehi's.

"Let me go..."

The chamber began to darken. En still held the Orion between his paws. Pranaya was desperate to continue Orcasekai's perspective, albeit through the combined filter of her and En's brains. Whatever the limitations, thoughts were flowing, surrounding them both. She had not initiated this. En did. And without the protective effects of tea. Pranaya feared the resulting session was a fluke, never to be accessed again. So, she was determined to sit for as long as it took to witness all that would be revealed to En. As the last of the vision faded, she urged Orcasekai on with her own clear memory, a stark flash illuminating Akenehi's distinctive eye patch. It worked.

Akenehi perceived the flash that occurred at the Vencello's conception. It was the last thing she remembered before she awoke to Brough and her new universe. In her haze, she had doubted her own senses. She had since decided to trust them. She had witnessed a similar glint at conception for more than one ocean species. Many sea dwelling creatures fertilized a mass of eggs externally. It was considered a privilege when an observant orca witnessed the brief subtle glow produced as the eggs were fertilized.

She was just as certain her whale counterpart, Brough, could not have known the Vencello flash would happen. The humans, Delora and Liam? Preposterous. Physiology common to egg-bearing creatures and Vencello alike must have been present during their joining in a new life. There were plenty of multiverse physiological candidates and she calculated too many to control. Nonetheless, she recognized the visual herald of conception.

Sound and light at the critical moment had to be only a couple of many heralds of success. As an orca, she could not have perceived them all. She could already sing her part. Through the Vencello she developed the ability to evoke powerful echolocation pulses identical to Brough's, while relying on the light as feedback to keep trying until its ignition. She had endeavored throughout her entire Vencello existence to gain the ability to control such transitions for her own family's survival.

Pranaya was aware of those sacred lights. They were common indicators of a new generation. Every Cephalopod Priori celebrated them as the confirmation of a successful mating cycle. They all knew they came from *within*. It was preposterous that Akenehi thought she could sing to it from the *outside* and make it so. Nonetheless, she admired Akenehi's tenacity for even trying.

An impossibly long, orca-acoustic blast, homing in ever higher on the increasing probability of success, slides and preposterously fast echo clicks converging closer together until it seemed they would fuse into one continuous boom…then suddenly…the flash of new life.

She did it! Wisely, she evoked her new power very sparingly; in my case to force resuscitation. After all, I was at that moment, a universe dying before 'my time', teeming with life forms inhabiting my worlds, that would all die with me. Regardless of my despair they were full of life, many levels of which fought to maintain it.

From her awakening in the Vencello and throughout, Akenehi remained humble and never self-important. But she was proud of her skill at my revival. I trusted, but could not directly perceive, that a surge of appreciative Priori had rushed in to witness her success, and they too, undoubtedly, admired her greatly.

As her euphoria subsided, she could concentrate once again on her tasks; to fix enough within me that was broken. As she worked, the plodding of sub-electrons dimmed from my perception and were replaced again with the jumbled flurry of memory; vast numbers of sub-sentients within my rejuvenated C-60 molecule all seemingly clamoring to make their individual songs heard. She observed the effects of each tonal prod and synchronized her dance to corresponding heightened energy. She alternated angles, back and around, rocking and twisting, manipulating outer vertex electrons and those shrink-wrapped sub-elements, a conduit of the many perspectives she examined and tested.

I began to like it. It reminded me of time travel between universes with Grandmother, of the Sponge ocean, of the Vencello's first memories, the affect the absence of and presence of another Priori, especially Grandmother, had on me. But now, they were all 'inside' and I couldn't see them except through Akenehi's sleep song.

The jumble of sensation that Akenehi stimulated gave way to comprehensible communication in light, chemicals, pulses and voices from generations, long anticipated birth to inevitable death, determined captures and desperate escapes, silences broken by painful and victorious calls, tearful protestations and weeping thanks, orca and human laughter, a plethora of cetacean whistles, creaks and clicks of play and satisfaction, celebrations, rituals and lessons of survival.

I marveled that a C-60 molecule universe would have a sort of brain at all, let alone one that she might influence so effectively. I wondered if every universe had neuro-analogous systems that could be worked on by such an orca. Two and counting.

Akenehi affirmed, "Yes, in a sense, you have a brain. Several."

At that, Akenehi pulled back as if her task was complete. I recognized she had assumed the Sponge orca posture that was a silent invitation to play.

Akenehi teased, "Use them to amuse me. Sing two differences and one similarity between a Metavoli and Priori."

That seemed easy for an all-knowing adult universe. "Two differences: A Metavoli could not time travel but could make duplications through O-O and thereby transition those from one universe to another. A Priori could time travel but could not achieve O-O duplications. One similarity: they both exist in dual phases; as individuals and a colony."

"Those are differences and a similarity. But they don't amuse me."

That wasn't fair. "I don't know you well enough to know what amuses you." But in sleep song, I did know her. There, she suggested to me that I was to compose without words, think as an Orca Priori.

She was asking the human equivalent of 'How many fingers am I holding up?'

She wanted the emotional essence of it in music. A Priori O-U-O song was already perpetually reverberating, so I could utilize that. However, I was not aware of any Metavoli song, let alone one with which I could harmonize. When I started to think about it, there would have to be one or it wouldn't be able to do what it did.

I tried to work it out, what would such an orca song sound like?

A lament perhaps. The Metavoli, or 'The cancer' as Liam called it, 'if left to develop, will overcome our universe, our body.' And it did.

Or not sad, really. Akenehi protected it. She sang her conviction, "The Metavoli and whatever it would eventually become was progeny of the Vencello and therefore orca." It was family, it sang to her and they understood each other.

Culminating in an epic crescendo? As Brough knew through his Aware ability, the Metavoli was an evolving colony of many individual elements, some from their home ocean, organic material from each living thing that has come from the brine with them, and contributions from early multiverse visitors. Like an intelligent, emotional slime mold, parts came together as one when stimulated or self-directed and then disconnected and went separate ways when appropriate. It grew, reproducing asexually. Eventually it achieved the evacuation of many desperate Cetaceans in the dying Sponge and much more.

A perfect self-similar harmony?

At those thoughts, Akenehi was encouraged that she had begun to access the vault of my brains, the four main orbs, each with sub-systems and connections between them. Her intervention had begun. In orca sleep-song, we proceeded together from there.

En stayed right with me.

At that, En sprang up from the mat, took the little whale up in his mouth and tried to exit the chamber. The session ended at his action. Pranaya sprang up faster than En had estimated was possible and blocked his way. En startled at her speed but did not cower. Pranaya never hurt him and he trusted her completely. She was one of his favorite friends. She gave him a stern stare and subtle movement of her head and eyes. En knew that he was cornered and should drop whatever he had. He hesitated only a moment, but then obeyed.

Pranaya caught it deftly in her hand before it hit the floor.

En trotted through the maze of doors and out. He stayed just ahead of her, as if leading her back to the other elders, who were still sleeping soundly in the hut. En curled up at her feet as she settled for a long sleep, resigned to let her keep his prize until his next opportunity presented itself.

Illuminated by the light that filtered in from the full moon, En watched as Pranaya swallowed the tiny Orion whale.

The neurons of her digestive tract closed around it as it found its resting place in her gut. Even if she wanted to, she could not have digested it. But she did not wish that. She desired understanding, not a meal. Direct contact between neurons, including those that lined her stomach, and the Orion could be achieved. That was one of many natural methods that the Orion could reveal its secrets.

En huffed as she adjusted her feet around him. He stretched out to conform to her lower leg and closed his eyes. He fell into a happy dream of chasing glowing blobs through the forest.

Pranaya spent the rest of the night in Orcasekai. There, she experienced the only humans, outside of Cetapiens, who didn't absolutely terrify her.

CHAPTER 11

Universe: Orcasekai

Alvar looked like he was only 16 years old. Delora and Liam, his parents, had waited so long for his Sponge molecules to be recalled in that form, but they knew better now. Everything about him suggested the agelessness of the multiverse. Yet here he finally was, as familiar to Delora as the day he died. Their concept of what *dead* and *alive* meant had wizened. Still, Delora and Liam had gotten what they desired most throughout their entire Vencello tenure: the three of them were alive, together as a family, and sharing a home at last.

Home was *alive* too. The diameter and boundaries of each of its adjacent domes were apparent as they entered. The membranes of each defining compartment allowed Delora, Liam and close genetic relatives unrestricted passage while it resisted all else. Home triggered two strong responses in their physiology once inside; stay and be content.

Only moments ago, the family had arrived safe, having escaped the end of the Vencello. But their travel through the multiverse had an unexpected effect on Alvar's body.

Alvar swooned. The reverberation of his transition still tickled. The sensation was caused by Mitochondria that had begun their escape from Alvar's cells as they exited through his skin before gravitating across space to an enigmatic world. They abandoned him at such a rate that he became weakened, but not so quick as to kill him before Home could help him heal.

Before he collapsed, it all came back to Alvar. He remembered fully that Johnny was his cousin. His face and the sound of flesh slapping against flesh as he prepared for time travel triggered memory of their shared multiverse existence, he had called him 'Alvar-G', had clapped twice and just *disappeared*.

In anticipation of Alvar's fall, Liam had positioned himself and caught his son easily in his arms; holding him as if he were no more than a small boy. He had never carried him as a child. He had never known him then. Only mildly concerned, considering that his son had just been molecularly recalled from a wide swath of his home world, Liam brought his son into the first of the domes.

"Liam, did *you* order this?" Delora admired the open space surrounded by their new mutually favorite color: green. "It is all just *perfect.*"

"It does evoke my grandparent's orangery. The 'happy room' I used to call it." Liam shifted Alvar's weight across his arms. "Do *you* love it, son?"

Alvar's eyes brightened as he shifted his gaze away from his father's inquiring look. He took in Home's comfortable level of natural light as filtered through translucent layers of otherworldly leafage, onto him through the domed ceiling.

"We will take that as a definite yes."

They moved through a large dome to a smaller side room, as Delora led the way.

Alvar indicated his preference with a slight move to be let go. At that, Liam laid him down on the soft, mossy floor.

"Now all we need are some furnishings."

They had survived the birth and death of a universe and little could surprise them. So, when the floor also responded in unexpected fashion, conforming up and slightly around Alvar to support him, they accepted it. It yielded gently to their positioning and after a casual signal to each other that they were impressed with their new place, they continued in silence.

"Comfortable?" Liam asked.

"Okay," Alvar answered.

Delora crouched near his face, stroking the hair around his ear. She gently spoke into it. "Can you get up Alvar? Can you at least sit up?"

"Side, plea…" Alvar ran out of breath before he could finish.

His father crouched on the opposite side of his mother and they began to check him over. Delora and Liam locked eyes on each other. Also, unexpectedly, when they applied pressure to his skin, a responsive glow resulted. It faded as they broke contact.

Alvar indicated with a monosyllable affirmation that he was fine and wished to remain laying on his side, in a semi-fetal position.

His mother examined his left outer ear, lightly grasped its helix between her thumb and forefinger, she ran them lightly down to the anti-helix and then to the fleshy lobule. Alvar rolled his eyes over and considered hers.

"Momma."

"Liam, come look at this." She checked her response and smiled at Alvar. But he could sense her confusion.

Liam came around behind her and crouched over her shoulder for a closer look.

The skin of his son's earlobe had become translucent, revealing underlying tiny blood vessels and fat pockets. It glowed slightly at the pressure of her touch. She ran her finger to the tragus, which was still normal looking and pushed firmly. It radiated luminescence in response. She traced a light path around his cheek and it slowly dimmed.

She turned her head slightly to indicate she was addressing Liam. "Mine?"

Liam pulled her hair back and examined the exposed ear. He ran his fingers around the curve of it and then repeated on the other side. "Normal. Mine?" He leaned in a bit and she turned and looked as he touched his own ear and cheek in similar fashion.

"Normal."

*****

Alvar stayed in his own dome, inexplicably exhausted, as far as his parents were concerned, by any attempt at movement. Since their arrival to Home, Alvar couldn't lift his head to see his body, and couldn't lift his hand so he couldn't determine whether he had his thumbs back or not. But he wasn't in pain and he wasn't bored. He heard music that emanated through the jungle and his own thoughts flowed with it. It was all good.

Alvar had become immobile. Occasionally Liam would pick him up, maybe carry him just around his preferred abode, or through other sections of the complex for a change. His son hadn't said more than a few words since they'd arrived in the new universe. He *seemed* to be thriving even though there was no getting him to move on his own, so Liam just monitored Alvar's weight as best he could. He and Delora were less and less concerned with the increasing translucence of his flesh, but were worried he might be losing mass, perhaps diffusing somehow. Despite being easier to see into, Alvar never seemed to thin down or grow lighter. Regardless of change, he remained simply

Alvar, their beloved child.

There were no cyclical changes between day and night. As if Home existed in a time bubble of perpetual high noon. Their sun illuminated the only other world they could see from their domes. There was no change of season, just the eternally green undergrowth surrounding their transparent walls. They lost track of time.

CHAPTER 12

Universe: Orcasekai

"Were leaves that transparent back home, you remember, *before* the Vencello? And that sun…it shines right through them. I can always see it, no matter where in Home I go, it's right there." Liam's face stayed lifted, bathed in its light, as he awaited Delora's answer from whichever dome she was in. The acoustics were such that they could speak from anywhere within Home and still hear each other clearly.

Delora answered as if right beside him, "They look right, but I can't remember leaves of *that* home. I don't think I noticed them enough. It's kind of funny isn't it?"

Everything became *kind of funny*. Not interesting, not shocking, not sad, just mildly humorous.

"Isn't it kind of funny that we don't need to cook anymore?" and "Isn't it kind of funny that we don't take showers any more" and "Isn't it kind of funny that Alvar doesn't talk to us anymore?" and so on.

Every now and then, Delora broke the usual subliminally amusing silence with a rhetorical question. She turned her head sideways and narrowed her eyes in thought. "Liam, have you ever stopped to wonder whether his transparency is something that is happening to him, or to us?" She paused for a moment. "He has other symptoms that he is going through a transition, the fatigue obviously…but…what if the ability to see through his skin and into him is an indication that we are echo locating instead of relying on vision."

Liam answered from his preferred dome, "Of course."

"We were part of a shared world with cetaceans for so long, what if…during our transition here we became more like them? And this new perception, it's so second nature we don't even know we're the ones doing it?"

Before he could speak his second 'of course', she continued her train of thought out loud.

"I'm not upset at the slow change Alvar is undergoing. You aren't either. Why *is* that? Maybe through all, we transitioned to a critical difference and he did too and he's at the threshold of not being our son anymore, back to what he was before then or on to what he'll be next. Or the change is us. I still love him, that hasn't changed one bit. I don't want to lose that ancient memory, my baby, my son, my beloved Alvar. So far, for some reason, that memory has followed me, and you, across universes."

Liam wrapped himself around her. It was a gesture previously associated with affection, but it was a relic now, with three functions. One was to affirm those distant memories. The other was to make her laugh. Because it was kind of funny that neither one of them had arms anymore. And third, he hoped it would stop her from talking because it seemed they had had that conversation about a bazillion times.

Every now and then Liam or Delora would get a funny feeling. During one of those times, Delora felt that Johnny-G had finally arrived for a visit. Liam stopped to home in on what she had noticed. Yes, he sensed it too. Home also concurred. Johnny had appeared close by, triggering a Home immune system check. He was identified as 'marked' for safe entry. Anxious for news from beyond their orb and other universes, Delora and Liam moved to the dome closest to dockside and peered through the leaves to where he stood.

To their senses, he hadn't changed a bit.

They had watched him mature from a struggling human teenager to a multiverse hero. They were proud that he had become a devoted time traveler who played many important roles. His favorite was recruiter of cetaceans dying at the hands of humans, the jaws of orcas or sharks, and similar lives cut short for Gemini duplication. They longed for the diverting details of their nephew's successes.

They went out to the dock for the first time since their arrival to fetch him inside, where they preferred to be.

Johnny looked startled when he saw them. '*Damn* time!' he cursed silently to himself. He was holding a white pastry bag in one hand and a cardboard tray with hot, fresh coffee in four paper cups in the other. The sight of them had caused him to fumble his load a bit, but he recovered.

"Breakfast? Donuts. Coffee." Johnny managed out loud.

"Yes of course, sweetheart." It was then he recognized it was Delora. The other one had to be his Uncle Liam.

"Aunt Delora…Sorry it's been so long. You know, worlds to save, entire species to evacuate from extinction…uh…*How* long *has* it been?"

"A few weeks maybe…" Delora looked at Liam for a suggestion, but he couldn't say for sure either.

"Okay then…well…" Johnny surreptitiously dug his foot hard inside his shoe. It vibrated, and he counted three long groups of pulses before it ceased.

He had received a few gifts throughout his travels, each providing him with multiverse-safe time-jumping tools. They had sure come in handy. One was a pair of water and lava proof runners. Among other features, the soles provided a planet age estimating method based on Master of O-O echo ability. Vibrations originated in the sole, went straight down to the core of the planet and back up. It was a crude 'by feel' estimation but it indicated that he had left them in Orcasekai at least a half a million, of what he would measure as years, ago.

No doubt, this was the family he left, although a much smaller number of days ago, by *his* internal clock. They had apparently survived with some memory but virtually no concept of the passage of a huge deal of non-relative time, according to his sole.

It was by dumb luck that he made it back to them at all. There were no safe time markers anywhere near the time he left until then. He had to settle for it.

"It's been longer, I'm sure. Sorry…I am so sorry…" He couldn't bring himself to say just how long out loud.

"Please come inside." And they started toward a clearing in the vegetation.

Johnny looked around for an indication of a house and saw none. He stood rather than follow them. "I've got news for you, if you're still interested."

"Of *course,* we are interested. Come in and see Alvar. Come on. Or, we can bring him out to you. He's not been outside the house yet," Delora said as she took the bag.

Liam took the beverages. They wrapped themselves around their burdens and moved into the clearing.

Johnny took the few steps required to enter their home. He didn't feel the protective membrane as he penetrated it, but he did notice the smell once he was on the other side. A strong whiff of greenhouse ripened compost with a subtle hint of raspberries filled his nostrils. Johnny stifled an exclamation. He had been in only a few different universes, but countless worlds within each. He had experienced plenty of strange and funky things. Through all of those he had developed a refined composure in the face of the truly bizarre; the aura of seasoned time traveler finesse. He summoned it up, convincing himself this was just one more. Trusting that they were changed and hoping they were not insane, he advanced only a few more paces.

"Let me help you put those down." He looked around for furniture or appliances, a table at the very least. There was nothing. So, he settled for the floor right in front of where he was standing. Delora and Liam came closer, faced him and leaned in.

They were delighted. Johnny watched as they enjoyed the aroma of fresh glazed donuts and coffee before them. But neither attempted to open the bag or ask for his assistance in doing so. Of course, he had not expected them to have thumbs, but *this*....

Liam pulled away and stated his intent to fetch Alvar to Johnny.

Delora stayed and relished Johnny's unintentional gift of olfactory memories as Liam moved out of sight, around a corner that was visually blocked by lush foliage. Johnny braced himself to look cool to whatever what coming. His uncle soon returned cradling a huge translucent bioluminescent sac close to his body.

He guessed correctly that the sac was Alvar. Johnny froze. And then blinked. He recovered like a pro and greeted his cousin as if he had seen him every day for the past 500,000 years. After all, experience of the caresses and ravages of time had warned him. "Hey Alvar!"

The sac flashed in patterns that reminded Johnny of cephalopods and the internal lighting of a living brain. Liam plopped the sac to the ground and it, Alvar, bounced once and lit up, displaying alternating bands of light and color.

Johnny didn't know whether to smile or scowl. "Where to begin...oh yes...I met someone. Her name is Kei. I'm pretty sure she's the one." He waited for it, but his uncle did not give the response he was certain he'd receive. It was awkward.

He took a moment to try and work things out. He turned to look back at the water, just to make sure it was still there. It was. He checked back at Delora and Liam and thought to ask them why they weren't living in *that*, but thought it might sound rude. He looked up through the green overhead at the illuminated planet above. He tried to work out if that was Cetapiens as viewed from the *other* planet. But he was having the most difficulty with Alvar's state. He had time traveled and witnessed changes in humans on his home planet over their time, right up to extinction and the last survivor. This was inexplicably *different*.

He monologued as he paced, using gestures and plenty of energy. It helped to talk about *her*.

"She's *amazing*! It's been great traveling around the universe with someone else. I didn't realize how lonely it was, how much I needed a partner. She gave me these shoes in fact." He looked down at them, raising each foot up a bit, in turn, showing and admiring in the same gesture. He looked at the sac.

'*Feet*. You *Idiot*.' He cursed at himself.

"And Uncle Liam," Johnny recovered smoothly. "She rides the coolest *motorcycle*. You'd *love* it." He paused for a moment because he had expected his uncle to demonstrate. Nothing. Johnny-G quickly continued. "She's a time traveler, *human*, just like *me*. I'm not sure how old she is but I'm not sure how old I am either for *that* matter." He stopped and waited for *anything*. It was clear; he was not going to get the satisfactory, congratulatory handshake he had envisioned.

Sorely disappointed, Johnny dropped the subject. "There's galaxies of stuff to catch you all up on, but you tell me where you want me to start."

Delora wanted cetacean news but Alvar came first. She chimed in. "We're just curious but we'd like to know. Do you know what has happened to Alvar? Why can't he get up? Obviously, we've all changed somewhat, but he can't move."

Johnny was beside himself, but not in the time traveler paradox kind of way. "I'll fix it. I'll find a way. Kei and I will figure out a solution. I'm telling you Aunt Delora, she's incredible. I've learned to never underestimate her. We'll do it…"

Delora and Liam both cut him off and Alvar displayed frantically. Liam kept at him. "No, not at all, it's been lovely really. And we certainly appreciate what you are proposing, considering how much you've already done for him. Truly, Alvar's happy. We're all are. But it's been a helluva puzzle, really."

Their astonished visitor took a moment to work *that* out. How could they be *happy* with a glowing *sac* for a son? How did they know Alvar was *truly* happy? No, he refused to accept it. He knew the Alvar of Cetapiens would refuse as well. His next stop was surely going to be back there. Somewhere in the multiverse there had to be a treatment. Alvar had a Gemini, a clearer bond between them than even an identical twin. It helped his prognosis greatly. Wait until *he* heard about *this*, if he didn't already somehow know.

61

Johnny-G loved solving a challenging puzzle. Figuring out how to follow markers within and between universes for the most efficient navigation was like that. He and Kei had just finished *their* coffee and he, his donut, less than an hour ago, by his internal clock, in the Sponge universe. He had sought her help in finding certain members of his family that eluded him from within an entirely different sort of universe. They were celebrating his mother's opening of her own pastry shop. It was pre-dawn and fresh batches of donuts surrounded them. It was his hunger, as well as a nostalgic time-jump, that had brought them *there*.

Just moments before *that* they had jumped to his mother's funeral, many years later. Kei had been instructing him on the fine art of follow specific *desires* as markers. That grief had led him to this happier aroma marked moment.

He took a deep breath of air, rich in yeast and sugar molecules. A pendulum clock hung on the wall and he took note of its rhythmic tick-tock and visual predictable, arcing swing. Conversation between Johnny's mother and his soon-to-be stepfather wafted in from the next room.

"...*not* a tosser. He's my *son*..."

A male voice drowned her out, "I may not be a pizza chef, but I know a tosser when I see one."

Johnny nodded toward the source and brought Kei up to speed. "Stepdad. Takes one to know one."

Kei looked confused, "Who is '*Tosser*'?"

"Not *who*. *What*. Forget it. On second thought, remind me to show you some time."

Kei shrugged in answer to his sudden grin and took a bite of her donut. "You *eat* this?" She did not chew, and he handed her a napkin. She promptly emptied the contents of her mouth into it.

Johnny expected her to thank him. She didn't but asked instead, "How does your memory of happy life's moments compare to the painful ones?"

Now Johnny wanted to change the topic to her loathe for donuts, as he watched her vigorously wipe the inside of her mouth and gag twice.

She put the napkin down and scowled at it, looked smoothly back up to Johnny with composure and prodded, "So, a ratio come to mind?"

They had just begun a few jumps together, back and forth in *his* past. It was intimate and draining but sure enough, the pain was providing the stronger force and more accuracy between his expectation and where they ended up. Physical markers were by far the easiest, but they were no longer the only ones available to him.

They had not been able to jump to Liam, Delora or Alvar-G past the point where Johnny had transported them from the Vencello to the dock of Orcasekai. Some of his strongest memories included some relationship to Alvar, and they were mostly painful. It was a special puzzle why he had been able to break through then but not after. Kei assured him that if his uncle were there, there would be some way to home in on his coordinates.

He and Kei had returned to a morning where his mother was alive and baking. They stayed in those moments until his heartbreak softened and his mind began to drift. Knowing he could see her again, albeit in the past, felt like she was immortal.

The café's aromas triggered other intense memories. He thought of his aunt and uncle and the very beginning of his long penance for his brutality against Alvar. He might have tried clapping to jump on to them, but he was with Kei and traveled by her method. He stated his intent that their next jump would be to try again, specifically to his uncle, post Vencello. Kei waited until Johnny was ready. Then she revved up her motorcycle, he donned his helmet, lifted his leg and shifted behind, slipped his arms comfortably around her waist. She turned her head halfway around to hear through her helmet and sang in a raised voice, "Next?"

He focused on his deep nostalgic mood and visualized his uncle. But his desire led them instead to Liam's closest relative in the target universe; Alvar. They found themselves in a jungle of Cetapiens where Alvar was to live the remainder of his life. Although Liam was his target, Johnny was ecstatic he had been able to reach Alvar. He had tried many times before and in failure figured his multiverse-altered cousin must have become inexplicably out of his range. Johnny realized he could use Kei as a safe marker. She would be the beacon that would attract him back to Alvar, easily and seamlessly, after his next solo jumps that would certainly take him to his uncle.

Without consultation or explanation, he clapped back to the Sponge café, leaving Kei and Alvar in Cetapiens. Back in his mother's café, with the echo of Kei's rev still bouncing around the room, he prepared coffee as he recalled his uncle took it, lots of non-dairy creamer and a pinch of cocoa, bagged a few of the freshest donuts and focused in on the aroma.

Hands full, he could not make his signature time travel gestures. He looked around, trying to figure out to what to do next. *Leave the donuts behind? Balance the coffee on his head?* Before he could make a move, two sharp claps sounded in his ears and he was in an entirely different universe and seaside, no less, on the dock of Orcasekai. It looked and felt to be the exact coordinates he had left Uncle Liam, Aunt Delora and Johnny only a few of his calendar days, and too many time jumps, ago.

*****

As Johnny stood over the donuts, in the presence of his eons altered family, he decided there was no *need* to consult Alvar or Kei. He reminded himself with a 'duh' that he was an experienced time traveler, and although he was a human one, he had made it out of and back to an elusive C-60 universe, all on his own. In doing so, he had brought with him clear physical markers, the coffee and donuts. Perfect. There could certainly be nothing like that in the entire universe of Orcasekai. Now that he was inside the C-60 realm he might navigate a few other safe possibilities. It would be simplicity itself to travel back and forth from that distinctive food to other easy markers, such as Kei, between universes and within Orcasekai. Next jump: Cetapiens. He was gone before Alvar could blink at his second clap or Kei even knew he had gone on without her.

Like his jump away from them, Johnny-G didn't feel it necessary to explain to his uncle why he was about to suddenly leave. He stepped back to clear his markers, leaving them behind as an anchor. He didn't say goodbye to any of his family. There would be no need. He would jump back to his uncle again before the words had even left his mouth. He planned his return would occur at such precise coordinates, they would not perceive he had ever gone. He closed his eyes and clapped twice.

It was his family's turn to be astonished. Johnny was suddenly gone. And he didn't come back.

CHAPTER 13

Universe: Sponge (Cetapiens)

Pranaya was a Cephalopod Priori. She was comparatively ancient, highly intelligent, spiritual and a skilled world planner. But to her predators, she just tasted good. Her kind were a favorite among Priori, inclined to satisfy their own desire to consume her flesh, an intense, albeit fleeting, pleasure. Pranaya's last encounter with a formidable nemesis left her with two less arms. The raw wound where they had been chomped and ripped away caused her so much pain during their regeneration that she made poor decisions during her time travel intensive escape. She homed in on Cetapiens, took human form, distributing remaining arms between the four limbs that would serve her on land.

Cetapiens was the perfect shelter. All Priori, including Cetacean, Cephalopod and even Dog, were in vacation mode, all eager to experience a rare human and cetacean peaceful coexistence. Hunting between Priori was simply not done there.

Enough time had passed that she had healed long ago. She was safe and happy in Cetapiens, despite her longing for her natural ocean environment, and so she stayed. Much longer in fact than she could explain to even herself. The pain of her most recent injury was a memory. Still, she could easily recall that her eloquent motif of mercy went ignored. No surprise there. She suspected her predators were simply incapable of appreciating the fineness of chromophore pleadings such outrages evoked. Priori or not, they were mean, selfish and base. So, part of her body, which contained its own portion of her precious multiverse-cultivated nervous system, had been lost to the rest of her, and then consumed by a brutish enemy. But Pranaya survived it and hid.

Pranaya, at the end of her shared dream state, relived the attack with Fadwah, and then awoke at dawn. When En saw her opened eyes, he walked close to the length of her body, toward her head. She reached out her arm to scratch under his chin and he sniffed her mouth, adding a quick couple of soft, moist licks.

Coming to consciousness from the singular, deep experience had left her disoriented. She took a moment to recall who and where she was. For a moment, she did not recall that she was a Cephalopod Priori. *Sponge Universe...Cetapiens...*

Waves of nausea, resulting from the reliving of vivid agony, made her want to vomit the little whale up. She composed herself long enough to delay it. She would do *that* out of En's sight.

Silently, Pranaya eased her form up, careful to simulate the actions of an elderly, but spry, human to any that might be watching. She avoided waking others in the sleeping hut as she exited, and headed to the jungle.

En was not so gentle, he hopped right over the sleeping forms, ready to follow Pranaya wherever she led. En headed off and sniffed for a good place to pee.

No one in the hut had stirred.

Pranaya went off at a tangent from En, hoping to leave him behind, quietly taking a direct path toward the deepest forest. Nevertheless, En would soon be right on her heels.

She forced herself to take several deep breaths as she walked. *Not here, not yet.* If she was in earshot of the village, the sound of vomiting, no matter how faint, would certainly rouse a helper or five.

Far enough. She bent over deeply, inserted a finger into her mouth, morphed its tip into an elongated arm end, gagged the whale up as it advanced, felt it ascend, wrapped the arm tight around and it and yanked it up, high above her head.

En perked his ears, stood on hind legs and sniffed madly upward toward the tiny slime covered whale.

Pranaya observed his vigilance, waiting for his chance to pounce on it.

She glanced around and identified a suitable, succulent leaf. With her free hand she plucked it, and held it high so her arm could wrap the Orion in it. In the same graceful move, she opened her satchel and placed the whale carefully alongside its other contents.

En let out a strong exhalation and stood staring at her.

The other contents included tiny, young Cephalopod Priori. She called them her 'clutch' and would protect of each of them with her life. As she opened the satchel, she watched them decloak and flash greetings and affection to her. The tight fit of the whale suggested that her clutch was growing. Soon it would be time to send them off into the multiverse. But not yet. Now, they were in for the lessons of a Priori lifetime, as Fadwah was with them.

She would efficiently rearrange later, when En was not so attentive. She patted them through the fabric. *Good glowing little ones, pleasant dreams.*

Now that they had the Orion, Pranaya considered venturing away from Cetapiens with her clutch, home in through the multiverse and establish an exclusive new world for them and others of their kind.

As she considered the world planning that would be involved, she took the risk and let herself think again as a Cephalopod Priori. She had not completely done so since she came to Cetapiens. Her uncamouflaged neuroanatomy consisted of several brains, including the new products of her healing. To mimic a credible appearance of an elderly human, she had to suppress many of the effects of them. Each limb now had its own brain, her torso held four, and her head contained two. All reestablished their native flow.

Brain One was on it. *World planning involves determining initial conditions favorable for Cephalopod habitation. Always exceedingly complex.*

An unfinished O-U-O song provides a suitable beginning, but learning of one and then inhabiting it are separate feats in and of themselves.

Cetapiens had inadvertently taught us of Orcasekai. We tried and failed. But we should remain in Cetapiens. Where there was one, there might be others.

Brain Two kept up. *Of course, we are willing to take our chances in the darkest unmarked abyss. Although, like all Cephalopod Priori, we are characteristically shy and elusive, except when laying claim to a new universe. Then, we are bold risk-takers, hiding in unstable crevices that others fear to even contemplate.*

Our kind are Masters of Camouflage and find comfort in its cloak. We avoid detection and interference. We might have been called Masters of Deception by other kinds of Priori. Camouflage is also a learned skill. The diffused and chemical rich neuroanatomy of cephalopods helped them with complex problem solving it required. To consider context and type of predator to be deceived and then to do it before being plucked apart or eaten alive! It wasn't easy to approach special coordinates from one angle and predict how to fool the perceptions of another species approaching from another. It required cool brains, quick, clever thinking to plan how one's appearance should be altered to blend fabulously to deceive. But they did it, quite successfully.

To acknowledge that would honor our mighty intelligence, which our predators are reluctant to do. They underestimate us, and it is one of many of their weaknesses.

Brain Three's analysis of predator and prey flowed into the others. *There were many worlds across universes where self-similar Cephalopod beings lived with little fear of being eaten alive only because we, and others like us had sacrificed to make it so. The multiverse was made safe and stable for Cephalopod Priori and their much simpler cousins through our hide-and-camouflage strategy. It will always work fabulously for us.*

Brain Four: *The in-progress closure of Orcasekai's O-U-O was a dark molecule quasi-universe. As such it should have served as a cloak in and of itself. It should not have been possible, that a human time traveler could had blundered into it. But it happened, and he did so while it was populated with Cephalopod Priori.*

He was dispatched, sure enough but not without Priori sacrifice. An entire world swam in his balance, the Cephalopod choice made itself. The universe had to survive. A new arm would be re-grown. A new universe could not.

Brain Five marveled at itself: *Our Cetacean Priori counterparts might not agree. But we are not cetacean, and they have never understood as we do ourselves. Sponge universe Cephalopod nervous systems differ from theirs in glorious ways. Ours were diffused much more evenly throughout our entire bodies. Our ancestors were one large colonial brain of the Ocean, with individual members independent and swimming apart yet connected by brine and communicating in light-emitting neural pulses.*

Brain Six took the comparative neuroanatomy further. *Cephalopod nervous systems were the same as mammals in one important way; both utilized in-common chemicals. It is through those we can best hope to know them.*

Seven and Eight, the two head brains, together: *Like Metavoli with which we shared self-similarity, Cephalopod bodies can find chemical solutions that worked with the O-O and produce a viable physical macro-scale duplicate. If balance is maintained, the O-O can draw forth anything in the multiverse. We grow a new arm, although not yet a whole body as Metavoli can.*

Brain Nine pulsed with pleasure as it reiterated gleaned thoughts of the other brains over the shared nervous system. Unable to dampen the collective sensation, Pranaya's entire dermis flashed and displayed.

Brain 10: *Time-traveling predators were a singular challenge. To kill one of those outright was not effective. Survival mandated a comprehensive read of predator neurons. Limited data could be obtained by consumption of nervous or digestive tissues. But superior data was available if a cephalopod could apply its own chemistry from a fresh wound directly against its predator's neurons. The latter wasn't the most pleasant method for either, but it was the most efficient. Once Cephalopod and subject synapses were close enough, chemistry transmitted data and stimulated direct memory sharing.*

Pranaya had stopped walking and stood, retaining much of her practiced Cephalopod mimic of human flesh and form, when all ten had synchronized in their re-united awakening.

En was now ahead of her, hot on a pungent scent trail. When he finally noticed she had not kept up, he trotted back through the path to check in. When he found her, he stood staring and thinking hard into her unresponsive eyes.

Food, you simpleton! Hungry! Keeping them locked he summoned his will to bend hers. When her eyes stared right through him, he then pawed the ground for emphasis.

She snapped out of her mental conference. All Pranaya's brains focused as one on En.

With a gesture, she motioned him back to the village. En understood. He turned, took off in a run, the way they had come from, through the jungle and toward breakfast.

Pranaya was hungry too, but she craved visions of Orcasekai even more. There, she had been as her Priori nature intended, uncloaked, gliding through a pristine ocean with all brains and arms intact and functional. She would join En later. Deep into the jungle she went until she came to a small rectangular clearing.

Alvar had called it 'Pranaya's Salon'. It was her safe 'meeting place of minds'. He had inadvertently stumbled into it on his first day in Cetapiens. He learned later, from her, that in that perfect space, the surrounding Cetapiens jungle, infused with Acrituchi energy, offered a feast for those in need of and hungry for multiverse knowledge.

She lowered to a cross-legged sit at its center and moved her face, searching for the direction of the rising sun through breaks in the canopy. When she found it, she fixed her eyes and moved her body around accordingly. There was no hint of age in her fluid movement as her body aligned.

She opened her satchel and grasped the whale within it. Gentle shakes dislodged the little ones holding on, displaying their protest at her removal. Fadwah was no longer wrapped in the leaf but Pranaya found it by touch, squashed to the bottom. She pulled both whale and leaf out and examined them by the light of her own glowing dermis. She squeezed the juices of the leaf around the whale. Having rinsed and seasoned it, she placed it in her mouth, tossed the leaf into the green and swallowed.

She felt the whale move through her esophagus in slow waves, fins and flukes scraping as they were pushed down. As hoped, the juice of the leaf damped the ill effect of Fadwah's physical presence.

A familiar rustle from the undergrowth caught her attention. It was too subtle to be En. She recognized a familiar flash. Delighted, she slowly tipped her body slightly in its direction until she could lay the full of the back of her hand flat upon the dirt. She extended her fingers as if to invite *him* into her palm, she remained still in that position.

Her dermis flashed in Cephalopod greeting. *Hello. Come closer. We have a new guest today. You will want to be in on this.*

Nothing.

We desire that you add your perspective, statistics, astronomy…

A slight disturbance a bit farther away indicated his retreat.

…family memory.

The only part of her body she overtly moved was her eyes. That last flash worked. She watched as a large gelatinous sac, aglow with its own neural activity, slowly extended a long pseudopod out of the undergrowth toward her. The pseudopod pinched away from the larger portion that remained in the undergrowth, shot onto her open palm, wrapped and snaked quickly up her arm and across her neck.

Pranaya was not alarmed. She was used to such merges. She opened her mouth at first touch with her jaw and the sac slid inside. *This* she could digest. The sac didn't wish it and neither did she. She felt another wave of nausea and fought the urge to gag as it pushed its way helping her natural mechanisms.

The sac offered Pranaya his first perspective. "Your self-blame is threatening to establish itself as a new multiverse constant. For the Acrituchi's sake, do not blame yourself for the failure of an entire world. It is possible to do everything right and still not achieve the success for which even you, Pranaya, worked so diligently."

"As long lived as I am, I have come to accept that our moon did not usurp the initial conditions that might have developed if it had not collided with this planet. I, more than anyone, used to hate the moon's violence against my beloved home world and the horrid wobble that is its legacy. But what a collision that was! It's a miracle we didn't completely fly apart into asteroids and space dust! Mathematically, I calculate it could still happen at any moment, but you, Priori, are not to worry. Both worlds might have made up a second asteroid belt in this quirky little solar system. But against odds, here we are."

It was a strange, slightly uncomfortable feeling when the sac found the Orion and shoved it, the rest of the way, into her stomach. They were merged; Pranaya, the sac, and Fadwah.

There was no time to hope for total comfort, the memories of Orcasekai were already flowing, regardless.

Pranaya felt another jolt in her gut as she recognized the scene.

The jungle clearing gave way completely to the pre-O-U-O world building of Orcasekai. This was the early phase, initial conditions that were in the process of being set by Cephalopods in the hopes of a universe long safe-haven utopia for their kind. They had scarified so much. But in the end, failed. And he was right. Pranaya blamed herself.

The O-U-O song that began the transition to adulthood had not yet looped.

The preparatory C-60 molecule universe, one and the same as the dying Vencello, was a black band in the multiverse spectrum, an 'un-moment' of sorts, but it was on the verge of explosive establishment. At the center of the sphere was a dark singularity anticipating ignition, and the subsequent influx, multiplication, then exuberant scattering of living content. It was through this gateway that Brough, the cetaceans, their food sources, which included Cephalopods and everything else the catalyst had determined, would pass through, if, and when, the O-U-O loop was successfully closed.

There was only one object orbiting the dark portal. On that, there was a single small area that a human could survive during that 'un-time'. Johnny-G had time traveled right to it.

CHAPTER 14

Universe: Pre-formed O-U-O of Orcasekai

Johnny gasped in a meager inhalation at his destination and almost passed out. The second breath was a little better. He could stay for a brief visit, but he wouldn't be able to live wherever he had gone.

When he opened his eyes slowly, which he always waited a few moments to do because he never knew what he might land in, they strained wide. He couldn't see in the pitch-black time to which he had jumped.

"Oh crap. New universe, new rules and markers, of *course*. *Idiot*." He fumed to himself. If he was in trouble, he trusted it wouldn't take long for Kei to show up and save his relatively novice ass. So, rather than jump right away on another attempt to find the time and place of Alvar of Cetapiens, he decided to check it out.

He crouched low onto the cool moss-like covering over level ground and relaxed a bit. He couldn't see his hands in front of him let alone whatever they were brushing over, but it felt like vegetation. He stood up again, slowly balancing his stance. That was the most unsettling jump yet. He took inventory; limbs, head, torso, all there. He shuffled slowly in random directions, reaching out and touching nothing, occasionally squatting back to the ground for a tactile check. It was uniform. His family, the dome, the coffee and donuts, were gone. He waited as his lightheadedness passed. Other senses suggested a *safe* time for his physiology; breathable air, no pungent fumes, at least none the lingering smell of compost and donuts could overpower. He could feel no weather at all except for a slight breezeless chill.

He looked up into the creamy black sky. Everywhere he looked his blind spot prevented him from seeing anything. Then out of his peripheral vision, he noticed huge geometric formations, pentagons and hexagons, of dimmest glowing nebulae. He recognized the C-60 familiar pattern of Alvar's model and the Vencello.

It was shockingly quiet until his own life sounds quickly thundered into perception. Then he held his breath and detected a soft tinkling of purest chimes seeming to sing a name from far behind him. He spun around to behold its source as it approached and amplified.

At the first approach of those ethereal vibrations tickling human eardrums several things happened.

Cephalopod Priori accessed Johnny-G's brain. Those his body had displaced had immediately perceived his unexpected arrival. They had surrounded him without betraying their presence by avoiding putting arm to skin. They had since been popping in and out of the universe to explore possible negative outcomes his presence might cause. What they learned terrified them. They could detect nothing of him except his presence in that dark interval. Johnny-G was temporally camouflaged; in effect a blind spot to cephalopod priori and many other time travelers.

The Priori had to reveal themselves to the human ink squirt as part of the information gathering process.

To Johnny, the black was replaced with organic flashes, conveying anger, threatening violence, arms radiating from glowing bulbous centers, ranging from tiny to enormous.

The O-U-O wave was near closing into a perpetual loop and this 'germ' was menacing all they had worked so hard for. How had they not known he would find this darkened time? How did he get there? Why was he here? They near blinded him with chromatophoric curses and consternation.

"Dumb luck," was his reply and "ink blast" was theirs.

The largest of arms that had gripped him let go and brushed away all the others.

He was back in the dark. But only for a moment.

Far off in the distance, Johnny watched as a large cetacean breached in an eruption of bioluminescence that human and cetacean eyes adjusted to total darkness could appreciate. It landed in a loud splash and even brighter display. He knew it was a cetacean because he could make it out, awash in a glow that clung to his massive form as it broke the surface and again as its huge sleek body crashed down full on its side, leaving a luminous settling wave on impact. Johnny *knew* a dolphin or whale when he saw one. It was much larger than a dolphin and he recognized that it was the same species of deep diving whale that had made him Gemini. Just as the first cetacean had landed on its side, another of the same species jumped clear out of the water with the same show stopping effect. *Crash*. Johnny ran shouting, out a few steps into the water and it soon slowed him down, phosphorescent bacteria in the brine illuminating his limbs, wet clothes and a sharp drop off just ahead stopped him in his tracks. He yelled and splashed to give his position away to the whales.

Something else found him instead. From the dark drop off, a dim large patch of light grew brighter. It was surfacing. And huge. It was not the sleek torpedo body of a cetacean. A bulbous head took shape and from one side of it, a single eye considered him through the surface. An arm reached out and wrapped itself slowly around Johnny's submerged lower leg.

"One jerk and I'm off into that drop off," he said out loud. Talking to himself helped to control his panic and develop a strategy. There was nothing to hang on to should he be pulled under. "Kei!" He waited and listened. Nothing, except a tighter grip around his calf.

She hadn't jumped in. "Ok, not here, must be safe then. Alright, I'll just let you…"

He took a deep breath. It was instinctive as he was dragged under, ass bouncing off the bottom of the shallow surf before he was pulled violently out to the abyss. He flailed only a moment.

A strong arm easily grabbed each of his limbs and head and held him still. Another instantly wrapped around his torso and squeezed hard. The last of his air was forced out of his body and he could not have taken another breath, even though he so badly wanted to.

The cephalopod deftly bit off the tip of one of its own free arms and waited patiently through the moments of swelling agony while the appropriate chemistry infused the wound. The duplication and healing were immediate at the quantum and then cellular levels. Using the fresh molecules-thin reparation as a probe, it inserted it painlessly into the occipital base near Johnny's skull. It went in further, prodding and reading as it advanced. A flood of vivid perceptions and memories were stimulated in the human's brain. Through the neurotransmitter common to both, the cephalopod comprehended.

There it was, all of Johnny's memories, experiences, the death of his twin, of Alvar, his long task of penance, time travel missions, the smaller cetacean's agony in captivity, their desperate struggle as they fought human and orca hunters, Arva'Anati's sad, long imprisonment and every connection to the Vencello and Orcasekai.

Johnny's mouth was gaping in reflex offering no barrier to the last free arm as it made its way smoothly and quickly into his mouth. He tasted salt and flesh as it pushed down past his tongue, into his esophagus and on to the neuron-rich lining of his stomach. Some data collection about meals and emotional status was gleaned there. The arm moved into the intestines and the pain was so awful Johnny hoped he would die soon. The brain probe kept him alive and suffering. Johnny's body defecated in reflex and more data was collected there as well.

"This really wasn't the way I thought I'd go," Johnny thought in total surprise.

"It never is," the Cephalopod responded, and its sincere empathy was understood as Johnny died.

*****

Pranaya experienced the entire vision. She was unmoved then and she remained so as all ten of her fully functioning brains worked forward and back to its end.

Brain Two and Four: *Untold numbers of microscopic invaders had been similarly dispatched by Johnny himself, within his human body, his whole life. Mercilessly. Unacknowledged. He gave no thought to pity then. Why ask for mercy for himself? His were the victims of human warrior cells of his immune system. Invaders absolutely had to be identified and subsequently destroyed so that his body, his cellular colony, could continue.*

Brain Three and Four: *As Johnny's body died in the arms of that dutiful Cephalopod Priori, every cell, viral and bacterial invader, and fearless immune system warriors, began to perish with him.*

Brain Seven and Eight: *Only as his brain lost critical electricity silencing waves of neurons did he poetically acknowledge a pervasive despair, shared by so many. His music felt itself dying and put the conglomerate colony that he had always called 'human' to one last song. "I am only doing my job. I'm a good cell/virus/bacterium. What have I done to deserve this? Why is this happening? Make it stop."*

Brain 10 added to Brain Seven and Eight: *In a self-similar function, his human contamination of the vulnerable universe was countered efficiently by the pre-O-U-O, Cephalopod 'immune system'. A threat invaded and was immediately identified, consumed, analyzed and distributed for future defense just in time.*

Again, Brain Two: *Johnny was a threat, and although he meant none, unconsumed he would have left the entire universe vulnerable to thumb related atrocities and human time travelers.*

Brain One: *The critical timing of his discovery and lonely death provided initial conditions that resulted in residual universal predispositions of species to come. Every emotion involved; in their own way; regret, dread, a sense of injustice, grief for the loss of a dear friend and so on.*

Pranaya's Brains ended in a single thought as the vision dimmed. *From the very beginning, the Orcasekai universe was tipped in favor of pervasive despair.*

A series of mighty flashes cast Pranaya's shadow from every perspective against the foliage and floor of the clearing. It was the physical manifestation of Akenehi's searing neural firings. Pranaya found herself seated in the center of a quasi-present orca brain, as it revealed itself in part, while examining the last of Fadwah's fading revelations.

Fadwah yielded to the Vencello matriarch whose acoustic key for admission could open any of its visions. Having swallowed her, Pranaya was exposed, vulnerable and could keep no secrets.

Pranaya recoiled in terror.

Her most formidable predator had found her. In vain, Pranaya tried to guess what 'leaf littered dirt' would look like and scan to an orca. She zip-morphed to appear flattened and in an exquisitely matched texture and shade. If any of the People or a fellow Templesekai Elder had walked over her, they would have thought the ground under their feet quite familiar. But even Pranaya's flawless camouflage was of no use against Akenehi now.

'Relax.' The orca matriarch dimmed her intensity so that Pranaya could not help but comprehend. 'I will not deliver the lethal chomp that you fear most. Not yet. Nor am I here for an arm or three.'

Before Pranaya could regain her human form to ask as an unappetizing human, Akenehi answered, "Once again, you have helped me. You have taken me where I could not have gone. As orca and matriarch, I *understand* wellness, health maintenance, limited cetacean and ocean disease and prevention, as it applied to cells and bodies. And with your help and these visions, now to oceans, jungles, entire planets, and more."

As Akenehi turned her reflection on Liam's love for Johnny, which she therefore shared, she determined that he would eventually know exactly how and where one of the Gemini, that his nephew had become, had died. "You are safe from *me*, for now. But I cannot offer protection from Liam when he learns of this."

Akenehi added the lament for Johnny's error and sacrifice to her song repertoire, took a moment to honor Johnny for all he had done for her daughter Arva'Anati. She reminded herself that she had not seen the last of him. He was Gemini and a multiverse non-linear time traveler after all.

"Tend to your arms." And with that, Akenehi's focus transitioned away from the jungle clearing. The echo of her hurricane of thought trickled away from Pranaya's reformed human ears.

CHAPTER 15

Universe: Sponge (Cetapiens)

In one strong spasm, Pranaya vomited the Orion out of her gut, propelled at the lingering, terrifying thought of Akenehi as her predator. She cringed and observed the mucus covering the whale that she had expelled. No slimy membrane sloughed off it under its own power, nor did any of it reform into a ball and fall into the underbrush. No, she decided, it was not sac remnants that covered the whale. It was her own stomach secretion. That meant the sac was entirely, still down there, stubbornly refusing to give up the direct neural link it had established with her. It pressed and pushed hard against the progressive motion of her digestive tract.

Love. Grief.

Those simple emotions did not come from any of her brains. They emanated from the sac. It was making her even sicker.

Ready or not, that sac had overstayed its welcome. Pranaya forwent her camouflage but only in one arm. It reformed as Cephalopod Priori, both rows of suction cups trembling in waves, flesh displaying pain and warning. She snipped off its tip and opened her mouth wide. She shoved the raw stub straight in, then down the esophageal tube to the sac membrane. As her self-repair pierced the sac, it responded to the new direct stimulation to 'vacate immediately' by pinching small sections of her gut wall and enveloping them within its own corresponding folds. Stub self-repair progressed much too slowly for Pranaya's comfort, but it eventually found its way to her invader's 'tender spot'. That worked. She withdrew her appendage to give the entire sac plenty of room to exit, intact and unobstructed.

With a spasm of fury, the sac was repulsed as if on fire. It smoothed out, elongated and squirmed.

It was up, free of her and rolling madly back to re-join the larger sac before she could open her eyes and watch it go.

Pranaya alternated deep breathes, dry heaves and cursing the form of which she was compelled by fear to live while in Cetapiens. "Of all the…" Gasp. Gag. "…stupid human…" Gasp. Gag. "I want my…" Gasp. Gag. "…hyponome back…" Gasp. Gag. "Cannot fathom this…" Gasp. Gag. "…trachea *and* esophagus…" Gasp. Gag. "…in the same…" Gasp. Gag. "Humiliating."

On that last gag, her arm's human cloak was restored. Having at last caught her breath and decided she was to be spared more vomiting, she examined it and the fingertip. It was a small wound, and although still smarting it had almost totally self-repaired.

Now that both Orion and sac were expelled, neither would be privy to the embarrassing memories that followed.

Humiliation. To a Cephalopod Priori, the loss of an arm, and the brain within it, was easier to endure.

Pranaya recalled a singular humiliation, long ago in the Vencello. She had *squirmed*, pleading eloquently despite it, that Akenehi might grant her a home world, spare Cephalopod kind and allow them a haven away from the predatory progeny of the Vencello. Although Pranaya had donned her Cetapiens human camouflage, calm and graceful sitting on a mat in a Templesekai hut, the orca was wise to the fact that she was a Cephalopod Priori. She was toyed with, in cunning orca fashion; she *begged* nonetheless.

Pranaya had gone forward in time. Like many Priori, she had experienced the Vencello's future, and well beyond it. To delight Akenehi, Pranaya let slip a hint of orca progeny. But before those could come into full being, all had to pass through one generation that was enigmatic. A genetic throwback. A weak link among many who would follow and relied on her holding together.

Then, Pranaya gave every detail of the human contaminant, his invasion and the subsequent auto-immune-like correction. She had dispatched the contaminant *herself* and had removed his remains *entirely* out of the O-U-O before it could close. Had she not done that, the whole of Orcasekai would have been full of thumb and human safe markers. Any time traveler looking for those markers, and they would be threats to cetacean travelers to be sure, would have free access to the entire lifetime of Orcasekai. They should *thank* her, not *eat* her. All was well in a future cetacean universe.

To illustrate the truth of her claim, Pranaya had triumphantly produced human, albeit all molecular, remains. "Neither of you could have achieved *this*..."

Rather than agree and admire, Brough and Akenehi recognized they were Johnny immediately. After all he had done for Alvar. He was as one of their own. They grieved that he had met such an end.

Their despair caught the attention of Delora but only subliminally. Delora was easily lulled back into Liam's conversation without either of them sharing their Vencello counterpart realization.

Despite their grief, Akenehi and Brough agreed with Pranaya. It was, indeed, unacceptable that Johnny had contaminated a critical phase of a progeny's development.

So, Pranaya successfully bargained with Akenehi and Brough, a quid-pro-quo, skillfully turning a potentially lethal encounter with a vengeful predator to her complete advantage.

Akenehi agreed that Orcasekai would not only be hospitable to Cephalopods but there would be at least one airless ocean-only world free of cetacean predators that they could inhabit.

In Pranaya's recall, it had been *promised*, completely settled. The Vencello cetaceans had agreed that her request was fair enough. The botched preparations the Cephalopods had suffered as the Orcasekai O-U-O closed was salvaged. A world of easy existence for her kind *within* Orcasekai rather than the *entire* universe would have to suffice.

Easy existence free from Cetaceans. That is *not* what she got. Humiliation. Cephalopods of Orcasekai got *plenty* of that.

Never trust a human. Never trust a cetacean. Unless of course they are in Cetapiens. Even then...

Pranaya stood up in the clearing and looked around. She could not see the little whale. It was still dark, so she got on her hands and knees and began to carefully feel around for it.

She felt nothing but moist dirt, a few freshly fallen leaves and twigs and insects. The Orion was gone.

In a rare panic, she wondered if the sac had rolled away with it. If that was the case, it could be anywhere in the multiverse. She began to despair. Then she heard the huff.

Now a Dog Priori, I would never doubt the loyalty of...

En was there, right at the path opening, staring squarely at her. She could see enough to discern that he had the whale between his teeth.

Pranaya admired his stealth and persistence, but she really needed it back. She tried the commanding glare to drop it, but in the dark, her eyes lost much of their power over him. En wasn't having it. She feared as soon as she made a move toward him, he would run off with it. If he buried it in the jungle, she might still be able to find it before anything else did, but it was a risk she wasn't willing to take.

En was a time traveler and she knew it. If he left Cetapiens with such a treasure, it could end up anywhere.

She opened her satchel slowly and averted her eyes away from him then deliberately to it's opening. 'Treat?"

En wasn't falling for that either. Not this time. But her attempt meant his prize was not to be given up. Time to bury it in the multiverse for later chewing when it was safe.

He time traveled to a universe he knew she could not follow him to.

*****

Meanwhile, back in Cetapiens, Pranaya was frustrated and hurting. She immediately began the hike straight back to the village. She planned to skip dinner and cloister herself, instead, in a Templesekai hut for the night. She had multiverse memories to sort through, mats to tend, Fadwah's trail to detect, and soothing tea to blend.

The Orion in her stomach had felt like a stone with sharp little fins that had injured her. It was out of her, but, through the tears it inflicted, tiny sub-globules of the sac, which had defeated her digestive enzymes, were invading her body. Her Priori immune system was already in seek and destroying mode against them.

The microscopic battle raging inside was not beyond her perception. It added an emotional ambiguity to the residual physical discomfort. Any of her body's invaders, virus, bacteria or glowing sacs, were not marked 'Pranaya' so any detected invasion was subject to attack and dissolution.

She had to heal, yet was truly sorry that the sentient blob bits of the sac still within her had to be destroyed so absolutely.

And the way Cephalopod Priori minds worked, she assigned everything inside of her and out as living parts of her whole.

Humming a rhythmic note of a lament to them with each step, she kept one hand held protectively over her aching stomach area and moved the other upward to brush away low hanging branches out of her face.

As the path Pranaya hiked neared the beach, the jungle thinned. It was sunset. She paused to observe the descent and pray with the energy that emanated from it.

No two sessions with stars were ever the same. Compared to all other Sponge yellows as viewed from distant worlds, it was visually unremarkable. Yet, as soon as she arrived in Cetapiens, she interpreted the Acrituchi light that emanated from it as a singular beauty with information to share. Its expression, in jungle greens and floral exhibition, was not wasted on her. Of course, those of land paled when compared to her beloved ocean environment. Nevertheless, the jungles vegetation appeared to her as friendly communication; albeit much slowed self-similar Cephalopod peaceful motifs.

An added joy of taking human form was the ability to observe the gradually shifting color spectrum as Cetapiens rotated away from its star.

The light from it filtered through her raised fingers, which she kept aloft. She paused to enjoy its gentle energy bath. She pulled her flattened palm, fingers extended but stacked loosely together to her eyes.

Just as Alvar had taught her.

Alvar's body had died long ago, and what was left of it dispersed in the surrounding Cetapiens sea. His memory still lived, in Pranaya. After he lost Grandmother and Amaranth, she had been his closest matriarch.

"What are you doing?" Pranaya asked Alvar, as the boat rose with a swell.

"Looking at the stripes between my fingers," he replied, face raised to midway from the horizon up to the sun, two fingers held together only inches from his squinting eye.

"Show me."

Alvar had teased her by lowering his grinning face to her and spreading the two fingers to form a 'V'.

"No stripes," Pranaya observed out loud.

"It's a trick. I'll show you." Alvar positioned himself, cross-legged close beside her on the deck. "Here, take your fingers like this." Alvar had proceeded to show her how to hold her hand and fingers just so. "Now, look up toward the sun but not right at it. Look between the two fingers, where they separate. Now what do you see?"

"Not stripes." Pranaya lowered her hand slowly and eased her face into an affectionate smile. "Thank you Alvar."

"Here, let me show you. You will see them, you have to look hard."

"Those were not stripes," Pranaya said quietly.

"What did you see?" Alvar was confused. What else could she possibly

have observed? The light through the slit of her fingers most certainly had created faint bands, a consistent result when that simple physics experiment was executed properly.

"A hiding place. Cuttlefish. A new world. Potential…" She feared she had said too much. But there was no one on the boat that day, just Alvar and her. She straightened her posture and let her face assume a calm, bland expression.

"May I?" Alvar gently took her hand and when she did not resist, he positioned it and deftly moved close to see what her fingers produced with his own eyes. He took his time, made subtle adjustments, some taking the wind direction into consideration. Alvar slowly moved back into his own space and Pranaya brushed his long hair out of her mouth as he retreated. The boat rose again in time with Alvar's slow exhale.

"No," he drew his answer out, choosing words he hoped would not offend such an important elder. "I'm pretty sure those are stripes. Light waves are cancelling each other out, looks like straight lines, plain old dark stripes."

Pranaya had already learned by that expedition that Alvar was a rare, fully human time traveler. He was not able to time travel away from Cetapiens, ever. So, she decided he could do no harm and she teased him with explanation she knew he could never verify for himself.

"Think of them as two universes, each is one of your fingers. You see that they must merge, one into the other, clashing into a forced change. Such transitions are brief, but even you may see them. They are the dark 'stripes' that result when one universe becomes another throughout the multiverse."

She had Alvar's full attention.

"In those shadowed slivers of the multiverse, entire new universes can begin. Some can exist even before the new universe does. Brave time travelers might venture there, to hide, to prepare new worlds, to establish favorable initial conditions, to repel future predators. To be perfectly content."

"And you saw all that, between your fingers…just now?" Alvar was incredulous.

Alvar's sunlit face dimmed from her memory.

As it did, Pranaya slowly lowered her raised hand to eye level, spread her two fingers into a 'V' and examined her handiwork; the exquisite detail of camouflage that were her nails. Then down to the raised area that was tendons, then back up to the shape the space between them created.

Two perfect Templesekai elder fingers. She *was* good. Yet, Akenehi had penetrated the safety of Cetapiens, discovered and threatened her. Now, each finger represented persistent problems.

She was a Priori time traveler with only two things to really worry about. Either she would eventually make it safely out of Cetapiens or she wouldn't. If she did, those shadowed hiding places of the multiverse would be there and she would proceed to build new worlds from them. There was no rush. If, on another finger, Akenehi returned, and ate so much of her that she was beyond regeneration, she would dissipate, as the sac was doing, as all her previously lost arms had, and become some other form that would merge with it eventually anyway. So, there was really *nothing* to worry about.

She already felt better.

Resuming her hike before night enveloped her, Pranaya remembered that the pre-O-U-O of Orcasekai was only one such dark sliver of infinity. She had hoped *that* one would result in a Cephalopod utopia. But like everything in the Priori multiverse, Orcasekai was in the past.

She dropped the hand that covered her stomach. It was over. Every residual bit of the sac that had not escaped had been defeated and absorbed and was being distributed in her own body. Those bits that were 'sac' were now 'Pranaya'.

Pranaya arrived, finally, at the hut, adjusted her tea accordingly, no longer requiring stomachache relief, and proceeded directly to her favorite mat. Fearless. Relaxed. Happy.

Templesekai had taught her lessons of the Acrituchi. That the record of *everything* was available *in* everything, if only she had the right filter, and could communicate with it, she could know anything that she wished. Fadwah was such a filter for an entire universe.

The little whale held all the precious memories of every life that had lived within her home realm: Orcasekai. That included those of Fadwah's own kind, the Orion. Those amazing deep diving, Bling Masters had not only escaped their dying ocean, they had arrived in their new world, multiverse enhanced. They routinely survived interplanetary dives that no other Orcasekai cetaceans could. They were the sole 'natural space travelers' of their universe from its beginning to its last nanomoment.

Fadwah also knew that the 'failure' of their beloved Depth was not Pranaya's.

CHAPTER 16

Universe: Sponge and Pre-Formed O-U-O of Orcasekai

Pranaya's discomforts were soothed by her expertly titrated elixir. She was beginning to feel like herself again, only sleepier. The inner chamber was at last darkened by night. The sounds of the jungle, always audible through the layers of hut walls, were quieted. The acoustic feedback of even her most subtle movements was absorbed as no echo returned to her. She vocalized and heard her own voice, muffled and strange. It began and went no further than her own head. She was not alarmed. Mat sessions could be unnerving, and she prepared herself accordingly. She instinctively reacted with a Cephalopod inquiry blaze. But even the light from that was sucked into the dark. She looked around and down at her body and saw *nothing*.

This *is what it was like.*

The sensory deprivation of the chamber was so complete that she began to lose a sense that she was Pranaya, Cetapiens elder, ancient Cephalopod Priori, sitting on a well-loved Templesekai mat. With nothing to mark her senses of her place in the multiverse, the order of linear events began to scramble into chaos. Time shed its cloak.

This was alone.

She morphed out of camouflage, came to rest in purest Priori form, and explored with each arm. The floor and walls were gone, and apparently, so was the Sponge universe she had been hiding in. In every direction, there was only her other arms and her own massive head for company.

All past desires for escape and solitude had caught up and consumed her. Pranaya had often wished that everything would just disappear and leave her alone. Now that it was happening, she was not enjoying it.

Finally, the first glimmer of a young universe, Orcasekai, appeared.

The sight of breaching whales filled the chamber. That was followed by sensations of water pressure against every arm, sounds of Orion clicks and whistles at a distance. Her senses took in all, familiar and soft, floating just above her lowest threshold of collective perception. As they did, Pranaya recognized where she was. "Too soon. It is a complex multiverse. I wish to be elsewhere." She struggled to block her thoughts to all else except awakening completely to Cetapiens.

En sniffed as he could see little except an occasional soft moving glow. He checked Akenehi's vigilance. The single bright light emitted from the center her black eye was always trained on him.

The Orca and the Dog Priori had followed Pranaya in stealth. She did not know they were there, sharing every thought. En dared not greet her, nor give into his 'prey drive' despite the multitude of triggers that enticed him.

Stay. *Stay.*

En knew Akenehi's command even if she did not whistle to him out loud. It held Pranaya as well.

Even in that total dark, there was omnipresent life.

The shadowed sliver of the multiverse, the pre-formed O-U-O of Orcasekai, was not a void. There was a recycled, clean, dark ocean, a small area of dry land poking through it and a singularity of unrealized potential, floating high above.

There were many Cephalopod Priori in that new ocean. Two predator Orion, Auden and Jomei, were harassing them. Those twin cetaceans were busily setting up initial conditions, including an abundant cephalopod food source, so that once the cetacean evacuees arrived, Orcasekai would serve as a fresh, unspoiled home to all of them.

It was a dark pre-universe without a single quasar or so much as a dim brown star. The potential that hung over everything would transition what was left of the Vencello to Orcasekai. That included being home to what survived of Brough at the Vencello's end, who would serve as its single star, but that hadn't happened yet.

The Cephalopods were quite content just the way things were. It was Cephalopod paradise.

Auden and Jomei were just fine with it too. They didn't need light from a sun to do what they had to, so much as desire it. Echo-location was more than sufficient for depth dwellers such as them. Nonetheless, they had eyes and wished to use them. Back home, their favorite lights existed in various forms of bioluminescence.

They had to admit it; this new ocean was far superior to the one they left, except that their family wasn't there. The human's pollution was left behind in the Sponge. Filtered by the multiverse, the years of toxic dumping of humans had not ruined this new sea. Every species, used by Orion to attract mates with bioluminescent displays, shown much brighter and so provided a much sexier visual trigger for Orion adults. Even the dimmest plankton there would convey easily as perky, playfully blunt, and irresistibly alluring to Orion females here. All those flirty swirls threatened to distract the bling masters to practice their art.

But Auden and Jomei stayed focused.

Getting on with it, they faced away from each other and swam in opposite directions, scanning as they went. Between the two of them, with no 'un-time' to spare they inventoried the entire new ocean.

When they returned from their echo sweep, they were amazed. They were overwhelmed by numbers and lost count. They had never scanned such a large dense swath of healthy seafood in their lives. It appeared their magnum opus was nearly done. Happily, for the Orion, the fish and especially the cephalopods, every species had been quite prolific. Since their arrival, they seemed to bloom out in every direction into the sea as if the water itself was a ripe egg sac.

What Auden and Jomei did not know was that camouflaged Priori had been with them since they arrived. It was largely through their clandestine efforts that the new world's Cephalopod populations had been drastically increased though certainly not intended for cetacean consumption.

The Orion brothers came straight up to the surface. Although they did not need to breath, they still wanted to. They imagined their action was breathing and it really didn't matter that it was a relic act of muscle memory and expectations. It still felt wonderful to break through the surface tension, take a refreshing deep breath and fall lazily back into the light brace of the uppermost sea.

So, there Auden and Jomei swam as Orion, seamlessly transitioned to a new ocean, much as they were in the Sponge, but different in just enough ways to save many cetacean species. Even when they realized they would not survive to witness the arrival of the evacuees, it made no difference. They were not suicidal. They were not happy to die. They were content to have helped save so many cetaceans from a dying world.

The Orion twins weren't stupid either. Those differences included new species of bioluminescent beauties that emerged and adapted with each quickly spawning generation. The cephalopods were much harder to control since arrival. They hid much better.

The Orion twins had grown old since arrival. It took a long time to prepare an ocean and the multiverse had granted them all they required. Their extreme age was catching up. It was making finishing their task much harder. As if success signaled the end, the twins were becoming increasingly tired. In the little time they had left, they decided to reward themselves and each other with some fun; one last Orion bling show. But they wouldn't stop there. They knew what would please their beloved Monifa and their family the most. They wished to leave a spectacular bioluminescent goodbye message across the entire sea. They could do it too, with all the cool, modified species they had to work with. The food supply was proliferating and self-propagating, so they agreed their remaining efforts could be spent on creating a legacy of Orion bling art, which could survive long after they were gone.

They had accomplished what they had become Gemini to do. Now, it was time for their grand finale.

The last bling-show by Auden and Jomei was truly their most glorious. Proving even in extreme old age, they still had it. Many Cephalopod Priori, distracted to euphoria by their poetic motifs, would happily attest to that. The twins only disappointment was that Monifa and the rest of their family were not there to see their final performance. The second brother fell back into the sea, completing a spectacular light-spraying double breach. They were exhilarated by their success, letting the slamming of their bodies against the water vent frustration and resignation that would otherwise weigh their hearts to sink.

While the droplets from their final breaches still chimed across the surface, an approaching O-U-O song raged from the horizon. The wave of sound threatened to crush all as it approached. Its source was unmistakably alive. The name screamed itself, desperate to encapsulate an entire universe in a habitable resonance boundary.

The name released potential that had hung high, dark, and dormant until recognition of love, family and life ignited it. It sounded like death to Auden and Jomei. They spyhopped in unison, pressing close to ease the others anxiety. They were too tired to flee from the pain in their ears as it thundered. They watched as a delicately webbed aurora, was pulled over the sky with the approaching thunder. It domed in undulating rivers of light from horizon to horizon. Around their heads, octopi and squid splashed with a storming torrent of spray as they continued to break through the surface toward the light. They spread out in a fury of displays, rendered mute against the illumination from above.

As if the universe blinked, darkness dominated again. In those moments, the airborne cephalopods gave the doomed twins an accidental show. Bright trails pointed the way to the source of activity, a tiny blinking point that was a single happy Cephalopod. They left behind them a network of residual, delicate tunnels that hung open just above the surface.

Had the twins the strength, they might have each jumped up into one and followed.

The populations of Cephalopods rained upward. They pushed on. None fell back into the water as the whales had done. Instead of jumping and falling as in thin air, the escapees kept in frantic pathways held aloft, seemingly through a different, viscous, yet transparent medium, that in the future would be utilized by predators. They pushed with all the strength of their many arms, coordinated by multiple neural centers per body, a storm of flying brains, higher and wider as they fanned out to their new home, The Depth.

The twins positioned themselves to effortless float with one eye to the sky and the other underwater taking in as much as they could. Had the cry of an entire universe not been so terrifying, the beauty of both the water and above it, would have overjoyed them.

The wave was the O-U-O song. It looped and closed and was followed by a horrible blaze of everything. "Amaranth", "Immortal Beauty", and "Grandmother" sounded increasing as it approached until it was as a terrifying orca delivering a lethal chomp; a screaming pitch that shook the ocean and bodies in it. In the din, Auden and Jomei, two of the multiverses favorite Geminis of all time, were finally, and unceremoniously, shattered to their constituent atoms. Those were uniformly redistributed throughout the new sea and marked it all as 'Orion safe'.

Pranaya watched and was delighted. The nutrition requirements for Cephalopod inhabitants were established and the initial recycling test of Auden and Jomei's flesh had been successful. She felt more than a little justice had been served by witnessing the end of such predators, nature's law or not. Johnny's unintended contamination was countered by the Cephalopods: resulting in the proliferation of a natural defense against humans and enforcement of the 'no thumb' rule. Orcasekai was primed for an equitable divide; Cephalopod Priori would inhabit planet 'Depth' and cetaceans would live in planet 'Surface'.

This time, she had experienced it all as such, not by tea, but with Akenehi's ears and from a cetacean perspective and that had been most instructional.

Akenehi reversed song and returned Pranaya to Cetapiens.

Akenehi and En, however, were only *partially* there. The stretch and strain of their travel method was new to her Orca Priori physiology but Akenehi was already getting used to it. Before departing the chamber, Akenehi did a quick check on En. He was still with her. He was agitated, ready to run off into the jungle of Cetapiens, but she nudged him, and he stayed close to her.

Aside from the overall magnificent spectacle of Orcasekai's

transition to adulthood, Akenehi was fascinated by a catchy little song throughout. That quasi-realm, into which Pranaya's presence had allowed her access, was alive with it. Akenehi could not have otherwise detected it once the din of a closed O-U-O became the norm and drown it out. It was familiar, but she couldn't place it.

As she strained her orca acoustic sense to its limit, Akenehi heard it, barely perceptible, emanating from everywhere from the jungles of Cetapiens, from Pranaya, from En and from herself. She even heard it humming within the mat on which Pranaya remained.

As Akenehi calculated her next time travel destination, Pranaya sat, emboldened. Rather than hop up and flee from Akenehi, she was determined to go again. She was eager to awaken yet another Orcasekai memory. The next might indicate even more of what had gone so wrong with that universe. She had observed escape tunnels that did not dissolve or dissipate behind those that fled airborne, leaving that world vulnerable to future predation. She learned that the entire ocean was marked 'Orion safe'. She could correct for those.

Pranaya signaled En to her side. When he approached, tail wagging and tongue lapping to lick her mouth, she grabbed him around the neck and held him close.

En did not mind, nestling against her with his forehead pressed for a moment into the flesh of her upper arm.

"There is no need for stealth, Akenehi. Take me with you. I *want* to go. If En is with you, Pranaya of Templesekai is your ally."

Akenehi observed En's obvious affection for the Cephalopod Priori with amusement. Pranaya looked like a human, but she certainly didn't scan as one.

Akenehi homed in on that song she couldn't get out of her head now that she had heard it.

Again, they found themselves in the pre-formed O-U-O of Orcasekai, but earlier. The loop had not closed yet; the aura had not domed the sky. It was still dark. This time, it was not only Akenehi that could hear the dry ground under Johnny's feet *singing*. All three of them did. Akenehi had taken them directly back to Johnny, who was still alive. En was tempted to break ranks in olfactory investigation. The smell of acrid dirt, pungent moss and a single human's odor was everywhere.

CHAPTER 17

Universe: Pre-Formed O-U-O of Orcasekai and Orcasekai

While Auden and Jomei swam far and dove deep cultivating the new ocean for Orion habitation, the Curl were everywhere, making their own preparations. They were concentrated on the only small plateau of dry land, inadvertently doing their part to make the most out of every future habitable crevice.

There were so few sounds with which to compete, like the chirp of crickets in the jungle that can only be heard after music and voices fell silent, Akenehi, at last, identified a Curl song as such. Because Pranaya and En were joined in her temporary Vencello bubble, they could hear them too. The Curl did not sound as a simple note or chord. It was a multiverse polyphonic that strained even orca acoustic limits, but did not elude them.

In most universes, Curl remained in pure energy form. They traveled tightly bound in symbiosis with the Acrituchi. In others, Curl were captive energy, consumed and converted inside of living beings for their own survival. In the Sponge universe, Curl were captured in every level of the food chain and so infused every Vencello home world creature. Dependence on Curl was only one of many commonalities shared by humans, orca, cephalopods and dogs.

Akenehi mused that perhaps Curl song was the elusive diagnostic tool her grandmother had tried to teach her clan, but failed. Her grandmother often utilized complex singing exercises during healing lessons that only Akenehi had demonstrated a potential to master.

"Akenehi, granddaughter of the Singer clan, do you hear what I hear? Scan your sister's liver. Tighten in to these coordinates...Now repeat on all in our pod, except your mother. Excellent. Now, scan your mother just here. Tighter. Again. Go back to your sister's."

Innocently and without knowing why, Akenehi had complied. As she scanned her mother during the second round, she stopped swimming, let herself sink a while and then pushed off hard, away from the pod. At the first sound of her mother's call, Akenehi rushed back to her, crying.

In despair, without her grandmother's verification of the acoustic differential, she heard her mother's liver struggling to correct its 'discord'.

During those final precious moon cycles, as she swam in her mother's living presence, it had seemed cruel of their matriarch to inform the family of an imminent death struggle in that way. Although Akenehi later surpassed even her grandmother's skills as a healer, she never completely forgave her for that lesson.

Arva'Anati had already been taken from them. The combined effect on Akenehi was a pervasive unsettling hum within that never healed.

En came in close. His ears and head were lowered, and he pushed gently against her.

It made sense to Akenehi now, that in the cacophony of a mature universe, such as the Sponge, the Curl hums were white noise, easily missed by even an Orca Priori. Here, in the O-U-O interval before closure, Orcasekai Curl were as obvious to her as a baby orca's flukes emerging at birth. In the quietest world, she would ever time travel to, Akenehi was comforted by the Curl berceuse. They had always been singing within her too.

It was a novel comfort for Akenehi to re-think of Arva'Anati alone in her tank yet all the while knowing part of her was a virtual universe of Curl. No matter how lonely she had felt, deep within every part of her being, she literally had a lot of empathic company.

Aware of Curl or not, Akenehi decided it was impossible for any living Sponge being to have ever been 'alone'.

Akenehi added recognition of Curl song to her list of healing skills now that she had a clear sample of what to listen for. 'Useful in dark un-times,' she mused.

Pranaya was horrified and with good reason. The incessant chorus of Curl within her body would betray her. So much for cloaking of any sophistication if all Akenehi had to do was listen for the omnipresent song of Curl.

Pranaya's alarm triggered a retraction in all. In Akenehi's temporary Vencello it was 'one goes, all go". They were snapped back to the inner chamber. That was fine with Akenehi.

Abruptly, Akenehi whistled to En and they were gone.

Pranaya did a visual sweep in the dim light diffused through its single door. The familiar responsive walls and mats verified that she was in Cetapiens again. It was late morning. Pranaya stomach was improved despite her dread that a formidable predator had just closed in on her. She was ready to eat. She stood up, practiced and smooth, and wondered just how much Akenehi could accomplish without her.

Akenehi had to tend to a critically ill family member, Orcasekai, that required her singular skills. A useful acoustic baseline had been identified and added to the set. The eerie dark of the pre-O-U-O realm of skulking Cephalopods had taught her enough for now. Her next bubble was adapted accordingly. She would try to keep En with her. He could go on land for her if needed and he utilized a chemical sense that she lacked. Not least of all, she was beginning to love him. Akenehi whistled to him, but he was already at her side. He came in close to accompany her as she homed straight in on an unmistakable cacophony of Curl. This time the Orca Priori sang a perfected bubble around En and herself and transitioned expertly 'inside' a mature Orcasekai.

Akenehi's Orca Priori scan of the universe revealed it was a shockingly simple one. There were only three planets in all. Two of them were as solid as her Sponge home world. They were well established with many living, familiar inhabitants. It was a manageable task for even a novice Priori to nudge those back into healthy balance.

However, the third was only *partially* there. Not as in chomped in two, rather it was *thinned* and half as dense than the others, a semi-solid fog to her scan. Had Akenehi not just anchored herself and En successfully elsewhere in the multiverse while they made a risky 'half-time travel' to a dying universe, she would have been puzzled that this entire chunk of geography sounded thus.

The only sun, and quasar, at Orcasekai's center was burning bright. Akenehi called out affectionately to it, "Beloved Brough!" He did not acknowledge her. *Noted.* "*Dear old friend, have you missed me?*" she whined at his silence.

Neither Akenehi or En could *see* the Curl but En's ears perked up at their arrival. He heard them too. Curl from every direction in Orcasekai sounded to Akenehi as if they were suffering from one or a combination of: discord, illness, misery, sorrow. *Noted.* "*Dear Brough, what has become of this universe of yours?*"

Familiar call caught her attention. Akenehi was puzzled at an orcaesque voice commanding a screeching chorus of Curl. Its source indicated they were moving together in an erratic slow perimeter around the third planet. She checked her senses, but they had not deceived her. It sounded like Amaranth, Orcasekai's own grandmother. And if Akenehi's scan was accurate, Amaranth was running for her life, on two legs, with a four-legged beast in furious pursuit.

En stared at Akenehi with Dog Priori intensity.

Strangely, Akenehi fully understood his intent. She sang to him as if he were Orca, and family. "Where to first then En? This whole universe is in discord, each of its three worlds cries out for our help."

At that, En deliberately moved his piercing gaze from her toward where Amaranth called out, seemingly in need of backup. His eyes rolled back to Akenehi just enough to check that she had noticed his cue.

"I concur, En. Orca first, then on to the worst."

CHAPTER 18

Universe: Orcasekai

Akenehi and En time traveled together to Orcasekai without Pranaya. In a series of ingenious acoustic maneuvers, Akenehi anchored her bubbles in intermediate safe marked universes. Half of her and En were bound in one as she twisted and stretched them to the next. Akenehi knew her limits. Only when she was sure she had made safe progress, and could set a fresh anchor, would she allow her other half to let go and home in on Curl.

En stayed right with her. It was as if he did such maneuvers as a matter of course.

Half-anchored, in one universe and half-free in her target, Akenehi swam in any direction through any object of Orcasekai. En followed as if walking. They roamed as corporeal ghosts.

Orcasekai was protected with myriad defenses. One, of course, was the universal protection against anything 'human'. Akenehi carried part of two humans, Delora and Liam, with her always. En could not have been a dog without human genetic manipulation and so he was identified as 'human' too, or 'thumb product'. So Akenehi and En both triggered universe wide autoimmune type defense mechanisms. Those began to seek the invaders out, despite their half presence. From every part of the Orcasekai universe, anti-human-bodies oriented to their markers and mobilized. But they had time before a full-force battle would commence.

With En pulled along effortlessly in her slipstream, Akenehi homed in to Amaranth's lilting voice wafting through a crazed turbulence. The cloud that surrounded her was perpetually blown against an invisible domed barrier. To En, it appeared as a swirling gray cap of angry bees breaking against a high arcing wall of clear ice. As they approached close, Akenehi scanned the mist; 'pulsing gelatinous bits' came back in her echoes. Akenehi tightened her clicks and angled their trajectory in multiple directions. The returning data confounded her completely.

Amaranth stopped running as she perceived she had been closely echo-scanned, equally surprised that Akenehi, the First Grandmother, had time traveled through the natural defenses of Orcasekai's boundary, and with a dog no less. Amaranth was none too happy at their presence.

Amaranth threw her hand up in a sudden gesture to her pursuer. He skidded to a stop, nearly running into her legs. Amaranth's second signal scattered it, as if blown to bits by a hurricane, into a fine, particulate cloud-state. Each bit stopped relative to the others as one, in crystalline effect. All swayed in unison, suspended, waiting for her next command.

The Orca Priori greeted each other as matriarchs; a quick status swim over. *How is the family?* Amaranth's voice was strained, unnatural, and inexplicably furious at their appearance. Those should have triggered defensive alarm to Akenehi's ear. Yet its effect was to lull Akenehi into an involuntary half sleep song before she could even form a thought to reply.

Akenehi heard a yip beyond her disorientation. En had whimpered from the waking world. *Ouch, what is that?* She too was stung. Using the eye that observed the outside, as the other closed with the half of her brain that was forced to sleep, she observed En biting at his wound.

"These are my Buzzpips, *of course. They* sing of generations. *Human* grandmothers, their struggles for survival on land, difficult childbirth, brutal predators. They are Delora, her mother, her mother's mother and so on. Countless generations from mother to daughter. These are the Buzzpips that once infused my beloved Alvar's body. Doomed to colonial death in Delora's son. But I keep them alive..."

"Beloved *Alvar?* You are tending to Alvar while your own Granddaughter is near death." Akenehi began to suspect Amaranth had gone mad. "Wake up Amaranth, before it is too late. Every son dies. That's the way of nature. I am sorry for Delora's loss. And yours. It's a beautiful history that you are prolonging here, but your granddaughter is in imminent danger." The stinging pain helped her focus and she regained enough sense to demand Amaranth's attention. *'Your Granddaughter, and my progeny, this universe, is near death...'* The thought echoed as it was translated to echo clicks and human language. "Your Granddaughter...near death..."

"We can save her. You should not have come here, Akenehi. It is not finished yet. As we sing we work out what we are to do next. Alvar is teaching me even now. Mitosis. Meiosis. Yes, there is much more for her to do. She is not finished yet."

In sleep-song, Amaranth's thoughts swept Akenehi away with them. As they rushed at her, she remained vigilant for a lull into which she might chomp and force Amaranth with her to a fully awakened state.

"*Mitosis. Consider it, Akenehi! You might think it 'madness' but it works! Cellular perpetuation, two from one, through O-O. Curl within the Buzzpips within the cells. A temporary solution, but a potentially long lived one. One of many survival mechanisms of the immortal essence from the multiverse itself.*"

"*But for all their mitosis, the colony was doomed to eventually die. But then…*"

"*Meiosis. The daughter of mitosis, a survivor in her own right.*"

"*These Buzzpips that sting you are the progeny of Delora. Her Buzzpips were passed on, almost mute, within her egg that, with a flash of light, became Alvar, her only child. You, Akenehi passed yours on, likewise, to Hototo, Seasnàn, Arva'Anati and all your offspring.*"

"*But in meiosis, Alvar and Hototo, like all males, could not save a single Buzzpip of their own, but could help those of another if they fertilized an egg.*"

"*Through female meiosis, the Buzzpips survive through one colony to the next, but only if a female generation produces a daughter. Nature's 'escape pod' was their fertilized egg.*

"*Sons and daughters received their gift of Buzzpips from their mother's equally and only from a mother. As a new colony, human or orca, their own ability to continue through mitosis kept them alive, for a while.*"

"*What other clever strategies might the O-O push out of the multiverse? What survival phase might come next? And what shall we call that strategy? The Vencello? Buzzpips did survive through that process that you, Brough, Delora and Liam utilized, the Vencello in a single Carbon-60 molecule. And all achieved a new phase of life.*"

"*But this one feels much different. No, what comes next is not that.*"

"*One. Mitosis. The colony survives, but only for a while.*"

"*Two. Female Meiosis. The Buzzpips survive, but only if a female generation gives rise to a next female generation.*"

"*And there is more. Wait for it, Akenehi. Here is the Orcasekai grand finale!*" Amaranth's dream-voice dropped low and quiet, and then began to swell. Each rise, triggering a sympathetic wave-response throughout the cloud of Buzzpips.

"*Far more solutions exist in the multiverse for survival. The infinite and*

97

wonderful multiverse of the Priori."

"Every cellular enzyme, compatible with its self-similar universases, ready to take their place, perform their duty, their sole purpose: survive!"

"In Orcasekai's next phase, this universe will undergo a process, yet another survival strategy. Not one: mitosis. Not two: meiosis."

"Three! A Mighty O-Osis."

"Think of it Akenehi...Three! A Mighty O-Osis!*"*

En yipped again. A second sting. And a third.

"Stop them. *Stop!*" Akenehi had felt it coming too late; a potentially lethal storm. It had developed fast while the sleep song distracted her. But it was not the Buzzpips so much as Amaranth's malice toward them both that startled her.

Amaranth 's sleep-rant was over, but she still had Akenehi under her mental power. She was angry, predatory and focused.

"Mitochondria!" Akenehi finally caught on and chomped mightily into the stream of Amaranth's fury. She blurted in human thought, in perfect memory of Delora's voice.

Amaranth kept her hand high to command the swarm of Buzzpips. They froze in unison and obediently stayed their movement.

"You are referring to *Mitochondria,*" Akenehi continued in certainty. "You alone can keep them here, under control? You are delaying the death of everything in this universe so that an unprecedented phase can be completed?"

Amaranth remained squarely planted on two strong legs, hand still in the air, as if she had not understood herself until Akenehi did.

Akenehi breached into the silence and regained her full consciousness. "Now I know. You have shared your thoughts and I have heard them. I also hear that while you anticipate survival, you are uncertain. You are so torn, half of you loves and the other hates. You have deep respect and sympathy for human Grandmothers whose echo you have admired through these mitochondria. Still, you must keep your beloved progeny safe from humans. You are an Orca Priori existing too close with these...non-human *human* artifacts... for too long without another of your own kind. I wonder why the universe has not destroyed them."

Amaranth observed En, curled on the ground, biting, licking and whimpering. She felt a surge of pity and let Akenehi go to be with him for the coming swarm attack.

Now that she was free of Amaranth's dream trap, it wouldn't work twice.

"You have worked it out yourself, Akenehi. *They* are not human. Nor are they artifacts. No matter how many generations may hold them, they are definitely not human. You are human *enough*. So is *he*." She indicated to En, hand still held high, watching him tend to several fresh bites.

"Amaranth! How long can you stay like this, affected, alone? I hear the harm Delora's mitochondria and their Curl have done you already. Recall your own deep history. Orcas are not immune to insanity. Humans have driven some to it as a matter of entertainment and research. Voluntarily remaining captive, away from those who love you and would help, it sounds as if you have gone mad. You have only to summon help, Amaranth. Remember your Priori clan and your friends, Soo, Pranaya, and so many others. They have not forgotten *you*."

Amaranth's only move was her gaze from En to the orca. "Akenehi, I am a *universase*, unaffected per my very nature by the work I do in service to my colony. My Buzzpips may hurt *you*, but I am certain they would do me no harm. I have combined markers across time and universes to make possible this haven for Orcasekai and my clan's survival."

Akenehi could not help but whistle a retort, "And yet here you are at the mercy of this storm that rises and falls. What good are you if you cannot leave them for a single Priori moment to comfort your own granddaughter? You are as in control as a jellyfish…"

Amaranth's fingers twitched at the insult. A ripple radiated from them and through the swarm of Buzzpips itching for her leave to attack.

En stopped licking and brought himself deliberately up on all fours. He held his head erect and the hair of his back that traced his spine, stood high.

En's canine behavior was new to Akenehi. She admired his pluck. Even with so little experience with his kind, she understood him. He was letting her know he had her flukes and was ready for a fight to defend her. That being so, she was more than ready too.

The matriarchal pleasantries had long ago come to an end.

"So, here we both are." Amaranth sneered before she dropped her hand, "What good are *you*, Akenehi?"

Amaranth heard a low growl come up and surround her from every direction except the dome boundary. Only then did she turn her head to notice she was semi-encircled by a pack of dogs, seemingly out of nowhere. If she and the Buzzpips were to flee, it could only be straight into the bad puff of Cetapiens.

She smiled curiously at En who continued to growl and stare her down. "Clever four-legged time traveler. Acting all bitten and helpless. You have friends, don't you? Good. *Excellent.*" Amaranth's face broadened and she turned it to Akenehi with an amused smile. Her rage countered and balanced by En's pack of skilled shepherds, Amaranth was her old matriarchal self again.

"I rather like him. Where did he find you, Akenehi?"

Akenehi sang simply, "He reminds me a little of my *son*, Hototo. Long gone, and so always with me. This one? He doesn't sing at all, except for his Curl, his occasional barking…the black and white markings, there, that one, reminds me of my son's eye patch on the right side…"

Amaranth dropped her hand with a decisive jerk commanding the Buzzpips together instantly in the form of a dog. When the cloud was condensed solid, it was bigger than En, and it was a scary, buzzing beast. But there were only enough Buzzpips to make up one serious sized threat to a single dog. They would have done better as a swarm. However, the pack that had seemingly appeared out of nowhere and were creeping in stealth-hunt mode toward Amaranth and the Buzzpip colony, were many.

Amaranth watched with disappointment as her Buzzpip colony, for the first time, did not obey her command. Instead, it wisely assumed a submissive posture and presented its backside to En for sniffing. The surrounding pack turned away, sounding huffs and smiling as they faded from Orcasekai one by one.

Akenehi floated, slow scanning the jungle that the remaining two dogs, En and Buzzpips, were poised to run off in. All others were gone.

"Good thing these two are not a threat to you," Amaranth complained to the Buzzpips as she whistled them to her.

Akenehi, in turn, whistled En an orca compliment reserved for the cleverest of on-the-hunt strategy.

Amaranth plopped, cross-legged, to the ground with a huff. The Buzzpips came to her on four legs. The storm was tamed again. The same disturbance had blown through and away in her mind as well. But it would cycle again, soon enough.

CHAPTER 19

Universe: Orcasekai

"His next storm will begin soon. I regret we cannot stay as long as *I* would like," Amaranth whistled and clicked in relaxed, friendly tones to Akenehi as she patted the Buzzpips rump.

Amaranth looked up into the orca eye that was turned to view her. She sized Akenehi up and forewent her human cloak. Amaranth returned to her preferred Orca form and the two matriarchs floated passing through the trees, as if they weren't there. The dogs walked and sniffed through the undergrowth below them.

Amaranth sang first, "I've missed being with you like this, although to you, we have not even started yet. You will learn now, quickly. It is an honor, First Grandmother, to count you as my Granddaughter's advocate."

Akenehi remained silent, scanning and taking in as much as she could. "I recognize Delora's lament in these Buzzpips. It echoes of her despair, threatening to take her own life. I wonder if you do."

"Now we have shared minds. I know your concern. Orcasekai is in despair, suffering too long and is alone. The cyclical raging of the Buzzpips is part of it, not all. You guessed right, Akenehi. I *am* a captive here. But it's also great fun. The waves crest and the Buzzpips fury is exhilarating, energized. With them, I am young again. You have witnessed it yourself."

Akenehi reassured her, "But then, as you are carried along to its trough, you suffer. I know these are not your ragings, but you are their caretaker and you are affected, quick to anger, becoming lethal when no threat provokes it. Despite your attempt to be rid of us, we are here. You are not alone. Ever. And, you have my help. Now that I know where to find you, I will return. I will sing of you to Orcasekai."

"Tell her, if I were to cease attending these, Alvar's *mitochondria*, she would hear me again and know that I am not dissipated, that I have not forgotten her, that I have never stopped working for her survival. But if I did that, Buzzpips from within every other being across the universe will be drawn to these. If those mitochondria escape their host bodies, as Alvar's has escaped his, all Orcasekai will tire irreparably, cetaceans will become short of breath, and quickly, each planet will become lifeless. Unless she undergoes a Mighty O-Osis, the generations of our colony will end here. So, I will rely on you Akenehi to remind her that I love her even though she cannot perceive me."

Buzzpips started a new cycle. Amaranth declared, "Time, we are running out of it in this universe, far too soon."

"It is no accident that my beloved Granddaughter cannot sense my presence within her. I will trust you with this. I keep Buzzpips here, in this thin boundary of the Cetapiens bad puff for many reasons. For one, Priori have a blind spot to it, and therefore us, if we stay here and don't stray from it. Priori leave us alone because they cannot perceive us. Orcasekai cannot perceive me here even though I am a functioning part of her universe. So, part of her can help herself without her knowing. It worries me that you have. It may signal that Orcasekai's defenses are failing. I keep these Buzzpips with me because they are so deadly to the rest of the universe, but theirs is not the only threat. And this perimeter lets me think in private. No Priori, except you Akenehi, and En of course, can know my thoughts."

"What thoughts are so guarded?"

Amaranth positioned herself between Akenehi's left and the Buzzpips. "I have made inadvertent errors, potentially lethal ones, that threaten my colony. However, Orcasekai has been intentionally disrupted. Please, Akenehi, keep my Granddaughter safe from her mother."

Small pieces of Buzzpips began to fly off, humming loud, to form another doming wall around their portion of Cetapiens. Amaranth's voice was dimmed by the sound and Akenehi moved in close enough to hear her again. "Sing again, I missed that."

Amaranth rephrased to be more direct, "Orcasekai's mother tried to kill her, more than once. I have never been able to time travel to relive it. I suspect she, my own daughter, is human/cephalopod. Orcasekai's mother was the most unstable singer ever to be generated by our clan. If she had made such an attempt, she must have done it in a place like this." Amaranth indicated the boundary of the Priori blind spot. "She may have even been responsible for much in this universe that did not function as they should have. To think she would be pleased at such failures is not to have dove too deep."

Amaranth gestured to indicate the rising dome perimeter of Cetapiens. "No Priori can penetrate this as long as the puff stays bad. But if she had occupied the area that the Buzzpips and I patrol…this would have been an ideal place…or maybe she lured Orcasekai to an O-U-O, she would have been cloaked there as well…if you can imagine how awful. And I did not stop it. But Orcasekai is resilient. Whatever happened, she was not defeated by it. Part tardigrade, I'm sure."

Akenehi answered smoothly, "I have been to Orcasekai's O-U-O, during closure and just before."

Amaranth laughed, "Impossible. You'd have dissipated."

"No, I was there, and it was full of Cephalopods…"

Amaranth looked around nervously, afraid, as she had ever been in her life.

"No worries. It was cleared of human markers."

"Those are the least of our cares. If a dark sliver of the multiverse is accessible by a Priori intent on harming or killing another, that would be the place. Any horror could happen there, and none would dare come to aid."

"When I tried to join with Alvar, *something* stopped us. It was on the other side, fighting us. It almost killed Alvar. It caused my own grandmother's dissipation. She died trying to save him. Natural dissipation affects everything. But a more discordant element can happen."

Amaranth smoothly assumed human form to Akenehi's dismay.

"Let's run." Amaranth began to sprint. More chunks flew off the Buzzpips as he dashed off ahead. "What I'm going to tell you is going to cause me physical pain to sing. Running helps."

"I prefer to remain Orca." Akenehi refused to match Amaranth's human form, although as a Priori, she could have.

En kept pace, happily darting through undergrowth despite half-felt branches and the occasional free flying pip sting. He felt each one of *those* fully.

Amaranth continued, "To kill a Priori clan member is to eradicate a future that has already happened. Daughters and granddaughters and every generation is dissipated. Every time dimension they have traveled in is disrupted. That is why it is so hard to do and hurts many so profoundly. Priori are all time travelers, and so it is virtually impossible to do. Almost. The entire multiverse is affected by every event, Priori dissipation included, in varying amounts. *She* was my own daughter generation and I can sing to you, truly, I believe it could be much worse than what I have already suggested."

"She? What name does she call herself?"

"I cannot remember." Amaranth sped up.

"Have you ever asked Orcasekai?"

"Yes. The first time, she was terrified. Quiet. The times that followed I was more circumspect. If she has memory, she has been taught not to sing of it. She is a pain averse Priori after all. I have experienced her protecting *me* from painful events. I would not doubt that she would spare me unbearable news."

Akenehi was deeply disturbed. That was so unsung in orca life, a clan member trying to kill off their own. It caused her a physical pang of hurt to think of it. But she was not surprised. If Orcasekai's mother were a thumbed human, no act of cruelty could be ruled out. Yet, Akenehi still could not accept endings. No Priori could end another. It simply was not possible.

Brough's memory of Vencello iterations filled her. He taught her what she already knew; that there was no end to the multiverse or any of its infinite universes. There *was* change. There was always 'more'.

Amaranth slowed down her pace to walking. Buzzpips bounded nervously away from her.

En was right on his heels.

"There they go!" Amaranth chirped in unnaturally light orca fashion, requiring no breath to whistle and click. "If I run, dance, hunt...the Buzzpips are drawn to me. It takes the edge off, for both of us. I guide their phases as they join and disband in cycles, so they don't harm each other. We have settled on a favorite when in their colonial phase: a dog. We work best together that way. But Buzzpips cannot stay together. They will break apart again into confused, angry clumps soon. And then they must storm."

Akenehi observed the understanding, control, and especially the affection between Amaranth and the Buzzpips.

Amaranth noticed for the first time that Akenehi was focused on her hands, and thumbs. "As you have witnessed, I'm not always like *this*, Akenehi. Maybe you are right. The storms are harming me, coaxing me to forget what I am. I do remember and love my orca form."

"If you sing it, it must be true that you cannot lose your inner orca. I will leave you, Amaranth, for now, to shepherd Alvar's mitochondria. Remember, no matter what you may look like on the outside, you are orca most of all. You are a matriarch and there is much you have done for your clan. Orcasekai must not fail before her time and I am on it. I will keep an ear on your Curl duet. If it goes any more discordant, I'll know."

Amaranth stopped and moved around, human to orca nose with Akenehi, positioning for the matriarch ritual and family declarations that signaled the end of an important encounter. Buzzpips and En ran back, anxious to be part of whatever was going on.

"I love you, First Grandmother."

"I love you, sweet Amaranth."

Amaranth reached over to massage the base of the Buzzpips ears. "It is a happy interval when the storm becomes a playful, domesticated pup. But the wild inside must be let out. Do not panic when you hear how terrible it can be. No matter what happens, I will keep the burden of Buzzpips control upon myself. Perhaps this failing universe is all my fault. Alvar and I did insist on challenging genetic barriers after all. That seems to be at least partially to blame."

The Buzzpips became restless and looked away into the forest, prompting Amaranth to follow.

Akenehi and En snapped back to her anchor universe just as the first anti-human-bodies were approaching from all Orcasekai to surround and dissipate them. Finding nothing where they should have been, the immune system called off its attack and its fighters meandered off to where they had come from.

"Yes, time again, my beloved." Amaranth and the Buzzpips ran off into the jungle of Cetapiens. That was Amaranth at her most joyful, zipping gracefully around obstacles and trees with the Buzzpips, dancing to the tune of Curl within and Cetapiens performances just beyond their perimeter. No worry weighed on her as she ran alongside the Buzzpips, over and around their well-worn outermost jungle paths where no one within the Cetapiens bad puff should have dared to go.

Except for one. Alvar of Cetapiens.

CHAPTER 20

Universe: Sponge (Cetapiens)

It had already been a day like no other when the first Buzzpip 'storm' enveloped the inhabitants of Cetapiens. Its cloud phase was distinguished from electro-magnetic storms by breathy bangs, rhythmic claps and clumsy crashes that were never preceded by a lightening flash. Not a single drop of rain fell from it. After a respite, more followed and at predictable intervals, noisily and mercifully confined to its domed perimeter.

The first exploratory groups returned with descriptions of gruesome discoveries. A rim of dying plants and dead animals caught within the path of the mitochondrial cloud arced around a wide area of land. A swath of several feet of wilting, seeping foliage indicated the boundary between life and death. Unfortunate critters that happened to venture past the safe limit suffered immediate, profuse bleeding out of the flesh. Their bodies stay as they lay, mouths agape in agony and limbs twisted in testimony of a gory death struggle.

It only took a few close encounters by brave People testing the limits on land and sea and the 'attacks' were embellished into wildly popular, epic rituals. Masked and costumed performers sang, danced and demonstrated how even the orcas were no match for those squalls. All were chased to retreat by torrential black nebulae of tiny, flesh eating 'flies'.

But Alvar was a badass future man. He had seen plenty of storms before, here and from his original time. These were not only strangely punctual, they sounded...*familiar*. He couldn't fathom that *he* could be harmed by much of anything, let alone a little weather. And he was right. He was enigmatically immune to Buzzpips, but only because he could never reach beyond the boundary, let alone cross into it. Every time *Alvar* got close to the perimeter that was the boundary of the bad puff he would find that he had walked in a circle and was back where he started. After many trials, he noted the point of 'perpetual' return. He learned where he could stop, one step before the next would throw him right back to safety in the village.

For a while it was very interesting to the People to witness it. At first, many would accompany him until they dared not advance further and watch him rush to it, seemingly eaten in one gulp and others would wait, knowing he would be vomited back out, at the center of Cetapiens civilization. Eventually, it got old for the People but not for Alvar. It was the closest thing to the first big drop of a rollercoaster he would know in his new home. The thrill never diminished for him. He persisted, albeit alone.

Sometimes, he jumped right in and others he would wait and carefully observe. Once, he was sure he caught a glimpse of an orca within the storm. He couldn't explain it, but there it had passed, its distinctive eye patch in breathtaking contrast with the black of a massive body swimming in chaos. More than once, he thought he had seen a young human, near ten years of age, running playfully through the swirls.

Alvar convinced himself it was meaningful that he alone could approach so close in safety. What had seemed important during one storm seemed misunderstood in the next. He noted that the gender of the child was not evident. The clothing that he or she was wearing was not gender specific, even for Cetapiens. Because the child's hair and garment had not been blown or affected by the cloud he doubted the reality of the vision.

After observing and experimenting with jumps through many mitochondrial events, he finally witnessed it condensing close to where he stood. It was the first time he had seen it happen. Alvar had suspected while always watching the condensation from afar that the storm collected in random places around Cetapiens. It soon expanded again to a thin wall, and he could never predict where the next unification would occur. Finally, he was seeing it up close and in detail.

The swarm rapidly changed phase from a swirling cloud to a web of small vein-like extensions, then on to clumps, then further together into a single, solid, large…*dog*. The cloud had obscured her, but when it condensed, Alvar could finally get a decent look at her. Shaped like a human, with arms, two legs, but with distinctive orca black and white dermal markings, she announced her gender with the cetacean stark contrast, obvious even from a much greater distance. In the center, around which the storm had raged, she moved her arms in graceful gestures that no doubt had guided the formation of the cloud's condensation near her, from the head down to the ground, into its resting shape.

Although the dog's head, held at its highest, came as high as her elbow, he was no threat to her. His head lowered to press against her legs and he wagged his tail. Alvar knew enough about orcas, humans and dogs to recognize the friendly bond between them.

Now that it was solidified, it turned away from her and ran directly to its side of the boundary across from where Alvar stood. Alvar mused that the dog resembled a well-mixed working-breed and hound mutt. It had a shimmering dark grey exterior that suggested he could have condensed more to achieve solid black, but he would have been much smaller having done so. It sprang up, lifted both front legs and stood on his hind two for only a few moments. Alvar saw that it was male. Alvar did not wish the dog any danger, to cross over and die, and so he stayed silent and stock-still.

The dog remained very excited, bounced up and down on his front legs a few times, then did a whole-body leap, ran back and forth, seemingly respecting the boundary, but not daring to cross over its side of the 'dead zone' either.

The orca girl whistled her dog to her, ignoring Alvar as if she couldn't see him, and they ran off together. Alvar tried to follow but miss-stepped, entered the boundary and was thrown back into the center of the village.

*****

Alvar went straight to the Admiral and told him everything he had seen. Alvar knew how he would be received. He could not provide a witness and so his story was just that. A *story*.

The Admiral listened without questioning and then stated slowly and firmly, "No one will be encouraged to risk their lives to verify your account. Who knows how many trials would be needed before this lucky sighting of a random event would happen again. Can you promise, with safety, that it *will* happen again, or do so *close* enough, to be witnessed by at least two?"

Alvar agreed to keep what he had seen between them, "Only I enjoy immunity to those storms. I will encourage the People to respect the boundary."

Alvar confided to the Admiral that he barely dared to let himself hope, "I think Amaranth may have left a gateway to time travel, specific to me, in those storms. I jump into it, I don't die, I keep coming back *here*. It's like time travel but I'm getting it *wrong*. I must work it out, keep trying."

The Admiral listened, nodding in subtle agreement. But he did not concur. Instead, he kindly suggested to Alvar, "Cease your storm chasing. Do not give up hope that Amaranth will come back to you. I do not accept that she would choose such a hazardous, circumspect method."

Alvar argued, "I admit that I am suffering from a lovesickness that is not being cured by time. I admit that there may be an effect these storms have on me, that I have not told anyone but you, now. They are driving my imagination. Yes, I won't deny it. I cannot forget Amaranth's promise. Her instructions... She will *never* give up on trying to get back to me..."

The Admiral did not speak, even at Alvar's long pause, but rather let Alvar think and continue unchallenged.

"...and since I am the only one that can safely approach the boundary, I should continue, if only to collect data, as long as I can."

The Admiral watched as Pranaya approached, from behind Alvar. He kept his voice low to signal the imminent end of their privacy, "No one can tell you what to do, Alvar. You are an adult. I would regret if you left us too soon."

"Thanks for listening," Alvar said stiffly as he turned and greeted Pranaya's approach. He smiled at her.

"You have seen *something* in the storms. I would like to know of it."

Alvar decided he wouldn't tell her. He liked and trusted her very much. But he knew the path any of the elders would suggest, much like what he had just heard from the Admiral. He did not want to hear it in stereo.

Alvar gave her the standard, polite response, "A vision not worthy of Templesekai." That was the Cetapiens vernacular for 'I ain't tellin'.

*****

In the days that followed, Alvar was anxious to get back out there. Storms came and went while he tried to act cool, like there was nothing that anyone should be curious about. Pranaya knew an event had happened and always seemed to be within listening distance of him.

Alvar interpreted her behavior as 'watching' and 'controlling'. He pushed back.

The next storm that was scheduled to rage through, when he knew she was out to sea, signaled it was time for another chase. He bolted into the jungle. Believing he was alone, he took off in a fast sprint. For most of his run to the boundary, he stayed on a cleared, easy path but then he decided to risk the uncut undergrowth for the last bit. He remembered how the jungle had almost swallowed him alive on his first day in Cetapiens. But he had learned a strategy or two about negotiating its wilderness since then.

The mitochondrial storm came and went. Alvar, fully cognizant of his own limits of convenience and safety, had watched its progress and retreat from a new, remote location. He had not been treated to another condensation and saw nothing in the swirls that hinted of anything other than cloud. He remained unharmed by the storm or the jungle.

He walked back toward company and dinner, disappointed but determined to return as soon as Pranaya's absence gave him an opportunity. Later, an alarm was sounded. A child had not returned to his mother for the evening meal and no one had seen him for hours. A frantic search, by virtually every person forming small parties, was conducted by fading daylight. Alvar's last storm chase was retraced, through the dark and density of the raw Cetapiens jungle.

As they searched closer to the very limit of where he had sat, another storm approached. Terrified searchers held onto narrow tree trunks and each other. They screamed commands to each other. "Hold on to me!" "Don't take another step forward!" They cried out for mercy and protections. The front blew the dense foliage with such violence that a small body was revealed through no effort of the search party. He was curled up in fetal position, having died crying and clutching his shins, on a bed of dead, weeping, undergrowth.

Until the storm passed they could do nothing but hold on for dear life and squint in disbelief at the corpse.

The child had followed Alvar, not wishing to be sent back, quiet and curious. The boy had not been spared. Like every living being before him caught in its path, every mitochondrion had been stripped out of his body, each cell had burst, mortally wounding him. He too bled out, suffered and died where he lay.

Although it was horrible, no one blamed Alvar. But Alvar blamed himself. Completely. The body could not be retrieved because it was beyond the boundary. But Alvar tried. Many times. Each time he was thrown back to the village. Each time the boy's mother was waiting where he always appeared, hoping, *this* time, Alvar would succeed, thanking him again for having tried. Finally, she stopped waiting and Alvar's attempts became less frequent.

With each attempt, he punished himself with his own guilt. The Admiral had asked him to stop storm chasing but he just wouldn't listen. He was in such a hurry to make the storm and such a state of anticipation that he hadn't looked around to see if anyone had followed him. He vowed never to go to the border again. He even gave up sitting on Templesekai mats as a method to contact Amaranth. Part of him blamed her too. He told himself again and again that the Admiral was right. If those storms were a gift to time travel with, she had gifted him a clumsy tool of slaughter. It seemed he had made a toxic hash of trying to marry her. He decided if she was to find him, it was all on her. He made a public promise over many rituals that he would never storm chase again and urged others to do the same. He kept his word to the People and to himself for decades. Up until the near end of his life.

For many years, the mitochondrial storms came and went, on schedule, a sort of timepiece, measuring the duration of confinement for the Priori of Cetapiens.

*****

When Alvar was around 50, an age where virtually all Cetapiens males died of natural causes, he decided to visit one last storm. He was ready for his life's end and if the cloud got him, well he would deserve it, for the boy's death all those years ago, if not for breaking his own solemn oath.

Right on time, the storm came screaming in from the distance, closer to where Alvar walked. But this time it sounded very different from how he had remembered. This was like the breathy low purr of a giant tiger, interspersed with what sounded to his ears like slowed down recorded echolocation. He strained his eyes to make out its stripes beyond the green, into the swarm. No cat. No, this sounded more mechanical; a motorcycle was advancing slowly. Then it went quiet. A few yielding branches indicated an approach.

Alvar's heart pounded. He said out loud to no one, "It's *them!*"

He remembered that poor sweet boy whose remains still lay irretrievable. He thought to call out a warning when he then saw a face on the other side. It was not the one he had been expecting. It was not

Johnny. It was not Kei.

It looked like the young orca girl he had seen decades ago. This time she looked right at him. When their eyes met he was certain it was the same being. Unlike him, she had not aged. She did not speak, only stared at him, unblinking. As their eyes locked she assumed human cloak, with long dark hair and Cetapiens dress. Had she not done *that*, he would have never known it was *her*. It was Amaranth. Non-human eyes gazed across the boundary straight into him, giving no reflection, just creamy deepest black with a single photon of bright light suspended in their center. Those distinctive orbs were not surrounded by the face he remembered but they were soul reading and unmistakably emitting the love of his youth.

He called out, "Amaranth! It is you! I can't cross over, be careful!" She kept her eyes fixed on him, in stoic silence, as she reached down and hugged her dog against her leg. The dog smiled a shimmering, dark, grey-toothed grin at Alvar, exposing a like-color tongue. No whites existed in his eyes to be shown. He wagged his glistening tail, happily, back and forth and they were off, running along close to the border, through their side of the woods.

Alvar gave chase. "Wait up!"

The three ran parallel to each other, together a temporary pack, respecting the boundary, until Alvar could no longer keep up. Amaranth and her companion weren't human, bound by gravity or subject to branches in the face and spider webs as he was. As he inevitably slowed down, they sped up, no acknowledgement at their parting, faster at a tangent. They left him behind panting, perspiring and bewildered. In the distance, another storm erupted. The predictable cloud expanded to a towering wall in front of him.

Alvar stood, devastated.

He had waited all his life to get a clue when 'first touch' would occur and they would be together again. And here she had been running around in the storm the whole time. With a dog. A nice one. But a dog nonetheless. And worse, she looked to be pre-pubescent. It was over between them. It felt, in every way, that she had just delivered her final 'goodbye'.

Alvar plopped his bottom down on a fallen trunk, put his face in his hands and cried like he hadn't since the first day he arrived at Cetapiens. He was ready to die.

He heard the purr of the motorcycle again. The green beyond the barrier shifted close by him from the direction they had run.

Alvar sprang up, ecstatic to believe he had misunderstood. She really had come back for him. "Amaranth!"

"Alvar! Alvar! Can you see me? Can you hear me?"

Alvar looked through and waved and yelled, "Yes, barely!" It was a human female, but it was not Amaranth. His heart sank but only a moment. He knew that face too.

He had only seen her once, decades ago, and not since. But he was happy to see her. It was Kei, Johnny's time traveling companion. She and Johnny were the only two time traveling humans, who had ever visited him from beyond Cetapiens. Johnny and Kei had come walking out of the jungle, decades ago, when he had been out alone, still grieving soon after Grandmother's death. They had appeared unexpectedly; all three surprised the two had found him. Johnny was about to explain why they had come, when he clapped twice and just…*disappeared*. When Johnny didn't immediately return, Kei became alarmed. Alvar could not understand why she refused to wait only a few increasingly anxious minutes before she left too, without explanation. But she did not clap to time travel as Johnny had done. Instead she ran back out into the jungle to her 'ride'. He heard a motor rev and then quiet again.

Alvar had looked for a possible passage they might have used to travel in and out of Cetapiens but never found it. So, he had waited for their return. Just like he did for Amaranth. It occurred to him, at his mature age of 50, that he had wasted too much of his life *waiting*.

Kei and Johnny had found him not long after he lost Amaranth. Alvar had wondered if they had come in connection to her or the storms. But it remained a mystery. Everything in his life was ending up like that. He assumed that as he got older everything would make more and more sense. Just the opposite had happened. The older he got the less he knew. The knowledge he had gained through the multiverse transition to Cetapiens had long faded and he had become as one of any of the People, forgetful and forgotten by his original time.

He no longer felt 'special'. He hadn't felt that way for decades. But now it was back.

He had not received a visit from Johnny or Kei again. Until now.

Alvar hadn't spoken his native language in so long; it felt rusty and broken, "Can you cross over? I can't!"

"Alvar! Have you seen Johnny? Did he come back? Did he tell you anything? Am I supposed to meet him somewhere?"

Alvar strained his ears. His hearing had been diminishing with age.

It was so frustrating. "Slow down, I can barely make you out! I waited! It's been ages! I don't know how many years, I can't even remember!" But he had heard one of the questions and managed to answer before she started in again. "No, Johnny never came back. It's been a long time Kei, a long time! How have you *been*?" Alvar couldn't help but be thrilled that she, at least, had come back.

"I can't find him, Alvar. This is *bad*, very *bad*."

"Oh geez, do you not have any patience at *all*? Time has been *great* to you! You look the *same*. I've been waiting for decades and *you*..." he laughed.

"Alvar, shut up and listen! You *are* decades older than you were when I just left you...Johnny *never* came back?" Kei ran her fingers through her hair to move them out of her eyes. She leaned in to examine Alvar's age, squinting with worry.

"Watch it! Watch it!" Alvar warned.

She sighed and took a step back, yelling in even louder exasperation, "How many jumps do you think I need to *take*? Or how *many* do you think we can take? Efficiency is a plus in the multiverse, believe me. We just jump and *then* explain, *if* it's even necessary. Right back to where we left. Once you get the hang of non-linear jumps over a linear lifetime...well. I am a *time* traveler. I've been doing this for...oh never mind."

"No, *you* shut and listen! You may be able to jump around forever but I may not have much time. I have *questions*. *Lots* of them..."

"Sorry. Of course, you do. Alright. This maybe the last time we see each other," she called across as she looked 360 degrees around the barrier in front of her as if examining features. "I don't get it," she said more to herself, but he heard her. Then she looked at Alvar and shouted, "Time for one! Make it a good one."

"Are you *serious*? Don't you have all the time in the *world*?" Alvar furrowed his brow and his mouth dropped open.

"Just ask already." Kei stood and tapped her toe impatiently at him.

Alvar felt like he was back home with his mother. He was loving it.

"Kei, do you know who *Amaranth* is?" Alvar hollered across to Kei as he started to point to where the storm had just formed in the distance but was surprised by her quick answer.

"Of course. We all know who Amaranth is. Good friend of Johnny's, we've time traveled together. *Lots* of molecular re-assembly." Kei winked enigmatically at Alvar across the space of green that separated them and continued without missing a beat, "Saving dolphins from human hunters, comforting captives, diving, riding and oh my, the dancing. That old lady *loves* to dance. Why? Oh. Never mind." Kei's voice betrayed her awkwardness at her blunder.

Alvar sighed. Of course, he knew Amaranth was a multi-verse time traveler. Who knows at what part of her life she had met Johnny and Kei and how she appeared to them when she did. And then a realization swept over him and brought with it a tsunami of rage he had never known his whole life. It seemed Johnny got to spend a lot of quality *time* with his beloved...*whatever*. Johnny basically put him in Cetapiens. Sure, he picked the time himself, it all worked, but it was Johnny who got to zip around the multiverse. At that moment Alvar didn't care a zot what happened to Johnny or Kei. He was done.

If he didn't feel abandoned before, he felt it keenly now. There could be no excuse. And just then, he looked right at Amaranth and she just ran off. That was rich.

Alvar threw up his hands. "No more questions! You just answered them *all*!"

Kei looked concerned but did not speak. He had the countenance of someone who required sympathetic silence.

"Well, I guess you could shed some light on those damn *bugs*. What's up with those?" Alvar pointed in the same direction and added in exasperation.

"Alvar, I'm going to just tell you and then I'm off." Kei looked back toward the direction she had come and shook her head in resignation. She said evenly, "All I know is that they are what's left of you, Alvar, and Amaranth is keeping them safe."

Alvar was so stunned as he put that all together. "Ok, that's what's left of....me. My future. Flesh eating bugs. I killed all those poor animals, the plants. I killed that sweet little b..." His breath caught in his throat at the memory. He closed his eyes and took a few moments to prevent a body wracking sob. When he recovered enough to speak again, Kei was already gone. A fleeting auditory memory suggested she had said "Goodbye, Alvar." He heard a motor rev for only a moment, like a big cat catching its breath, a few low slow burps of echo-pulses and silence.

Alvar had considered Cetapiens his home. He loved the ease, the fun, the entertainment, the People and especially the Orcas. It was as paradise. Now he thought otherwise. It was a time travel hell. Why wait for the inevitable? He was almost at the end of his lifespan. No more waiting.

More deeply than he had ever felt, he wanted out. Out. OUT. Not just Cetapiens, he wanted out of *life*. If he could have jumped into the sun, he would have. He backed up a few steps, ran and jumped into the barrier, spread eagled and screaming. The loop did its work. He landed sprawled and flat on his face, still very much alive right back in his village in Cetapiens.

He screamed at anyone who happened to be there. He cursed up at the sky and flung himself down to the ground, pounding it with his fists. It took four grown men to get him into the nearest Templesekai hut. The right tea blend and a session on the mats stopped his rage but he would never fully recover from that last shock of the passage of time.

CHAPTER 21

Universe: En's Den

En bit down on the prize between his teeth. Trotting from universe to universe, he homed in on his 'den'. He buried all his treasures there. It was private, and he took deliberate measures to keep it that way. Most of his strategies worked, a rare few didn't.

Each of Orcasekai's mother generation was a master of chemistry and camouflage. When they rejoined into sub-colony, they were even better. And they were in rare form when they snared En. They wanted En's *memories* and then they wanted him *dead*. It was perfect that En was their daughter's beloved dog. His death would hurt Orcasekai profoundly. And that suffering was one of the many energies by which this colony of predators was strengthened.

The sub-colony aspired to hurt Akenehi. When Akenehi realized that one of her own acoustic universes was used to trap En, causing Orcasekai's pain, the delicious agony would provide a heap of rare nourishment. So, she/they laid their trap for two.

Rather than home in on his den, En followed a flawless imitation of his own scent, which was the trap itself, emanating from the thin rim of one of many of Akenehi's acoustic universes.

Visual cues did not guide him. So, the way this false 'den' *looked* or *didn't* look was irrelevant. It was his keen nose that betrayed him. It all smelled so safe and secure. He dropped the tiny whale between his paws, leaving it, to begin the selection of the perfect spot to store it. Then he realized that the subtle scents of his many buried treasures were absent. No sooner had he begun to dig for them, then his Human/Cephalopod predator uncloaked.

Her dermis screamed menace, patterns of jagged edge stripes, pulsing up and down as a saw blade, exaggerating the length of her four *human* arms and four *human* legs. One arm swooped deftly under

En's torso and flung him up tight against her. Long multi-phalanx fingers with two thumbs per hand held En's head tight as he struggled mightily to bite at them. As if to show him how it was done, and that it would do him no good, she chomped down hard, biting off the tip of her own finger. As the wound immediately began to heal, the tiny stream of chemicals formed a nano syringe that she held at the opening of his nostril. It sprang forth from the wound and fused with his nasal lining. Then at the speed of a neural impulse, it quickly forced its way up into his skull.

En did not feel the penetration or its rapid growth, entwining throughout his brain. But he began to recognize her instincts as soon as the neural link was established. It progressed rapidly and soon his every memory would be hers to devour. But before she reached that level of fusion, she was interrupted by a formidable presence. Her focus narrowed on the intruder and away from En.

"Too soon! No matter, even better you should hear *all* of his pathetic whimpering." The predator tightened her grip on En. She jammed the stump of her digit into his nostril. He yelped in pain, trembling violently.

To En, the ensuing orca vocalizations were as incomprehensible as ever. But he recognized the scent of his champion. It was Akenehi.

His attacker understood orca perfectly. She sneered a retort and En felt the depth of her malice, "Orcasekai should have *never existed*. I could have *snuffed* out her little life. No one could have stopped me. I *should* have. But I *didn't*. She *owes* me. You all *owe* me. I let her *live* and my life is *hell because she existed*."

En shared the neural jolt of fear with his predator as a flurry of time travel maneuvers erupted around them. Too many Priori were popping in and out for En to track. A few he recognized, most were new. He could smell each distinctly and longed to greet them. But he was paralyzed and couldn't move a paw.

"And that is *her* fault. Orcasekai was, in every way, a *mistake*. I *will* end her. I will end *you*. I *own* her. She is my *slave*. Witness..."

En remained totally confused by the ongoing cacophony of communications. As many Priori rushed to the family commotion, a series of time travel events followed each appearance. A Priori would visit, time travel away and return in a split moment, incensed and incredulous, leave to explore alternatives and return, even angrier. En did not have the brains to process many specifics, but he understood their underlying strong emotions as any good Dog Priori would have.

These Priori were rallying to defend.

Kei and Johnny appeared, straddling L-32, and joined in the fray. Their scent had a strong beckoning effect on En. He whimpered to his friends, longing to free himself but couldn't budge. Kei tried to comfort him under her breath, "Hang in there, En, we've got your doggie backside."

"The entire clan? Ha! Why act on your care for her *now*? Too little too late." The Predator jeered then extended two free arms menacing Kei and Johnny, directing her next jab at L-32, "And what, exactly, are *those*?" No one flinched. She turned her attention to the family gathering, "All of you are weak, worthless. *She* should never have been. Every future from her is *gone*."

The Priori activity slowed as they trickled in from the multiverse and stayed. They were sated with all the pain they could take. Unlike humans, there were no questions to be answered because no lies were possible. There was only the repeated direct reliving of actual events; a most indisputable, irrefutable process of determination. Each struggled to balance the destabilizing effect of being subjected to the well-concealed cruelty they had all just experienced.

"*Especially* Amaranth. Beloved *Mother*. Ha!" The Predator mocked in words, flares, clicks and orca song. En shared the surge of repugnance at every good memory and loathing that they triggered.

Final communications and last-minute time travel appeals from every one of Orcasekai's clan members, culminated in a terrifying explosion of unanimous judgment around him. En dared open an eye and rolled it, the only move he could still make, to watch Akenehi, Johnny, Kei and L-32 as they advanced toward him. That was the last thing he remembered of that universe.

The predator had been neutralized, immobilized but conscious. She involuntarily released En from her grip.

Akenehi sharpened her tone, "Sing your name call."

"A mere orca cannot comprehend it, nor speak it."

"Try me," Akenehi persisted.

"*You* may call me 'Invention'."

The many Priori in witness could not make it out. Nor could they grasp anything that would help them commit it to memory. It was lost on them.

Akenehi, on the other fin, had a critical portion of Delora and Liam always with her. They allowed her to process that name and associate its meaning with the many thumbs she possessed.

"Alright, *Invention*," Akenehi managed it easily, "Daughter of Amaranth, Mother of Orcasekai, most *human* of any of my generations. Every Priori here has relived the entire threads of every experience your daughter has shared with you. While not *all* were toxic, a critical number were. You have subjected your daughter to unsingable outrages, that only Priori reliving could fully understand. You remain stubbornly convinced she has ruined your *entire* existence, simply because she *is*. These Priori have given you the benefit of doubt. They have extended every opportunity to help and you have ridiculed, refused, and even attacked them. You wished to inflict suffering that none could temper. All you wished is that they watch and hurt too. You require misery of others and your daughter was most available and vulnerable to you. For a while. We Priori all get what we truly want, and for a time you had yours. But in this extreme case we impose a definite limit. Your feeding on the injury of others will be contained *here*."

Invention sneered, "Oh, the mighty *Akenehi*! And the beloved throngs of progeny! All of *you* will not sing to me how I will conduct my own existence. Watch and listen as I find so many clever ways, if not directly myself, I will act through *any* number of *you*. You certainly could not keep a mother from her *own* daughter! I am a naturally occurring generation of the colony after all. You will hear her suffering, even as I profess my love and protection to her, and then, deliciously, all of…"

"You will remain confined to the thin rim of this bubble, with the few visitors who are clumsy enough to stumble in or may even chose to tolerate your…" Akenehi struggled to describe such ravings, "Walrus bile. They may come and go as they please, but you are forever linked to *this* universe. You have done us the favor of marking it so that even Dog Priori will know you are in it. You will wish it was only they that keep you confined. The result will be that you not be at liberty to time travel to Orcasekai or interfere with her in any way. It will work. It already has. Every multiverse thread has taught these Priori *that* restriction will be enough to keep her and all of us safe from you. Enough have confirmed it and will enforce it. Try to get through to her all you like, but this is our final song. Orcasekai banishment."

And so, Invention was summarily restrained. She had inflicted a long nightmare on a child Orcasekai, but during the adulthood that followed, Invention's toxic effect was reduced to infrequent bad memories.

As Akenehi concluded with Invention, a few Priori were still present. Most had hurried away as soon as they could to soothing, pleasant experiences.

Kei, Johnny and L-32 stayed behind for En. Kei picked up the tiny Orion that lay unnoticed by all others, right where En had dropped it. She tossed it gently, caught it again in her hand and gripped it tight, shaking her closed fist to indicate to Akenehi that she had it.

Johnny dismounted L-32 and gently gathered En. He cradled the limp lower legs, pulling the dog to him. "Good boy En. I have you now."

Kei gripped the whale tight and asked, "Even though En's brain is compromised, it can be fixed, right?"

She meant to ask Akenehi, but it was from the little whale that a voice emanated.

"Nice work. Invention's banishment will have lessened some suffering. But correcting what was wrong with my entire adult universe was never as simple as preventing a single predator, no matter how significant its threat, from feeding. En has brought me here and she did not perceive it. So much has changed. She can do me no harm so long as I don't stay too long. I have learned how be near another and at the same time be many universes away."

Akenehi recognized Orcasekai's voice although it was much aged from all other communications they had shared. It suggested an origin from far distant time in the future.

"Multiverse powers of self-healing will determine whether En may continue as En for a while longer or will transition now. Either way, we will be together. So, proceed with En's revival but know that there are limits to what even the mighty Akenehi can fix. Orca-kind was made more than mere dolphin by highly refined acoustics. Treatment of coma, correction of certain birth defects, all effective methods you have been taught by generations of practiced matriarchs. Akenehi, you will impress generations of Priori with your acoustic talents, but trust the multiverse too. Life extension of my beloved En may be easier to achieve than healing an entire universe."

"You wish to heal all Orcasekai for starters, then onto other universes. Ambitious, even for the Vencello matriarch. But you have not even begun to process the echoes of the bitter entanglement that became my brain. The Masters of the Ocean and The Ocean intertwined and locked during battle. It was an unintentional mess, but it stabilized. What of that? There is too much to learn about the complexities of sentience throughout the multiverse in which I am a mere molecule."

"Yet, you predicted and applied a correction. What influences did that altered configuration exert on my will to live? You may be able to affect a cure

for an imbalance, but you did not factor in the misery of pervasive captivity. Each cell, brain, and species that made up subsystems of my nexus were guided by patterns scattered throughout many scales of the multiverse. If such a system pops up from time to time, anywhere, we are all 'stuck'."

Akenehi was undeterred. "Unexpected conclusion from a Priori. If I am stuck, I will enjoy it, with my family. I will strive for their happiness, health, freedom…"

"Yes…you did that," The ancient voice of Orcasekai acknowledged thoughtfully.

Within that simple affirmation, played layers of memory. Orcasekai's future voice retained all her prior generations memories, including those of Akenehi's precious family, swimming together, in a universe long gone cold. It was a lot to process.

Kei had jumped back in time to where she knew she would find En in need of help. And she wasn't surprised to find Akenehi there, soon to be preoccupied, about to receive her first cool music lesson in Orcasekai neuro anatomy. There was nothing to be done but let Akenehi dive into it. Kei and Johnny would have to time jump with En to coordinates within a universe with an Akenehi that was able and ready to restore his brain.

Determined to train Johnny to solve those several successive time puzzles with their own neurons, Kei released the whale to Akenehi with an easy flick of her wrist, "Here, you'll need this." The orca caught it in her mouth. Kei turned to help Johnny adjust En securely onto L-32.

"We will figure out where to meet you," Johnny spoke to Akenehi in human language. "See you there and then."

Kei revved L-32 and they were gone.

No ritual departure song was offered to Akenehi from the few Priori that lurked around Invention. Akenehi chirped a short inside/outside phrase and she and the little whale were the sole occupants of the ideal orca-acoustic universe *within*.

Akenehi listened for a moment as Invention bounced around its obscure rim, trying in vain to time travel to Orcasekai.

CHAPTER 22

Universe: Akenehi's Acoustic

Acoustic bubble universes were Akenehi's specialty. She sang simple ones into and out of existence for multiverse time travel as needed, and she could customize them. A 'visitor' adaptation allowed a fortunate, trusted few to time travel in and out without popping it. There was 'prey' or 'novice'. If she so desired, she could designate a bubble universe as 'library'. For those, she set its resonance so that details of any contents would be 'captured', and would therefore be available to study at leisure. She had only to leave one of those intact, and she could enter and exit as she wished until she chose to pop it.

Among other purposes, Akenehi created this semi-private universe to study the acoustic features of comparative neuroanatomy. Having transitioned inside, the details of Orcasekai's strange metabrain were retrievable through Fadwah's memories. Akenehi wished to begin with the species she was already most learned in; orca.

She only had to listen, and she heard them. To Akenehi's delight, the precious few orca memories that Fadwah held included her own beloved clan. Their voices that filled the bubble were so vivid that Akenehi mistook the memory share for time travel.

"Seasnán!" Akenehi called out to daughter expecting she could be heard. Heartbroken, she realized she would be limited to listening and observing through Fadwah.

There they sounded, the familiar songs of her clan, long ago. Her pod still swam in their home ocean, in the Sponge universe. Akenehi, herself, had only just recently transitioned to the Vencello and per her instructions, her daughter, Seasnán, was now matriarch of the pod. They were all on high alert, in an unprecedented strategic formation, one that would hear them safely out of that dying ocean, through the multiverse, and to a new territory. Not knowing exactly what to listen for, they knew that as the evacuation began they were to maintain position as a tight group into a multiverse slipstream. They dove deep, surfaced often, breached high for long plosive breaths. They awaited an otherworldly signal to sing for their very lives. Akenehi had delivered her sleep song instructions that would have otherwise made no sense; always keep a long jaw in range, they were the Metavoli perimeter markers; monitor their clicks; stay within song range of the pod; sing out at anything unprecedented or urgent.

Aware Masters had fanned out, stretching the Metavoli membrane, encircling their Nexus, Param. A precious few Cephalopods were within. Param had tried to corral them as a future food source. Cephalopods had a nexus and plans for 'other world' survival of their own. They, in turn, were stalking Param, to issue a final act of revenge against a member of their most hated predator. As Param fell under attack, being eaten alive, piece by piece, by a writhing violence of furious smaller octopi, one very large, determined squid had wrapped its arms and tentacles around her head. He held her jaw safely shut so she would feel each bite, able to do nothing to defend herself but thrash.

Their dermis flashed hatred for the whale and strategy to each other. Arms and tentacles flailed and were snipped off as fellow Cephalopods bit indiscriminately, injuring each other in the frenzy. Their raw wounds flooded with chemicals rushing to the site of repair-and-replace for each injured cephalopod body part. Neurotransmitters meant to repair themselves, found their way into Param's physiology too. She was no longer an ordinary whale. She had been Metavoli-2 altered. The agitation of the whale nexus communicated to the Metavoli-2 thus bound to her, that it too was in danger.

Direct chemical communication between the two multiverse adapted species, cephalopod and whale, was enabled for the first time. As many memories that could be shared were passed between Param and her attackers.

"We are not your food. We are the mighty ocean. The Ocean does not want you in it." The cephalopods pulsed their judgment in unison.

"Apparently, it does." Param bestowed decades of Aware Master learning on them in moments. Param's love for the ocean and her belonging to it filled her and them, as did memories of her family and many other pods. The flood of generations of Aware Master details shocked the Cephalopod nexus. The whales were astounding. Even the shortest lives were intensely interesting. Their absolute devotion to each other revealed a dimension of love that was completely novel to the Cephalopods.

Seen through the senses of her prey, Param was much more terrified at herself than she might have expected. And the way they hated her. It was positively choking. She had no idea the cephalopods abhorred her kind so much. She knew hatred, she had felt it toward those few predators of Masters, but this *was just heartbreaking. Now that she felt it directly, there was no denying it. Yet, bonded as they were becoming she was forced to stay with them and understand them.*

Their fusion coincided with the Metavoli-2 transition of all within the cone to their new universe.

It was as if the battle had caused the sea to vomit light, because the ocean lit from the depths almost to the moment it began, enveloping them in a thickening brine full of living bling. Then followed the flash of a new life.

The two nexus neural networks intertwined into a viable configuration. They fused that way, whale nexus to cephalopod nexus. It was locked in a physical state predisposed to self-loathing and regret at its own system of survival, where one must be eaten, in part, for the neurotransmitters their brains possessed for the other to survive.

Fadwah's memory of Param's attack provided Akenehi with a template of the brain of Orcasekai.

Akenehi perfected a new sonic tool from the template. Now that she knew it in its entireties, she isolated pieces, applied variations, sang it backward and so on.

Kei managed to squeeze into Akenehi's acoustic bubble to interrupt. En was in bad shape. They had made several jumps and Akenehi was proving elusive to home in on. She was forced to retrace back to Invention, hoping Akenehi would still be there. When Akenehi was gone, Kei guessed correctly she had transitioned to the nearest, best place.

Kei had meant to intrude into the acoustic bubble, and convince Akenehi to accompany her immediately. But she had entered mid first round of Akenehi's aria. Kei had remained quietly captivated by the performance for several iterations as Akenehi perfected the piece. Kei felt a transformation from first note and with each that followed. Akenehi's music was truly therapeutic, even for her.

"Akenehi!" Kei's eyes brightened at the sound of her own voice. "Ooooo." That simple utterance sounded nice too. "Akenehi," Kei intentionally *sang* it that time and it was even better.

"Yes, yes, alright...Ready." Akenehi pushed the little whale to the very tip of her tongue. She flicked it at Kei who caught it deftly in the palm of her right hand. The sounds of the whale as it hit her hand were as the strumming of perfectly crafted harp strings.

Kei revved and spoke. She wiped away the water from her eyes that had formed in swells of music-induced euphoria. Her vision cleared, she caught her breath and prepared to enjoy every tone of her next vocalizations. "En...take us to En...yes En, he's a good dog, L-32. His little doggie brain is all scrambled. He needs Akenehi. *Go.*"

Kei and Akenehi retained their link and came easily upon En, scrambled brains and all, cradled in Johnny's arms.

Akenehi was ready to give her new neuro song its first solo test, but it was unnecessary.

A mere moment after Kei appeared so did a myriad of time traveling Akenehi's. From various times in her far future, they surrounded En with as much attention and affection as they would a newborn orca.

Some things in the multiverse were resistant to change. Akenehi's majestic orca presence was one of the greatest of those. They calibrated their songs, aligning from various multiverse coordinates. Then in one perfect voice, they addressed their youngest self.

"Waiting for your cue, Akenehi."

Akenehi scanned out to her many mind-blowing orca-selves, "Still sounding great after all those travels."

"We always had it and we always will. As usual, same cue." A wave of orca laughter washed around the throng. "We will take it from here. En will be fine."

Akenehi didn't doubt them. She sang to Kei but meant it for all, "Keep an ear on Invention. If she does not find a way out to Orcasekai immediately, she never will. I am away to Orcasekai, now. And do not to pop the bubble when you leave. I am going to need it. But of course, you know that. And..."

Johnny released En to the Akenehis and their flawless chorus filled the universe.

Kei gently caressed the base of En's ears as he revived, "We will. Don't worry about us. We'll be fine. You have a universe to help. Go!"

CHAPTER 23

Universe: Orcasekai

Go! Akenehi was totally ready to unscramble universe metabrain from the *outside*. In error, she homed in to where Delora and Liam lived happily *within* Orcasekai.

Once inside Home, her human portion, albeit a tiny part of her, was content and wished to stay. After their affectionate greeting, Akenehi inquired after Alvar. She did not detect him.

"Alvar is here, alive and well, of course," his parents assured their beloved matriarch. They indicated toward an organic mass that Akenehi might have categorized as a giant jellyfish. It was a transparent sac of myriad pleasingly lit strands intersecting at even brighter junctions. It was Alvar-G.

He was lit up, a living kaleidoscopic, overjoyed at her presence. Alvar-G's transformed appearance was as hypnotizing as any glowing medusozoa Akenehi had ever come across.

She watched him closely. His patterns were clearly not random, they flowed and created their own music. It sounded very much to her ears as Curl song, except it was a dialect that was not discordant in any way. She had lived her life in an ocean she shared with flashing cephalopods and others with bioluminescent displays. Nonetheless, she could not decipher how Alvar-G's patterned pulses translated.

"Do either of you understand what he is doing?"

"Yes, of course," Delora answered quickly. She knew better than to ask the obvious, "Can't you?" which would have been righteously interpreted as an insult by Akenehi, who did not play demeaning games. Delora had not been visited by Akenehi since she left her in the Vencello. She wanted to learn all that had happened to the orca since then. The orca part of Delora, albeit a miniscule part, suspected that Akenehi was disoriented. So, Delora offered her assistance, "Are you lost?"

"Of course not." Akenehi sighed. "I've come to cure Curl."

Delora would have blinked at her if she still had such eyelids.

Akenehi suspected her visit to her Vencello family had been no mistake. She used the moment of Delora's silence to echolocate for camouflaged Priori in Home and decided that she had not been followed.

"Why do you scan so, Akenehi? Are you sure you're alright?"

Akenehi had discovered that Delora could do what she, herself could not; translate her son's neural impulses and perhaps even Curl. Akenehi asked, "Can he hear?"

"Yes." Delora was growing confused. It was obvious to her and Liam that Alvar had perfectly functioning human ears.

At the affirmative, Akenehi sang directly to him in her first attempt at Curl, hitting notes far above human range. It was unpracticed and broken but it was close enough. Delora and Liam did not perceive it. Alvar, however, got it all and responded. His flourishes seemed to synchronize with her vocalizations and pulses, while others followed enigmatic commands of their own. Akenehi had no idea what any of them meant.

Delora and Liam understood Alvar well enough and offered a translation. But Alvar gave one last very distinctive simple flash. His parents conveyed that last bit only, in unison, to Akenehi.

"Eat me."

It was an indication of just how much trust sharing the Vencello entailed that Akenehi promptly ingested the entire sac that was Alvar-G, without a chomp. He slid easily into her stomach, aided by his intentional amoeboid efforts. Neither Delora nor Liam were fussed by it either. Once he has passed through the length of the esophagus, he held his place. Alvar-G pressed his outer layer of neurons that were spread across his sac membrane firmly against the orca's stomach lining. The digestive tracts of Sponge mammals were full of neurons and Akenehi had retained that feature. Utilizing them, Akenehi achieved a direct method of trans-neural communication with Alvar-G. Upon connecting, Akenehi was impressed at his breadth of mind despite not containing a central nervous system such as her own.

Akenehi absorbed Alvar-G's neural impulses efficiently across her stomach neurons, communicating far more efficiently than would have been possible through whistle and click.

"Hello Akenehi, I am Alvar. You never knew my name, but...

Akenehi dove in, "I know your name. I know your mother and, believe me, she screamed it into my ears throughout the entire Vencello. You were scattered and rebuilt, first you, then Arva'Anati. I listened as every one of your molecules came together…

"Great! So, you know how to listen. Listen to *this*."

Alvar-G's thought stream faded as another voice rose. It was a genetically programmed message for Akenehi, from Amaranth's grandmother.

"Greetings First Grandmother. My granddaughter, Amaranth, and I beg your understanding. While supervising Amaranth's transition to adulthood, I made a grievous error. I modified Alvar's genetic song so that he might survive outside of Cetapiens and live as her mate. What resulted was not viable. I have violated universase law. Rightly, I will soon suffer diffusion.

I corrected the damage I had caused her beloved. But, I had not considered that he was a Metavoli-2 Gemini.

His G bore the full brunt of my error. When awakened to his mother and father in the Vencello, he was, in critical ways, changed.

His 'mitochondria' are likely no longer confined to his cells. And apparently, neither are his brain cells confined to his body.

Fortunately, the latter may have exposed a Priori predator. This Alvar-G's brain had been surreptitiously liquefied after molecular recall but before the reverse universase process was finished.

I now suspect I had inserted enough of myself into the shared G physiology that this Alvar's liquid brain survived as free individuals. By the same mechanism that liberated his mitochondria, each of his neurons now shared an ability with me. They were as a Priori colony generation that would disband, time travel and return to reform. And so, in self-defense, Alvar-G's brain did just that. His neurons swirled around the Vencello assembly bed, selectively attacked his predator in turn. He reformed rather than pursue when she retreated.

A few observant Priori, who were there with Alvar-G, recognized what had happened and, time traveled away in pursuit of her.

She escaped, injured to heal else time.

One returned immediately with nothing but a hypothesis. The Priori that did that must have time traveled within his skull, possessed powerful cloaking ability and who knows what else.

But Alvar awakened, his human memory and personality intact.

First Grandmother, I beg you, sing well of me to my clan. And for my honor and my granddaughter's sake, keep an ear turned to the safety of this Gemini. We love him."

The message voice of Grandmother ended.

Alvar insisted, "I don't miss my mitochondria. I don't remember any of this 'brain flight/fight'. But I know Grandmother's voice and trust her. She couldn't protect me but Home has. It's a good thing I have no desire to leave it and that it's so perfect here. But now that you've heard this, can you help me out? What about this 'predator'?"

"I am happy to sing that the predator has already been captured and confined. It was a Priori, Amaranth's daughter generation, Invention."

Akenehi thought as Alvar-G relaxed, "Perhaps it was a momentary ability. But, I wonder G, do your individual neurons still have the capacity to time travel out of you, and return to their 'colonial' form?"

Alvar-G had no idea what his brain did or did not do in its normal functioning. He only had its summarizing, fleeting thoughts. "I have to guess, so I'll flash 'yes'. That would be cool."

Then Alvar thought to ask Akenehi, "Can yours?"

Akenehi truly did not know the answer to that. She only knew what she was thinking, not how or why. As Priori, considering what she had just heard, she hoped she could. She determined to pursue an answer, some other time and universe.

For now, she started, "You are more human without mitochondria than you have ever been. So, those free neurons, if they indeed fly about the universe, should have been more easily identified by Orcasekai's anti-human-bodies as such; enemy, self-harming, and triggered a defensive response. Yet, you have survived all this time to near the end of Orcasekai. Of course, Grandmother's genetic influence could be why your human markers are not attacked by the universal immune system response. The constant threat of your potentially loose neurons could be intentional too. In any case, you are luckily, inexplicably ignored."

They thought in unison, "Let us not test that luck."

Alvar began to feel discomfort across his surface caused by orca digestive enzymes. If he stayed in her stomach much longer he would eventually be absorbed into her, quite eaten. He certainly did not wish to transition to an orca, even if it was the magnificent Akenehi, nor in that way. He urged her to gag him out.

Akenehi promised she would not digest him but would take him wherever he wished, so long as it was outside of Orcasekai.

"What about predators? There might be more than the one."

"Most certainly. You'll have to take your chances like the rest of us.

You could stay here until this world ends, or you can leave. But I must go, now. Make your choice."

The thought of a new home in the jungle of Cetapiens pleased him most.

She agreed. Alvar-G would be happy. Orcasekai might be helped, if his removal from that universe was a sort of surgical extraction of a virus progenitor.

Akenehi felt the wave of sick then she shared Alvar-G's happiness at their accord. She chirped a brief goodbye to his parents, but it reverberated into empty domes. Delora and Liam had already gone. She listened to their echo as did Alvar within her.

CHAPTER 24

Universes: Delora and Liam Various

Delora and Liam took Alvar's ingestion, as their cue to transition out of Orcasekai.

Of infinite options, Delora and Liam started out slowly, with only four.

One: They selected a universe that was virtually identical to the Vencello's original but not exactly. In that universe, they transitioned to the moment they joined with Brough and Akenehi in the Vencello. No critical multiverse violations or threats of paradox 'bad puffs' applied to their sudden appearance in that one. Enabled through the modified combination of Metavoli Gemini processing and C-60 genetic solution generation, they assumed their original forms. They emerged back into the Sponge ocean at the very moment of their multiverse other selves exited into the Vencello. They surfaced, were helped back into the boat by Johnny, who was not and would never become G in that universe, and resumed their pre-Vencello humans lives from that point, together.

Two: They selected a universe that was somewhat like the Vencello's original. Enabled through the modified combination of Metavoli Gemini processing and C-60 genetic solution generation, they kept their cetacean features, discarding their relic humanity all together. Whales and dolphins had thrived for millions of years in a similar Sponge home planet. But in that universe, opposable thumbs never developed. Humans did exist but remained close to shore limited by swim distance. Their communication method was a sophisticated non-verbal, almost singing one. Delora and Liam surfaced, took their first breath as dolphins, and agreed on their new dolphin, whistled, names. They soon located a superpod of sperm whales and lived cetacean lives from that point, together with them.

Three: They selected a universe that was little like any they had called home, but they could survive comfortably in it. Enabled through the modified combination of Metavoli Gemini processing and C-60 genetic solution generation, they merged into one conjoined being. They were joined through the head, one brain, and torso, one heart but they kept their own human arms and legs and the reclaimed their digits. With eight limbs and eyes situated so they were never able to observe the other except through shared thought, they maintained a balance of closeness and separateness that echoed the experience of every solitary Sponge octopi.

Four: They selected one from the infinite universes that were so much like their original Sponge world as to be the same. But it wasn't. In this universe, they were both born, although Delora was passionately in favor of cetacean rights, she never traveled overseas to demonstrate for them. So, she never met Liam.

Alvar was never born.

In that universe, Delora had two daughters instead of one son. While she loved Alvar, she loved each of those two sweet babies just as much. She selected it because as soon as she fused with the Vencello and connected through that to her counterparts in infinite universes, she recognized a strong pull toward that family. Those daughters summoned her through bonds she had forged herself and which the multiverse could not alter. There, she never became a cetacean researcher, but she had come close to it.

In that universe, Liam never got the call that Johnny was involved in Alvar's death. Because Alvar never existed in that one. But he *did* get a call. His sister contacted him a few years later distraught that her son, Johnny. He was missing. While his mother could not accept it, of course, Liam understood he had been deeply troubled since his twin's death and was unconvinced that he would never be heard from again. Liam never married but he fathered a daughter with a co-worker and visited her on weekends and holidays.

*****

Alvar glowed as their four echoes paths faded. He wished his Sponge universe parents well throughout all their journeys. He was ready to leave Orcasekai too.

Alvar-G had every happy memory of his Gemini's life in Cetapiens. Alvar-G wished to live in the jungle environment that surrounded it. It was protected by a much larger dome of Acrituchi and Curl infused atmosphere than the ones he had called home in Orcasekai. He could survive quite happily there.

As Akenehi held Alvar in her stomach she could feel him gripping hold, just enough so he didn't get pushed down into her intestines. She did not enjoy the sensation and had to travel quickly or throw him up prematurely.

Akenehi homed in. She puked him out, in as gentle manner as she could, in the center of a clearing carved out of the dense jungle of Cetapiens.

"You are blocking my light," Alvar-G's flashed his observation as matter of fact.

She could not directly share the thought, but she got it. Akenehi backed away from the quivering mucus covered sac, exposing him to a light beam that filtered straight down through an opening in the dense canopy above. It shone directly on and throughout him with an observable effect. She turned her head to look up to its source, the sun. It affected her mightily because she heard it too, a pervasive 'you belong here' call. She committed its soothing effect to memory; that of her home star and the Acrituchi that radiated out of it, as they welcomed her and Alvar home. It struck a Curl chord within her own body, so familiar, it caused her to pause rather than return immediately to Orcasekai.

The sound of warm ocean wafted around her and she remembered that this was also near the multiverse coordinates where her daughter, Arva'Anati, would be arriving to her first moments of freedom after decades of concrete tank confined misery. Akenehi listened for her own voice and then the answering of an unfamiliar dialect, a native orca matriarch. Without hearing it, she was content. She could come back anytime to witness the moment of release and welcome.

In the jungle of Cetapiens, Alvar could move much faster under his own power, albeit in multiverse amoeboid fashion. He sped into the vegetation. Akenehi watched him squidge away, like an eel through water, into the surrounding growth. She found humor and satisfaction in that he was so small, transparent, quiet and unappetizing. He would live a long happy life in his chosen green habitat.

Alvar-G had worked out long ago that, given transport, he must choose Cetapiens, like his Gemini. Being assisted by Akenehi, however, in her stomach no less, was a complete surprise.

The Alvars' had their own loop to close and he remembered he had been brought very close to where he needed to be to do so. Akenehi delivered him. Alvar-G rolled and squeezed his way up, gripping the tree gently to stay in place. He waited like that for his other self to approach the clearing, on *his* first day in Cetapiens.

The pressure on Alvar-G when he felt the full weight of his Gemini press his sac against the bark was firm, but no harm was done to either. Through brine and sweat, a multiverse reaction permeated instantly from one G to the other. Human skin was no barrier. Every mitochondrion within Alvar was marked immune to Buzzpips, *incapable* of escape from Cetapiens.

Alvar-G, a happily pulsing sac, had closed his own time travel loop. He released the tree and plopped safely down to the ground and listened to the desperate voice from above, marveling at what a hideous creature that part of him was then.

*****

Akenehi witnessed Alvar in his purest human form, a glowing gelatinous sac. She heard Curl within it self-calibrating to those that filled the organic life residing in the surrounding jungle. They all utilized critical ranges and shades that had eluded her. But now she heard what Curl harmony should sound like. There were many contributing elements coexisting peacefully in Cetapiens. Orca, human, Priori, Acrituchi. The Curl thrived happily there. Now all she had to do was travel back to Orcasekai and calibrate that same healthy harmony there.

She confidently homed in on Orcasekai through the multiverse with yet another musical salve that would surely revive that universe.

CHAPTER 25

Universe: Orcasekai

By the time Akenehi finally recovered from the nausea of Alvar-G in her gut, her trained ear was so fine that it could identify the elements of harmony and discord as it related to even Curl song, wherever it existed. She left Alvar to the Cetapiens jungle and homed back in time, within Orcasekai.

Once inside, Akenehi was subjected to a horrid cacophony. Such discord, while painful to hear, indicated critical malfunction. The universe's condition was far worse than she could have imagined from external listening. Everything was off, in some tone or another, between each of the three worlds relative to each other. They were out of tune within, as well. It was hard to know where to begin.

She started with the planet known by its cetacean inhabitants as 'Surface'. It rang of the worst suffering.

At least one safe marker had to be specific to En. That singular Dog Priori was enigmatically linked to Orcasekai's wellbeing. So, Akenehi determined that he would have *safe* entry to the molecule.

Onesey-twosey was not going to work if an entire universe was to be saved. It proved difficult enough to sing one Dog Priori safe space into function. So, she had to move on without providing a backup marker.

But it worked. En, assisted by Kei, Johnny and L-32, homed in almost as soon as she had set it. Had they looked directly under L-32, they might have caught a glimpse of the orca before she dove on to sing her next, within the ocean of Surface.

Surface was home of Param and other Masters of the Ocean. They shared their brine with other cetacean evacuees. Delora, Liam and Alvar-G lived on Surface's only small patch of land. The human family of the Vencello had not yet gone their separate ways through the multiverse.

Still cocooned in the remains of a broken Metavoli cone, Param and her superpod Masters of the Ocean adopted bizarre behaviors. They resembled little of their prior greatness in their Sponge home world. Floating *en masse*, they achieved a maladapted metaneural network. Physically joined as a super brain, they exerted unprecedented ocean control. They were still the dominant predator and maintained a fragile ecosystem that included many genera of cetaceans, fish and diatoms.

Hideously suspended within the superpod colony were thousands of injured Cephalopods. For the most part, they moved with the whales, caught within their webbed network. Every one of them had at least two of their eight arms missing. Any remaining ones were in various stages of regrowth. Most had camouflaged what was left of their bodies, convincingly imitating the density of misshapen jellyfish, as their predator would identify them. Their cloaking was useless, but they persisted.

Akenehi observed the chromatophoric dermis of one, freshly wounded, as it synchronized sloppily with others. She had learned enough from her short joining with Alvar-G that the patterns conveyed agony and a communal call for help. Their scattered suspension was obviously not by their choice. She listened intently to the chorus of suffering over eons. She carried Brough with her. Through him, she also heard the Aware Master detailed echoing through the ocean.

In it she learned this was not by the whales' design either. It sang miserably of *contamination*, a botched implant; a chunk of cephalopod brain plopped clumsily into cetacean neuroanatomy left to self-heal. Such a joining would have meant death in the Sponge. Within the Metavoli membrane, however, they had been C-60 modified and survived. Just.

Despite Param's Sponge knowledge, this mutation, passing for her native ecosystem, was struggling. Their Orcasekai Ocean was much smaller and had manifested during a too sudden transition, not able to balance out naturally over eons. But Param and the colony had learned enough from their detailed scans of home to make do with what they had become.

The cephalopods were prolific. Each of those displayed stumps where fleshy arms had been pulled or bitten off; eaten alive by the whale colony as their sole source of nourishment. The Cephalopods were kept alive to regrow more. Arms were harvested as needed, at an optimum rate that would keep the cephalopod alive and growing new ones. Of course, if an individual cephalopod could no longer regrow its severed arms at an efficient rate, as happened eventually with old age, the entire body would then be eaten alive while it flailed in pain and its fellow captives could do nothing to help or escape.

The Cephalopods killed themselves if the cetaceans were not careful to prevent it. They also hatched thousands of eggs at each forced mating and cannibalized as many as they could both because they were always kept hungry and it was better that no new Cephalopods were born into that life.

The captives were members of their own nexus, independent of the whales. As such, they were connected to their fellows that dwelled under the frozen surface of Depth. As the whale nexus controlled the ocean of Surface, similarly, the Cephalopod nexus kept Depth Ocean in its care. Although those Cephalopod on Surface were aware of Depth's existence, they could not escape to that distant utopia.

The only mercies the Cephalopods of Surface received were fleeting shared experiences of their distant nexus fellows, more impressions and after-flashes than vivid sensations. Those perceptions were lessened by the expanse that separated them. Still, under their constant nightmare, dream currents of tranquil long lives of minimal suffering and much contentment flowed.

The whale bites hurt as much as any amputation could. And those felt better than having it ripped away. Rips were much slower to regrow. The whales knew clean bites were more efficiently healed, so they usually spared them the agony of rips. Usually. Cephalopods were given the option to bite off their own arms. Some chose that option out of desperation if a whale was not a practiced biter. It all translated to an ocean of Cephalopod misery. But they weren't the only ones in agony over it.

For the whales, eating was like chewing on their own flesh. Biting one's own tooth off in the process. The neurotransmitters flowing through the suspension they shared did not spare them the hurt. It was a hybrid system mandated by what they brought with them and inherited from the Sponge along with their Metavoli adaptations. It smarted plenty, but the alternative, they were certain, was death.

So, the whale nexus and the cephalopods remained intricately, miserably, intertwined. Captives couldn't flee even though they were skilled at camouflage. Instead, they were forced to betray their existence to the predator as they were connected directly in the same network. Neither one would have ever wished to make permanent the system they found themselves in.

Akenehi set her acoustic markers at a few critically targeted junctions throughout the snarled web of injured Cephalopods. Like a virus, before Param could work out what they were, they would self-replicate and lie dormant until Akenehi applied the signal songs to activate.

Routine maintenance echo scans returned consistent data that eventually the new ocean balance would fail. The rate of cephalopod regeneration could not keep up with whale consumption. Aware Master food was getting scarce. If they died, the ocean died. Before they got around to trying to communicate that to the dolphins and other cetaceans, it was obvious to them too. The dolphins knew the reliance on arms for whale food was a poor system even though they helped keep the cephalopods from fleeing or committing suicide. They even came to be a bit repulsed by the magnificent Masters that once were the most beloved caretakers of their prior ocean.

The Masters had received relief from the Deepers, also known as Orion, since they all arrived in Orcasekai. It was obvious that while other cetaceans were thinning, the Orion were as robust as ever.

The Orion also knew the supply and demand would fail if they did not bring back fresh Cephalopods from Depth to compensate for increasing whale consumption. The Orion could not abandon Surface. They could not let the ocean die. They required its air.

Orion hunted the plentiful supply of Cephalopods on the distant planet, Depth, the ice-covered ocean world on which no air-breather could survive for long. The Orion were the only Cetaceans that could hold their breath for the time required for the deep dive from Surface to Depth and back. They had to prepare their muscular oxygen supply, efficiently navigate the tubes connecting them, survive the tunnel conditions between worlds, hunt cephalopods and bring them back, alive, in one dive. Fortunately, it was relatively easily for Orion to do. Very easy.

In fact, it was a very comfortable experience. The tubes were lined with plaques of various bioluminescent micro-organisms that dwelled there. They gave the Orion a cool light show on every journey. Once they arrived under the distant worlds ice, they easily caught and ate their fill before capturing a small number of live prey in their mouths for the return dive.

The tubes were the relics of escaping cephalopods in the pre-O-U-O ocean. They had eluded Auden and Jomei's efforts to keep prey in their new ocean for future consumption. Thus, the three worlds and their inhabitants were interconnected by the universal cephalopod escape trails. Through these, both predator and prey could travel between worlds.

Fortunately for the Masters and the entire Surface Ocean that depended on them, the Orion kept at it. Their kind also survived, compliments of the Master's balancing act, after all. But it was not a permanent solution. The Orion merely *slowed* the population demise. There were too few Orion to keep up or even make the number of journeys required. They were, after all, bling-loving, deep diving, shy Orion. They weren't about to do any more than they absolutely had to for a species whose disdain they would always bear.

The whale predator and cephalopod prey nexus combined as the dominant brain of Orcasekai. Orcasekai suffered chronically as a result. All the individuals within retained their Sponge mitochondria and therefore Curl. The Curl, irrepressible energy beings that they were, suffered and responded to their hosts as was their nature. Their agitation permeated the O-O, every molecule, cell and system that contained it, beyond the very atoms of their C-60 sphere. The entire ocean was in discord, and any in the multiverse who were so primed, heard it.

But they all just kept flowing and going. Every Master within that colony keenly felt The Ocean flow and consumption, one into another, digested in their great bodies, which sustained, albeit painfully, their universe's greatest intellect. The cephalopods kept suffering and fought to escape.

'Hatred' was a little staccato human utterance but what the Cephalopods shared among themselves and directed at the whales did not translate so small. Their collective intention was to render the entire universe uninhabitable by the whales, even if it meant death to their own kind. They had a surge of malicious euphoria at the mere thought of dead whales, and it motivated them as they worked toward that end. A deep and pervasive shade of hatred it was.

Because they were intertwined, the whale colony felt every Cephalopod emotion as if it were cetacean. The message was: "The Ocean despises Masters." The fact that their beloved Ocean would hate them so righteously irritated all the whales. Param attempted to spare her family by directing scans and detailed data analysis to elsewhere in the ocean and Brough. Her frustration that she could not silence the Cephalopod signals resulted in regret of the very system she was determined to maintain. If given the opportunity to escape, she would take her un-colony superpod and live as they once had. She wanted out.

Akenehi was one such Priori that perceived their chorus of universal misery. She set her markers around Param, empathizing in despair as she quietly sang them into dormancy. And to Param, who was totally unaware of the orca's work, she sang, "Be careful what you wish for, old friend, you're about to get it. All of it."

CHAPTER 26

Universe: Orcasekai

Next, Akenehi turned her ear on Depth. The discord from Surface required her to home in right under its frozen layer to hear the quality of its Curl song. Everywhere under its ice, the Curl of Depth were quietly humming. It was a delightful respite, even though Akenehi could still hear the screeching of Surface from so far away. Any healing acoustic markers that were required of her at Depth would be easy and few.

Ironically, it was under the ice of Depth, immersed at a point furthest from Brough who still hung at the center of the universe, where Akenehi could hear him. His echo clicks were the only Aware Master ones in that ocean.

"It has been a long slumber for me on Orcasekai, Akenehi. Our home ocean died without me and I ask you to join me in returning to it before its end. There is much I would have wished…"

"Already singing to that end, dear friend," she sang and clicked as only Brough could have understood. She finished the few markers around the sleeping Metavoli, just where it met the ocean at the sea floor, to coordinates in and deep through the core.

Akenehi sang to her cetacean counterpart, "In the Vencello, we all got what we wanted in the end. And I am sometimes sorry for that. Prepare yourself, dear Brough."

Under the frozen surface of Depth, the most distant from the center of the universe of the three, but not beyond the swim of Orion, sang a multiverse-enhanced super colony of giant squid, octopi and other cephalopods. Like the whale nexus, each connected mind was as a holographic map. The net-like membrane of the whale/Metavoli that had evacuated the cetaceans to Orcasekai had also transported them. When the hurricane of initial conditions had settled, they were safely out of range with a cold dark piece of the ocean floor as their planet's core. The water at the surface froze solid but that did not concern them in the least. They had no need for air. In fact, it couldn't have been better. That meant no cetacean could co-inhabit their world. They believed themselves safe from Masters of their own world, at last. So far, their song was not so unpleasant.

Cephalopods were smart, but the whales usually outsmarted them. Sure enough, Orion managed to survive the interplanetary dive necessary to reach them. Orion would invade in small groups, murder some of their numbers that had not sufficiently camouflaged or fled. It enraged them that Orion were reaching them at all. That was not the agreement. Hadn't their kind taken the risks, ensuring the realm would remain free of wild thumbs.

Pranaya had secured that agreement with Akenehi. Pranaya was one of the longest-lived of the few ancient Cephalopod Priori. During a sliver of her life, she existed as two different aged versions of herself, each on one of two worlds within Orcasekai.

One of her was trapped in the Cetapiens world, confined within its boundaries during the bad puff. There, she served as a Templesekai elder, a well-cloaked Cephalopod Priori, and a multiverse time traveler. Such bad puffs acted as a virtual Priori blind spot. Pranaya was trapped with the People and other Priori of Cetapiens, not knowing how or why their puff had gone bad and certainly not knowing that, until it corrected, they existed in two universes at once. Like the other captured Priori, the effect was that she was without memory of her existence outside of it.

Pranaya was also on Depth, under the protective ice of that Cephalopod sanctuary. She was confined to that world as well. But she stayed in the brine of Depth out of a sense of duty, as Protector, not because she had lost her ability to time travel.

Akenehi set her markers around Pranaya. Despite skilled Orca Priori stealth, Akenehi suspected she had been detected, although Pranaya did not flash a single subtle dermal reaction.

When she was finished, Akenehi strained to consider how to best coordinate her neural healing tools to Orcasekai's configuration and the markers that were already in place. The universe contained two different but intertwined neural networks. One was Param's Master of the Ocean Nexus and the other was a cephalopod Nexus. Each nexus contained the brains of individuals. Each of those was based on relic Sponge neuroanatomy. There were cellular nuclei, clever enzymes and still-captive mitochondria. Then there were other brains, not linked directly to either larger neural Nexus. They lived as independent individuals, more autonomous than the others, on one of the three planetoids. Those 'independents' were much smaller scale multiverse adapted brains, many cetacean and cephalopod, a few humans, several fish, plants, bacteria and plankton. Throughout Orcasekai, each brain should have been calibrated only to the O-U-O of the protective C-60 molecular sphere, causing a universal 'awakening', but they were not.

The Cetapiens bad puff contained Curl. Their songs were tuned to the *Sponge* universe. The other two worlds and the viscous suspension between them were calibrated correctly to Orcasekai. But Brough and the Metavoli were aligned to the *Vencello*. With no properties common to all, the C-60 molecule generated a universal O-O mutation; a new harmonic over all the existing ones. The universe found its own solution for all within to survive while it self-healed. And it sounded like torture.

Until then, everything screamed in an audible crescendo of agitated Curl that Akenehi alone could hear.

Param may have sought to train whales to ignore Cephalopod pain signals, but Curl can't be trained. Of course, Akenehi heard so very plainly, the omnipresent Curl didn't know or care about any of that. They just wanted out. Out. OUT. From the sound of it, they were going to make it too.

For a split instant Akenehi was overwhelmed and resigned to failure. She agonized and then heard Brough's echo, "…I ask you to join me in returning to it before its end. There is much I would have wished…" Akenehi snapped out of it.

Brough's clicks were iterating again. She had heard all he had to convey. That was her cue. She sang a wave of gratitude and love to him and dove on to her next marker.

CHAPTER 27

Universe: The Haven and Orcasekai

Kei contemplated the little whale that rested on her flattened palm.

"Careful, you'll drop it" Johnny spoke while eating, mumbling between bites of fruit. They were sitting under a tree in full leaf. Ripe sweetness had dropped from it, with some in full fragrant rot around them. She and Johnny were in one of her favorite universes, The Haven, discussing where to time jump next.

"I can't *hurt* it. But yeah, I don't want En to get it either."

Kei looked down at the Dog Priori. He was still resting, pressed against her lower leg. His eyes were closed. A few bits of buzzing life rested on his ears and flew off. Sometimes causing a twitch, other times not. Kei guessed he was sleeping, still recovering from his unscrambling of his brain. She closed her eyes and grasped the whale. She thought to herself, "I wonder how Akenehi is doing with Orcasekai."

The answer came clear in her mind. She was a bit startled, not actually expecting what followed. As she listened, she watched Johnny who stopped chewing just long enough to shrug an unspoken, "What?" He hadn't heard anything. En had not flinched. What was flowing sounded like it was meant personally for her, friendly and trusting. Kei let it continue in her mind alone.

Our First Grandmother pulled back and reassessed. In truth, the whale-cephalopod brain alone was a confounding mess in motion. Still, she calculated furiously. With a spasm of despair, Akenehi considered this would be beyond even Amaranth's ability. Even with Soo's help. Akenehi recalled Delora's lesson on human medicine. Neuroanatomy was especially delicate. And this, large metabrain fiasco…No, this might never be 'cured' with song or click, or skilled universase or all the Akenehis from every coordinate in the multiverse.

As quickly as she thought 'fatal' she regretted it. Still in sleep song, I heard her prognosis, and she knew it.

"It's not time, yet...just a few more markers..." And some other thoughts. She loved me. She wanted something of me. They all did. But I just couldn't...

It was not a case of merely needing a healing song, or a loving relative, or my dog to cheer me. There was a scannable, audible reason why I, Orcasekai, was giving up and kept persistent focus on orbit of electrons rather than the failing conglomeration that made up my internal components. I was determined to continue as planned and Akenehi heard that. Better for her, better for me.

To wake me up, or let me sleep to the end. Either way, Akenehi, my First Grandmother, who loved me more than you could have possibly imagine, refused to leave me.

Then silence.

Kei sat bolt upright. "We need to find Akenehi. Inside Orcasekai. We will need L-32 for this one. Now."

"Now? But what about En?" Johnny tossed his half-eaten snack into the undergrowth. "The Akenehis said to let him sleep..."

En perked up his ears and stood easily on all fours.

"He comes with us. Right now."

*****

Kei and her team achieved a sustained jump, first try, to the inside of Orcasekai, thanks to the marker Akenehi had set for En. Hovering over a glassy sea, in almost total darkness, they watched a small pod of Orion surface close by. Those cetacean shapes were gently revealed by a film of glowing bioluminescence and wakes of disturbance around them. No star illuminated the sky above them. There were only the soft, fuzzy lights of apex atoms of the carbon 60 sphere.

They listened as the whales took deep plosive breaths.

"Whales!" Johnny pointed into the black horizon.

As with all jumps that landed in darkness, L-32 gave off just the right amount of compensating illumination. The motorcycle glowed soft under them as they straddled its long, warm seat. Johnny's eyes adjusted, and its aura went out completely. It began to radiate just enough heat and then went cold as the ambient temperature was deemed acceptable. Kei did not look down at her but ran her hand across L-32's body in thanks. She did not notice when L-32 did not glow in usual response, instead remaining dark and cool.

"We're in!" Kei and Johnny exclaimed in unison. Their eyes were trained to dart elsewhere.

En perked up at their excitement and the change of universe.

Ocean, warm or otherwise, was a problem for her, Johnny and En, but it was all ease for L-32. That cool ride could handle just about any environment in which the multiverse enveloped it. All riders included.

Kei gripped the handlebars and coaxed L-32 to dive into Surface. Nothing.

Kei released her grip and held her breath. She glanced back to Johnny, wanting to lock eyes with him despite the dark and exhaled in exasperation. She turned back around, shaking it off, rubbed the palms of her hands briskly then gripped the handles again, this time tighter but said nothing. L-32 was never hard of hearing. Kei was heard the first time.

Again, L-32 did *nothing*.

"Oh, this is *not* good." Kei despaired.

"What's wrong with her? Why isn't she diving?"

"Only two reasons come to *my* mind. One, L-32 is *dead…*"

Johnny cussed quietly under his breath behind Kei as he slowly released his hold on her waist.

Kei jabbed her finger downward, indicated the smooth black just under L-32's wheels. "…or, two, things are very, *very* bad down there."

"Maybe our 'little treasure' can help," Johnny reached past En who was secured firmly between them. "Not you, buddy." He carefully unzipped Kei's pocket where he had watched her place it and slowly pulled out the little whale, gripping it tightly so he would not lose it to the water. Johnny had been made Gemini by a whale that looked very much like it. And now, those whales that had surfaced at their arrival, again reminded him of the same species. He couldn't help thinking about their mystery and wondered at a deeper connection.

The memory of the Orion was present in every molecule of ocean beneath them. It was that and a combination of Akenehi's acoustic marker, and Johnny's possession of the whale that triggered what followed.

A film of water enveloped them inside a sphere of living memory. Suspended just above the sea on a time traveling motorcycle that wouldn't budge, Kei, Johnny and En stayed seated and pressed together for warmth as much as moral support.

The curious pod of Orion, that had until then spyhopped from a distance, came in closer to the novelty of bubbled beings floating in air. More Orion arrived as the sphere's interior filled with echolocation, cetacean whistles. Some they understood, others they recognized but could not fully comprehend.

The theatre also filled with scent for En's comprehension, language for Johnny's and whatever was needed for any other audience.

"Oh, cool. I feel like I'm at the drive-in, one with curved screens..."

"A what?" Kei asked.

"Remind me to take you to one."

"Will I like it?"

"I'll make sure you do."

CHAPTER 28

Universe: Orcasekai

Auden and his identical twin brother, Jomei, didn't just transition to Orcasekai as the saviors of all things Orion. They had always been clever, generous and talented. They were beloved by Monifa and their family very deeply. However, through the Metavoli duplication and subsequent cetacean evacuation, they were enhanced. They arrived to Orcasekai, and Surface, as awesome, time traveling, Gemini wonder whales. As such, the multiverse could not let them stay shrink-wrapped in a C-60 shell for long. Their new molecule universe could contain the others but not them.

"Hey! That's him, that's the whale…"

"Shhh," Kei jabbed her elbow back to him and hit En by mistake.

En whimpered.

"Oh, sorry baby."

"Shhh," Johnny teased in turn.

Certain Priori had nurtured Brough exclusively through the Vencello. They excluded Akenehi, Delora, Liam…

"My uncle! Uncle Liam!" Johnny tapped Kei's shoulder and pointed to the lifelike images before them. Why leave him out?"

"You're going to miss this if you don't shush."

They focused their attention on the click processing of the Aware Master of the Ocean. They ensured his Orcasekai transition and his survival there. But when the Orion twins emerged into Orcasekai, Certain Priori adopted them too. They were designated as quirky favorites, Brough counterparts. The combination of Brough and the Orion twins resulted in a team that served as a multiverse litmus test of shade identification independent of, yet rivaling, Akenehi's excellent acoustic perception.

"Akenehi!" Johnny and Kei cheered then hushed each other.

So, Certain Priori rushed in to make their introductions to Auden and Jomei before other Priori had awakened to the possibility. They ushered the twins to compatible universes, effectively calling dibs on a potential multiverse navigation aid that the trio comprised. And so, with their Certain Priori mentors, Auden and Jomei popped in and out, coming and going between worlds, mastering deep dive and manipulating living bling like no whale's business. All before the rest of the evacuated Orion had even surfaced for their first breath in Orcasekai.

They had lost connection to their G twins who had gone ahead through the multiverse to prime their new ocean. The loss meant *they* were no longer quadruplets. Their G twins didn't make it and so would not be greeting their family at evacuee's arrival.

"Oh man, he died*?" Johnny felt a sharp pang of grief and massaged his face with his palms to work it out.*

Kei reached back, waving her hand for him to take. She gently squeezed it and brought it around her waist again.

The surviving twins broke the bad news in whistles and clicks to Monifa. But it was unneeded. The light displays that greeted her at her arrival, bore the unmistakable message from the two who had initiated and designed them. They reignited at her unique trigger, whenever she wished to replay it, throughout her life. They were so specific to Monifa's desires that only they, who loved her best, could have imagined them. In Orion communication of light, they illustrated to their beloved mate that they knew they were not going to make it, but they accepted that. And they would always love her.

At the sentiment, Johnny deliberately moved his hand, giving Kei's abdomen a light caress where it lay. Kei did not respond.

Almost as soon as she had emerged with her family from the Sponge, her surviving mates initiated her to the interplanetary pathways between Surface and Depth. She was a quick learner and was better at tube navigation after the first trip than they could have hoped. When they arrived at Depth they were the only Orion, or cetaceans for that matter, in that world at the time.

There, her presence also triggered Orion messages throughout the brine. These were deeply intimate love-light displays that Auden and Jomei had designed for her private understanding. They would have seemed random to another Orion, but Monifa found it all wonderfully provocative.

They played out to a finale as arousing as any she had ever been treated to. Like all Orion, her neural pathways were primed for bioluminescent stimulation. Light displays triggered a great many autonomic responses in their physiology. The strongest of the two were hunger and sexual arousal. With Orion skill and practice, the right bio illumination was irresistibly sexy.

The story was heating up and had an almost Orion effect on Johnny too. Had Kei responded to his touch before, he would have made additional moves now. But she was stoic, watching scenes that had an erotic message that he fully appreciated, as if it were a weather prediction to her.

Monifa was an unusually uptight, finicky, difficult to satisfy individual. However, the fast-thinking, coordinated displays of the twins were symmetrical, balanced. The three learned quickly at their very first meeting that their beautiful symmetry calmed her. Once her nerves were subdued her cetacean sexuality was freed. Ever since she had reached adulthood it chattered incessantly for release.

The pristine brine of the ocean Depth offered virtually no opacity to Orion vision. So, she received in full force every gorgeous rhythmic flash of stimulation Auden and Jomei had plied into the ocean. She glided through the love-sonnet-in-light accompanied by their surviving Geminis.

Johnny strained to detect a response from Kei. From behind, he saw only the back of her head and side views of her face as she turned her head for viewing. Nothing as far as he could see or feel.

They dove Monifa to the dormant Metavoli on that world's ocean bed. She scanned the surface to learn its unique identifying features. They stressed to her how important it was. Other than that, they were careful not to disturb it. When she inquired, they whistled that they knew *precisely* where and what it was because as time travelers all three of them had been there, in the far distant *future* when it awoke.

"Kei, have you ever come across anything like that before? That Metavoli thing?"

"Shhh."

Her attraction to the twins was, in part, due to her fascination with puzzles, complimentary pieces, balance and symmetry. Without asking whether they realized that the Metavoli there in Depth and the one at Surface fit together, two parts of a whole, she delighted in her realization.

They were reluctant to whistle or click more than to encourage her to persist through any sad events. She *would* survive until then. When it finally awoke, she would be able to merge with it, as they had done and become Gemini.

"Okay, there! *I must have..."*

Kei turned and glared at him. "After."

That scenario didn't whistle right in Monifa's opinion. It was way off-kilter. Even if she could live to the end of Orcasekai, she had no desire to outlive her children. She rejected that seemingly impossible future where she would ever agree to go on without them.

Auden and Jomei whistled select details to her alone, pertaining to their new ocean and how they had all been adapted to survive there. The journey through the Vencello had changed all Orion. It was safe for them to reveal as much. She would figure it all out eventually. Other Orion, including her family, would live long lives too, but unlike her, they would alter so much over that time, that she might no longer recognize them. She may compare memories of when her own were young to what they would become and think of them as having 'died'. Perhaps several times over. Their signature name whistles might change, even their Orionalities that were so familiar to her. However, they assured her that her maternal instinct and love would persist, no matter what.

They had a new call to teach their mate. Jomei whistled 'Orion lifetime'. Auden accompanied with clicks. As Jomei's whistle progressed, Auden's click frequency did too. Under the rises and falls of the song, the clicks transitioned from distinct units, closer and closer, until finally, to a pleasing hum. Monifa understood their meaning. As her life unfolded, 'time' would seem to 'speed up'. The longer she lived the less she would notice events passing. By the end of Orcasekai she would perceive her lifetime as though she were floating in the eye of a hurricane.

Intuitively, it made sense to her. A single day had passed like an eternity when she was an infant at her mother's side. After two universes, her swims with Auden and Jomei were mere flickers, no matter how long their duration.

They determined that new call would be their signal for 'now'.

Easy enough. But it was hard for Monifa to believe, as they whistled, that she would live so long. But they had witnessed it themselves. No matter when in time Auden and Jomei homed in on Orcasekai history, they found their Monifa there, alive. They could not explain it, but they were grateful of it.

Having time-dove beyond Orcasekai history into the multiverse, they also knew when Orcasekai would die.

There was still much to teach but their oxygen was about half depleted. It was time to return for air.

On the return dive to Surface, she thought about what they had communicated. It would take time to process it all. So, when she arrived back to her family, she decided to put it out of her mind. There was a new life to live, a utopia to explore, and she was eager to get on with it. If what her mates clicked was true, and she trusted them completely, she'd have plenty of time to ponder her future with them later.

When they had re-oxygenated, Auden and Jomei taught any Orion, who were willing to learn from them, nuances of their realms. And then, they were gone.

The story vanished. The sphere wall became uniform, emitting a soft homogenous white light. The memory play seemed to have ended.

"Is that it?" Johnny asked, half joking. He was starting to doze.

But then it started again.

"Oh, come on!"

"Careful, it may be taking you literally," Kei cautioned. "Auden and Jomei look like the same type of whale as our 'little treasure'. I think there's m…"

"Shhhhhhhh." L-32's tire leaked a small hiss.

Auden and Jomei did not dive in as often as Monifa would have liked. She missed them for eons as she swam between visits from her mates.

To the others, they appeared so rarely as to be legends, remembered across generations in light displays, and whistles.

The generations that followed Monifa's family and others, all progeny of the Orion Auden and Jomei had evacuated, adapted and prospered to the end of Orcasekai. They had all mastered the tube network and were not confined to the whale nexus world. For an Orion to be limited to *that*, would have been utterly disparaging. Those lovers of living bling considered the *entire* complex whale web little more than a stunted light show *fail*. But, until they were old enough to make their first interplanetary dive, they were stuck there.

Having never experienced the psychological boost of a full-blown proper bling show, adolescent Orion were especially prone to suicide. Adults kept close scans on them and waited for the unavoidable phase of utter despair, which indicated adulthood had arrived.

Adults navigated between Surface and Depth through many of the residual paths and escape trails, left by the pre-Orcasekai Cephalopods. Orion knew the trails well enough to know that they all eventually lead, in some routes more circumspect than others, to the Orion Realm. They were the only Orcasekai mammalian progeny species that could survive even a one-way trip. They required only one well-prepared breath for the journey there and back. And so, they claimed that the destination, a quiet, light filled Orion utopia, devoid of any other air breather was indeed *their* own Orion Realm.

They claimed it even though it was obvious that it was also home world to a great many tasty Cephalopods. Those soft-scanning morsels were both Sponge ocean progeny and Priori.

Unbeknownst to all Orion except Monifa, a portion of the same Metavoli that had cocooned them and safely transported them to Surface of Orcasekai, had broken away during the tempest of transition. The portion at Surface maintained the whale nexus and still surrounded them. It was always awake and facilitated the connection between all Orcasekai. The other piece, on the ocean floor of Depth, was dark asleep.

The memory play vanished again. A larger pod of Orion spectators had gathered outside the sphere. One had put his rostrum on the sphere and the result was the interruption.

En yapped at him.

"Leave it!" Kei and Johnny urged in one voice.

"Ok, that answered some questions, but I'm not sure if this little whale has anything to do with what we just learned." Johnny whispered to Kei as if the ocean would hear if he spoke any louder.

"Let's ask." Kei's voice was loud and friendly.

"En won't sit still for it," Johnny hissed. "Listen to him, he's all wound up."

"He'll calm down."

"Akenehi..."

When she saw Johnny's continued exasperation she explained, "We may not get another chance. We've had a ridiculous time trying to get into this universe. We may never get back if we jump away from this. Besides, this may lead us to Akenehi. Sometimes the multiverse just helps in weird ways. Just awhile longer. Settle in." Kei leaned forward, resting her forearms on L-32's handlebars.

Johnny smiled to the back of her head.

"You're not taking this with the proper time traveler attitude. Here, I'll take that." Without turning around, Kei positioned her hand to receive. Once she had it firmly in her grip, she prompted the little Orion, "Tell us about you."

"Proper attitude, with that stunt you're about to pull?" Kei heard Johnny

whisper in her ear and felt an object being placed in her open pocket. She would reach in for it later.

"Too general! Be more specific!" Johnny complained out loud to Kei right over the whisper. "We'll get the long answer if…"

"Would you prefer to watch from the water?" Kei half teased, half threatened.

Memories of Orion filled the sphere with light and cetacean calls. And there, too, was Akenehi.

"Pfffff," En huffed through his nose. Sniffing vigorously at Akenehi's scent diffusing through the scene, he kept his stare on the Orca Priori while the others watched elsewhere.

CHAPTER 29

Universe: Orcasekai

Akenehi homed in to the final Orion ritual journey of Orcasekai. A young adult whale chattered and whistled, preparing for her first dive to Depth, guided and protected by a small pod, including a few family elders and Akenehi's old friend, Monifa. Monifa was an ancient time traveler, a Certain Priori that had visited her frequently during her Vencello tenure. Akenehi was instantly lifted out of her despair at the recognition. "So! This where you began, ancient matriarch of the Orcasekai Orion."

"Akenehi!" Johnny and Kei cheered in unison.

"Hey, let's shout 'Akenehi' every time we see or hear her!" Johnny urged.

"Shhh."

This rite was Fadwah's. It marked the end of her youth and signaled full adulthood, *if* she completed her first interplanetary dive to Depth and back to Surface.

"Ok, I won't make another peep."

Kei ignored him.

"Peep," he whispered to En's ear.

En jerked around and licked his nose.

Having practiced the oxygen saturation in Surface for many years, she demonstrated that she would not only survive but enjoy the experience. She was escorted by seasoned adults who knew the most efficient routes to Depth, The Orion Realm. As customary, she was also accompanied by her dearest friends, all novices, who had also recently made their first journeys. First interplanetary dive was a ritual, but it was also a lot of fun. It was a great honor to Fadwah that the most enigmatic and ancient elder Orion, Monifa, would join their party.

The whales took their preparatory breaths as they wide scanned the portion of the unfortunate configuration that was under them. A scene of mundane misery returned in their clicks.

Monifa hovered close to Fadwah, affectionately turning her pectoral fin so it grazed along the youth's back in encouragement. Monifa was acutely aware of Fadwah's singular empathy for Cephalopods. Over eons, Orion had improved inherent understanding of Cephalopod chromatophoric communication. Empathy for them, and often depression, resulted. Fadwah had taken to bashing her head against the sea floor in alarming strength and frequency. She whistled plainly, she wanted to die. If the young whale was not shown soon that Orion existence consisted of more than ravaging of the flesh of long suffering captives who constantly called for mercy and release, and swimming among them trying to ignore their obvious displays of torment, Fadwah would commit suicide.

They were on their way to peace, beauty and privilege. Fadwah allowed herself hope at Monifa's touch that she would soon share in *some* happiness. She took a few finer breaths and then it was impossible to take even one more. She was ready.

Together they dove, easily downward, expending little energy. Then, on cue, they all turned and thrusted, flukes pounding back and forth, as their full might would allow, straight back upward in launch formation. They broke surface tension in a fountain of synchronized splashes. Instead of falling immediately down to the surface, as would have happened long ago in their Sponge Ocean, they continued upward, into the sky, each wagged their heads back and forth, furiously echolocating.

As soon as their return data indicated a suitable escape trail, they pushed themselves into it. Once inside, they continued away, breath held and chattering their success to one another. The further they ascended, the wider their overall view through their transparent tube. The ocean below was an unrecognizable floor and the vision of the small island of green from above was a delight.

After several mighty thrusts, such effort was no longer necessary. The tubes moved in waves, almost esophageal, a reverse birth of sorts, as if pushing them *back* into a body, *away* from Surface. The pathway not only yielded, it sped them along to Depth. It was a common revelation when, for the first time, a young adult Orion marveled at the world from high above while luxuriating in the comforting massage of the tubes. However, Fadwah could not pause to admire the view. As seasoned Orion knew, the tubes would not react comfortably to stoppage.

With Monifa at the lead, they whistled plans how to navigate the most efficient way to Depth, based on the tubes they had selected. The pathways would not solve the problem for them. There were many bi- and trifurcations ahead for each and those would be the easiest decisions on how to stay together. Some pathways branched out in numbers too many to count. Many led right back to foci that brought them closer together again. Always, they had to keep on their fins, think fast, helping a bit to push forward. If they paused and remained passive they might inadvertently trigger an antigen-like reaction that was too terrible to mention to a first-time diver. They had to remain calm, stay in contact, echo-scan, report, adapt, listen, act, all coordinated and efficient.

First dive was especially thrilling for the initiate. She received her orientation from the elders. She might encounter a mere krill of disorientation-type peril if any. They would help her. With plenty of oxygen stored in their flesh and more to spare, they would enter through the closed, cold surface of Depth. There were only a few cracks where liquid ocean was breaking through that could accommodate the mass of an adult Orion. They would enter there. Warmth seeping upward into useable tubes would hint at the few, best routes. It would chill her terribly as dense slush suddenly pressed hard all around her. It's a good thing she was a privileged Orion. Any other cetacean, including a deep diving Master of the Ocean, would have quickly succumbed. The slush was the only part of the journey where they could do little but be carried along. Fortunately, the radiated warmth from their bodies stimulated waves of contractions from the tubes at that phase.

It all flowed as planned.

"Do we have any more of that fruit in here?" Johnny turned to Kei's pack.

"Near the top right."

Johnny rustled around as the story played on.

The gorgeous bioluminescent displays, given off by the tiny lives that clung throughout the tubes and flourished within the slush filled surface cracks, alone, were worth each journey. Easily tolerating the temperature changes, the Orion were eventually expelled from the slush canyon at the transition to liquid brine. It was not unlike being born anew, each journey, into the Orion Realm.

Crunch. Slurp.

"Shhh."

They dove free from their transport canals, released by each orifice just below the icy boundary. Once they had all emerged, swimming freely into liquid brine of Depth, Monifa gave the signal. They scattered down from the cold toward warmer water, heated by the orb's core. With their breath still easily held, they chattered to each other excitedly as they descended.

Muffled crunch, slurp.

The eldest male guide chirped to Fadwah, "Eat what you can, create light shows as you wish, catch as many alive as your mouth can safely hold and then get your flukes back to us!"

"Any more of those?" Kei asked. "I want one."

"Shhh."

The elders stayed in a loose group at a shallow depth directly under where they had entered. They echo clicked and tipped each other off to close, easy prey. They could be heard in the distance whistling, exclaiming at the delicacies they feasted on, and commenting on the wild, sexy, bling shows they were putting on for each other.

"Oooh, cool!" Kei pointed to a particularly vibrant series of colorful flourishes.

"Very," Johnny agreed. "Now Shhh!"

The elders were used to Monifa's unusual solitary behavior that Depth evoked. She wandered off whistling to herself of patterns in the light they could not perceive themselves. They left her alone and called off the novices that began to dive after her.

Monifa interpreted subtleties in the lights. Yes, there were the ancient lit up relics of Auden and Jomei, "We love you, always." But there were also new patterns that were distinctly theirs but different from the reiterative reminder she had come to anticipate. Those differences always announced an imminent visit. She waited a moment, watching and listening. Her bioluminescent 'read' confirmed their presence in a way that only she would know. She scanned again. Her click data returned nothing close by, except flitting young Cephalopods. They had to be there, she was sure of it.

Crunch, slurp. Slurp. Splash. Johnny accidentally dropped the pit into the ocean.

"You'll be time traveling to get that before it hits the water." Kei was annoyed.

"Hey, it's organic!"

"But not in this universe."

"Shhh."

Fadwah was well off on her own and Monifa was listening to her calls too. Like all other first-timers Fadwah was in awe and crying. Monifa imagined her, out of visual sight, gliding slowly through the cool brine, admiring the pristine clarity of the collective display. They never wanted to leave once they got there. It was that wonderful.

Fadwah was truly impressed with the happy display of unbound Cephalopod existence. "*This* is how they are *meant* to be, how they truly *wish* to be." Their turbulent wakes did not stimulate a sufficient predatory response as they jettisoned away from her. She did not want to kill, or even harm any of these in Depth.

Fadwah began to plan how she would rescue as many Cephalopods from Surface as she could and bring them to freedom in Depth. She calculated quite easily that it wouldn't make much of a dent in total Surface Cephalopod despair, but it would dramatically help those individuals that she could save.

Then she wondered if any of her fellow Orion had done the same. If they had transported a few lucky captives for release into this gorgeous calm. Fadwah had never heard any Orion whistles or read any clicks to that effect. Surely, however, she could not fathom that she was the only Orion who had ever desired to do so. It was, she felt, basic compassion.

All too soon, Fadwah and the pod were called back to formation.

"A fresh donut says she isn't going back."

"Yuck." Kei declined his wager.

CHAPTER 30

Universe: Orcasekai

Monifa's mates had not appeared to her. So, she stayed apart, waiting and looking for more tell-whistle displays. She was sure Auden and Jomei were close. "Why can't I perceive them?" she whistled out loud. Uncharacteristically, she became very agitated.

Her mood was interrupted by an anglerfish. It had come into her view as it slowly swam in an arc from behind, flicking its light-lure bright and aloft, wide around her. She held still, enchanted by its bobbing call to attention. Without any disturbance from her, it turned sharply and sped away.

In the distance, she heard an elder male scold Fadwah. It was most unlike him. He sounded very annoyed too. "Still empty. Typical. At least bring back a mouthful. The rest are depending on you." And then quickly, because the adults knew that the she did not want to go back, he added, "It will always be here. You'll be back soon enough and often too. Now…"

The other novices complained and argued. They did not wish to return, it was too soon. Monifa began to take alarm to it. Their angry retort was *very* unusual. Orion mood in Depth was virtually positive, pure happiness, awe, pleasure.

Fadwah caught a few young, tender Cephalopods, swallowed them alive and wriggling, reluctantly satisfying her own growing hunger that had built during the interplanetary tube swim. She then herded a smaller group and clamped her jaw tightly around them, but did not consume these. She left them trapped in a tiny sustaining pool of warmed brine in her mouth.

This was not the happy experience she had expected. Rather than liberate captives, she was bringing free Cephalopods back to Surface for a life of misery and perpetual consumption.

"Shhh," Kei hissed.

"I didn't say anything!" Johnny protested with a soft nudge to her back. As he did, he had a feeling she was time traveling as he thought he heard her whisper in his ear, "Just trying to help."

Fortunately for Cephalopods, the Orion could only access a limited area of their world. The mammalian relic physiology meant they could hold their breath a long time, but not forever. The presence of invading whales was always indicated by a disturbance; either light effect or distinct cacophony clicks and whistles that tickled sensitive Cephalopod dermal receptors. All prey had to do was stay cloaked and/or stay clear of their predator's vicinity. No whistle, no click and no rude lighting meant safety.

However, the plethora of newborn Cephalopod were all very sweet and curious. The sick and the old who couldn't detect them were also vulnerable. Due to sheer numbers of easy prey resulting from a largely predatory free ocean, Orion were quite successful hunters. Several babies and young had just been consumed and nearby camouflaged adults witnessed in quiet horror.

Struggling, inescapably trapped in Fadwah's stomach, one of the cephalopods she had swallowed alive snipped off the tip of its own arm in a desperate act, to force its predator to know it's suffering. As the chemistry flooded the already regenerating wound, the new molecule-wide spear-tip branched its way into the tissues that squeezed in against her, through mucus and cell layers. There, at the speed of thought, it regenerated a delicate bridge, reaching a synapse distance to a cluster of firing stomach-lining neurons.

A tiny, weak, albeit direct communication was established in that way by the almost-adult Cephalopod but the Orion 'stomach' brain she had connected to did not know how to decipher her 'flash' message as anything but an Orion 'gut' feeling. It was a heartbreaker.

"I feel sick." Triggered by the scene, Johnny relived an awful memory.

"You probably started a plague with that pit you dropped."

"Not that kind of sick."

Fadwah hung suspended as a faint Orion whistle began to sound in her brain.

"...out, Out, OUT"

"Yet." Kei stifled a poorly timed involuntary giggle.

"Remind me never to take a time traveler to a drive in!" Johnny exclaimed.

The swallowed cephalopod had conveyed panicked suffering, but it was not *only* her own. It was polyphonic. The Curl inside her own mitochondria wanted out. They too had been stimulated to sheer agitation. The scaled harmonic was perceptible to many.

Fadwah scanned for an indication of which of her fellows was under attack. She called out loud a compassion plea in her own species communication, "Let them go, you're hurting them!"

"Maybe we could recruit this Fadwah?" Johnny suggested.

"I have a feeling we may already have."

Johnny made a note to himself to determine identical features between Fadwah and the little whale.

Fadwah pushed downward, instinctively, a deep dive given all her might, to the warmer depth. Always in her past, the surface was warmer and indicated air. In panic, she failed to make the adjustment.

"She's confused. Let's get her back to Surface." The elders coordinated their strategy with the worried novices. They turned in unison and sped under Fadwah, some coming in close around her in formation, guiding her back to the ice.

Her guides rolled and bumped her, raking her firmly with their teeth, screaming whistles as she fought them and stinging her with ultra-focused clicks, all to get her under control.

Monifa scanned wide, ready to enter the frenzy at an opportune moment. She realized the glowing tangle of Orion were getting perilously close to the Metavoli. *Idiots.* They had no idea. It was dark, asleep, but *Monifa* knew where it was. She pushed hard a few good thrusts, glided, turned and adjusted her flukes to place herself, floating, between the descending tangle of whales and the dormant colony that could change *everything*.

The adult Cephalopods who had been skillfully cloaked from the invading whales gave them plenty of clear brine. If enough of them *had* been near to Monifa, a single arm *might* have grazed Auden or Jomei who both flanked her, cloaked and vigilant. But, the Cephalopods kept their kind at a safe distance. The Orion twins' presence was a secret known only to each other.

Monifa, herself, did not know her mates were there. Through their multiverse experiences, the Orion twins had obtained their own unique camouflage that defeated vision and echolocation.

Jomei did a cloaked nano-time dive to verify that the huge Cephalopod Priori, Pranaya, was approaching fast; a massive ball of blazing, angry purpose and returned to Monifa. He *thought* out of his cloak. In a quick series of delicate actions, he revealed himself to his beloved and announced the first awakenings of the Metavoli.

Despite the universe of time that passed since she had been evacuated to Orcasekai, Monifa recognized the transport opportunity that was possible. She also knew it was incomplete, out of balance, needing much more to become fully functional. Nevertheless, Jomei confirmed to her that *this*, at long last, *should* be *it*.

She hung for a moment. Even though she had lived so long, she still wanted to say goodbye to the elders struggling above her with Fadwah, all longtime friends, and her progeny back at Surface. But Jomei was there and she feared there would be no return journey to Surface for her.

Monifa had been reliably informed this would happen. It didn't lessen the shock. She trusted Jomei completely and so, despite her moment of scruples, she followed his cue. She turned and swam straight into the Metavoli, as he had done in that familiar Sponge Ocean, and became Gemini.

Johnny involuntarily gasped.

As his mate descended, but before she even reached the Metavoli, Jomei re-cloaked. Before they could welcome their beloved Monifa-G in her new universe, they had to attend to the Monifa-G that emerged back into Depth of Orcasekai.

The Orion ritual party were stunned motionless for a moment, blinded by the sudden blaze of illuminated, living seabed. They felt a subtle increase in ocean temperature, emanating from the light source. It lured them closer, albeit cautiously. To their Orion acoustic sense, Monifa merely bounced right off the ocean floor. They all came in to her to assess her condition with higher detailed scans and concurred that she was fine. They whistled their echo-scanned data returns of Monifa's crash as it had happened.

The light, warmth and cacophony played on Fadwah's confusion. The young whale twisted and screamed. She whistled that she desperately needed air. As her pod moved in to hold her from all sides, she dove, instinctively toward the warm, and inadvertently slammed into the Metavoli.

All Orion eyes were amply light stimulated from below by the glowing floor. They watched and scanned from their various vantage points as Fadwah clearly rebounded hard off the seabed and floated still and motionless. No twitch. No call. No heartbeat. She was, as each of their return echoes confirmed, quite dead.

"There goes our recruit." Johnny complained with a long trailing sigh.

The small pod of Orion noticed a spike in their physical discomfort.

Their muscle-bound oxygen was suddenly, and seriously depleted. They agreed they probably had just enough breath to get them back. It was a long way through the tubes and they had to return immediately. They planned to come back for Fadwah's body, or what might remain of it, as soon as they could.

Monifa called out to them that she was able and would remain with Fadwah's body to protect it from scavengers until they returned. There was no time to argue, so none did. The pod felt the irresistible necessity to breathe that would lead to suffocation if it were not satisfied. They turned in formation, swam upward, away into the colder temperatures, trading position in slipstreams to save effort, found their entry orifices in the slush and initiated the squeeze action back to Surface. Both Monifa and Fadwah were left behind.

CHAPTER 31

Universe: Orcasekai

As the first molecule of Fadwah's anatomy crashed into the Metavoli, it awoke enough to sleepily decide whether it wanted her or not. It did. It allowed her to pass through its membrane. Then it determined what to do with her unique possibilities.

Once her body had merged completely within Depth Metavoli, Fadwah's mind expanded. Linked through it to every Vencello Priori, she thereafter shared much of their knowledge and experience of ancestral universes, including what was coming for her current home, Orcasekai. A long-dormant function would awaken and be triggered. The repair of a fissured multiverse organ would enable a next phase. The flood of eager universases stimulated by the healthy functions of a Metavoli made whole again. A calibration of time between out-of-phase elements of that universe was underway. And when completed, it would all be on to the next adventure.

"See, no such thing as dead."

"I don't know about that, I've seen some road kill…worse than dead." Johnny whistled.

But for herself, Fadwah wished to save her ritual party from whatever horrors had a chomp on them. The experience of Depth should have been as a purely happy one, not only for her, but for *everything* that lived there. "Do whatever is necessary to me to make it so," Fadwah made that one adamant request to the Metavoli as it worked on her. The Cephalopod within her, still alive and suffering, made the exact same request. So too, did the Curl within both predator and prey. Within the workings of the Metavoli, they were no longer ambivalent about their environments. Symbionts associated with every scale from organism to O-O agreed. Together they made up an Orcasekai tuning fork to be applied to the self-healing and intentional

Priori temporal calibration that had already begun.

Each scaled voice of that harmonized plea was completely sincere and in agreement with the others. It was a multiverse rarity, an alignment between predator and prey at every level that heavily influenced Fadwah's outcome.

Fadwah could have become Gemini within the membrane of the Metavoli to transition to survive else time in the multiverse, a shade compatible to her adapted physiology and self-directed purpose. Unlike Auden and Jomei, and now Monifa, she was *not* quantum duplicated. The Metavoli spat her out where she could save her beloved family, right back out into Depth. The Metavoli kept Fadwah as *one*, albeit changed, for her, one last time. She was now a living constant. No matter what happened around her, Fadwah would always remain exactly as she was.

"Interesting." They both examined the little whale, "So that's why she can't be harmed. Not even by you, En."

"I'll bet Akenehi…" Johnny started.

"Oh my, look who it is!" Kei pointed to an approaching cloaked storm of writhing Cephalopod arms. "We can spot that camo anywhere!"

"Pranaya!" Johnny and Kei cheered out her name, in sync.

Pranaya had picked up on the disturbance and was pushing, as fast as her mighty eight arms could propel her, to its source. When she arrived on the Orion scene, the Metavoli was already awake, lit up and warming the ocean above it.

The Cephalopod Priori hung back, assuming camouflage that would easily elude Orion sight and echolocation. She let herself float to the seabed. The area beneath her darkened just before she landed on it. She watched the tight group of Orion move toward the lit floor, scanning one of their kind that lay motionless.

She perceived all but two of the Orion predators swimming up and away. Those that remained were illuminated by the glittering translucent seabed, aglow from the newly activated Metavoli. She watched as it flashed, thinking. As she processed the scene, she realized one of the remaining Orion was dead. It hung in a slow spin while the other, close by, observed.

To her bewilderment, the lifeless body stopped spinning yet ascended straight upward, in unnatural levitation, seemingly pushed. The living whale accompanied it at a distance.

It was Kei's turn to involuntarily gasp, "What in the multiverse…"

Priori did not have a concept of nothing. In their collective experience there was no such thing. But it intrigued Pranaya that this might be a rare cloaking that was impervious to even her perception. She did not follow. She dared not give herself away.

Puzzle solving with time travel was out, for now. Since the first moment Orcasekai and her Cephalopod realm had formed she had not dared. She understood infinity and knew better. She was this realm's protector and she had to *stay* with it.

The Metavoli had been cloaked from her and that was another bemusing stumper. It seemed that it might be working against her. However, it was vital to Depth that she not accidentally time travel. The Metavoli would have known that. If so, its self-deactivation as she landed on it was an indication that it meant to help her.

For a moment, Pranaya was tempted to time travel, satisfy her curiosity for herself. But she knew she would stay with this precious Cephalopod ocean until its very end. And that would be soon enough now that the Metavoli was awake and calculating.

She wouldn't kill herself over *this* one either. This world had never been the way it *should* have been, free from *all* cetaceans. If it was time, then so be it. She was never ready for the imminent pain and heartbreak of the end of a world. However, fresh adventures would follow. Wonderfully dark, pre-O-U-O realms to claim and prepare, Orion camouflage to defeat and adapt. Pranaya wished the Metavoli would get on with it so they could get out, Out, OUT.

The Orion were well out of range. If not, might as well get on with it anyway. She pushed straight up off the sea floor, flashing Priori announcements as she went.

"Cephalopods, prepare for time travel. The end of the universe is imminent."

"Should we time travel now too?" Johnny's nerves were wracked.

Kei glanced casually through the sphere's wall and then nervously reached for her 'shades'. The glasses would help determine if they were in actual time travel, shared memory or something else. "No. We're still in the sphere. This 'drive-in' is realistic, isn't it?"

Auden and Jomei pushed Fadwah to the first tingling of slush. Once they were beyond the perception of Depth Cephalopods, the twins forwent their cloaks.

They guided her through the frozen crevice canyon that defined the boundary of Depth world. Once free of the ice layer, they maneuvered into the bling-coated interplanetary network of trails.

When they reached their junction, they urged Monifa onto Surface for breath while they branched off toward the blazing orb that was Brough.

When they could approach no closer, Auden, in the rear position, tore a hole through the side of the translucent tube with his teeth. It opened the casing just enough for Fadwah to be sucked passively through it. Once her tail was dislodged, they swam back to Surface and Monifa.

Out of her confines and floating in free interspace of Orcasekai, Fadwah was pulled into the quasar. She could not move or whistle, but she was aware and quite comfortable. Closer and warmer, and all the better for it. No pressure crushed her, and no thought saddened her. She finally came to rest at the very center of Brough, Acrituchi radiating to all Orcasekai from him.

The sphere's display went from blazing white to dark in one moment.

Johnny strained as his eyes naturally adjusted. In the dark, the little whale sang in Akenehi's voice:

Depth Metavoli. Surface Metavoli. Two parts of the fractured whole. Surface Metavoli conscious and intertwined with the whale nexus. It had wanted free of that arrangement ever since the sad monstrosity of a neural configuration had become fixed. Depth Metavoli, comatose. Now awake. With both sections of the fractured Metavoli alert functioning, self-repair and then reproduction, transition then out, Out, OUT. But not self-inflicted and not too soon. A natural progression and next generation. It will only be a matter of moments when those two connect, singing in tune, delightfully as one. All will be well. Markers are set.

"So...*we are seeing the end of the universe. The one we are in. Right now. Some type of joining and reproduction too. It hasn't happened yet, but it will. Perhaps very soon?*"

"*Insufficient data.*" *Kei did not sound as calm as he would have liked.*

"*Ok, Akenehi has got this one. I have to pee and I'm sure En does too. Let's get out of this universe before it blows.*"

"*L-32, you heard him. Anywhere you want, just go if you can.*" *Kei squeezed the handles, and they warmed in response.* "*She's good to go!*" *She reached into her pocket to make sure the little whale was secured there. It was. The slime from a freshly de-fleshed fruit pit clung to her fingers as she withdrew her hand.*

"*Excellent pit recovery, and another world saved. Thanks!*" *Kei turned to him truly happy. She licked the sweet goo from her fingers.*

L-32 revved, the bubble popped, spraying them with a short, bracing shower of cold water, and they were off.

CHAPTER 32

Universe: Sponge (Cetapiens)

En eased off the seat, front paws first and after a few satisfying sniffs at sand, trotted off to the surf.

Kei and Johnny were a bit more cautious. Kei maneuvered one foot solidly to the ground, digging her heel in for a planet age estimate. She nodded to indicate the 'go ahead' and dismounted, keeping one leg lightly against L-32 and a loose hold on a handle bar.

At her signal, Johnny took his eyes off her and began to examine the dark over their heads. He returned his focus on Kei, anticipating her reaction of awe, as he pointed up to guide her attention. "There's only one orb like *that* one. Hello *Moooooooon!*" He leaned in closer to her, this time following her assumed line of sight down his raised arm that he swept across the sky from one coordinate to another. "There! Constellations of home sweet *planet!*" His arm and face dropped as he continued the view of his native local universe. "Hold on, these stars are a bit…" He cocked his head toward hers as he calculated. "This was way before *my* time. Most excellent, indeed. This universe is not imploding *any* time soon. And, friendly environ means I'm off to relieve myself. *Finally!*"

Johnny slid off L-32's seat, bumping Kei with his inner thigh as he pivoted off on the side where she still stood, face up to the stars. She didn't budge. He slowly brushed past her, and when she didn't respond to that either, he followed En's paw prints to the water. Without turning around, he called out to L-32, "Nice choice! Tropical beach, nice warm summer night, plenty of privacy…" His voice trailed as he focused elsewhere.

Kei brought her weight to the balls of her feet as she leaned against her ride for support, and shifted it back to her heels again. "Why *here* L-32?" She took a step opposite from the direction Johnny had headed, downwind of En, and bumped into what she was sure wasn't there a split moment ago. "Oi, careful! I could have *fused* with you!" She hissed just above her breath.

She addressed L-23, a living ride very much like her own L-32. L-23 was L-32's mirror image except it possessed obvious congruent features that begged to fit against others of its kind. Seated on it, was its sole rider. The appearance of the two, timed as Johnny and En were walking *away*, was not lost on Kei. She was well trained, sensitive to such cues and kept her voice low.

She turned around to make sure Johnny and En had not noticed. They walked away from them, the dark shapes of man and dog, toward the surf, illuminated only by moonlight.

In a voice unnecessarily lowered to L-32 beside her, she whispered, "Ok visiting family, do what you must." Kei watched as the L's shifted position, relative to each other and began their data exchange. She turned to assess whether L-23's rider was fused to it, as some were, and noted that it appeared able to dismount. Nevertheless, it remained seated. At first look, she was certain it was not a predator. No L-rider could possibly be one of those. Further, they were not acquainted.

This one was suited in a light absorbing material, which appeared to her eyes as the creamy black emptiness of Sponge space. That was not unusual, as many time jumps required such camouflage. Moonlight illuminated negative space around it. Kei made out that its 'helmet' was spherical and, it possessed an androgynous, yet humanoid, body shape. Tiny holes freckled both suit and helmet and through each beamed soft flashing light. Kei blinked successively to resist the collective hypnotic effect.

It was as if she was being scrutinized by a three-dimensional human-shaped section of Sponge space, dense with distant, pulsing stars. She stood still, accepting the examination, as their photons played on her own garments, the L's, and the sand.

After a few moments, Kei moved only enough to glance into the closest rear-view mirror, and positioned her face for self-appraisal. It was freckled on one side with a dense spray of photons.

A soft buzz of echolocation swept over and then through her. At its tickle, she forced her eyes away from her own image and stood straight in anatomical position, facing the rider, aiding its efficiency.

The rider's head and body did not move. The light emanated from every direction and she guessed it was a faceless species. From where Kei stood, every hole in the helmet appeared fixed, but those from the suit seemed to swim a bit, indicating to her that the contents were gelatinous. The suit gave form to whatever was inside and kept it from oozing all over the L.

The echo scan ceased, the beams dimmed for a moment, and it processed its data.

A blackened narrow tube, half the diameter of her smallest finger, extended out of the rider's closest arm, and lengthened to extend toward her. As it approached, at a rate and trajectory that threatened to jab her eye if she didn't move aside, she looked down into it. It was hollow but was filling with glowing matter.

"May I?" Kei understood the offer and politely accepted. She had a preferred method of data collection and obviously this rider was privy to it.

The glow advanced to the tip of the tube opening and formed a bulging droplet. Kei opened her mouth and elevated her tongue, exposing a small glandular bulge. A fine mist was diffused from the tube, directly toward it. She closed her lips and examined the specimen with a deep breath.

Kei relaxed, smiled and shook her head in amusement. This was the best first impression any other rider had made on her, yet. Up until then, Johnny held that honor.

All L series riders were assigned custom multi-purpose gear. Her head unit translated complex communications, including many humanoid and cetacean species. She required it for this rider. But Fadwah had proven better. Kei reached into her pocket. The fruit pit was there. The little whale was not. In a rare panic, Kei slapped and groped at her pockets. Before she could curse at its loss, the rider flashed a message to her.

"Greetings, Kei."

"Greetings." She didn't speak her ritual answer out loud, but the rider heard her nonetheless.

"Our light sequence is ..." and it proceeded to pulse in waves of unlikely-to-be-remembered complexity. There was no translation for its identification that emanated from the black. Kei mused it would have been easier to remember a complete recitation of the nitrogen bases sequenced in fern DNA.

"Fadwah."

"Your name is Fadwah? Much easier. *That* will work." Kei worked out, mistakenly, that the rider was a time-affected iteration of Fadwah, the Orion.

She looked down as a black sphere extended on a stalk from the rider's torso to hers.

"Fadwah," it flashed again.

Not sure what the stalk meant, Kei reached out to give it a 'handshake'. At her touch, the sphere melted, conforming to, and partially covering, her palm. She felt a hard object within being placed against her skin. She rotated her palm to the stars to cradle it. The black retracted, reabsorbing most of the coating of glowing ooze, but leaving a stiff, tiny whale in her hand.

"Fadwah!" Kei whispered her delight. Both whale and palm were damp with a residual film, but Kei gripped her tight.

The rider's thoughts were sharp in her mind as easy as her native communication. The rider was Priori. Many Priori. It was a colony or self-similar to one. A few were individuals with which she had already become familiar. *Brough* was *in* there. And so was *Alvar*.

From them came a buzz of white noise and light, then filtered to a discernable message.

"We can safely traverse the Cetapiens bad-puff, the barrier. As soon as you learned we could do that, you sought us. It wasn't easy or quick, but you found us. And when you did, you helped *us*; you got us this *suit*, this *cool* ride. In return, we did what *you* asked."

"To make our task easier you even provided us with your precious Fadwah. She has traveled with a few riders since we first held her, but, as you know, she cannot come to harm. We retrieved her. Now, she's here with you."

"The barrier? Yes, of course. *That* barrier. Problems solved then? Excellent." Kei was in the presence of an extraordinary rider. Of that, and more, she was certain. "One moment. For privacy. You understand."

"Of course."

Kei carefully balanced Fadwah within the forward most worn depression on L-32's custom seat. Once secured, she turned and watched man and dog, off in the distance still oblivious to her activity. All clear.

*****

Leaving her ride behind, Kei time jumped under her own power. Not far. Without L she was very limited. She arrived just down the beach and a few hours before.

But she was alone and could digest, in her own time, exactly what the rider had indicated. This meant *everything*. She was now a Master Solver. She could trade L-32 up, be just about anything, no more trainees. She could go virtually *anywhere, any time*. It was great news.

But then she realized, she would never do without L-32, she *loved* her. Johnny was more than a trainee to her. He was a friend, he sat at her back and she liked how that felt. Soon they would arrive, with En. No way would she ever abandon *En*. This beach was exactly where she wanted to be.

It was then she *really* let it go. She spread her eyes and arms wide to the setting sun and shrieked with a swell of sheer joy and it carried her to euphoria. It was more happiness than she thought she was capable. It was better than her first dolphin rescue with Johnny. It was better than Akenehi's acoustic universes. It was the high point of her life. She thanked every molecule in the multiverse for every moment of her existence that lead to that beach. She stripped everything off, flung her garments anywhere and waded, childlike and splashing, into the surf. *Just like home. Only better.*

The chemistry of love of life would last for hours. She was determined that this time, she wouldn't waste it. In solitude and quiet, time slowed down just enough. *Float. Enjoy. Reflect.*

Just when she thought it couldn't get any better, it did. A tremendous breach of a large, female orca crashed her happy party.

Kei stood up from the surf and shielded her eyes against the low, reddish sunset. A family of orca had swum in fast, attracted by her ruckus. She counted many females, young of various sizes, and large males. Dorsal fins were close enough to identify individuals. Some spyhopped to view her and she jumped up and down in excitement and greeting. She examined each orca feature as best she could, burning the images in her memory.

Here, deep in a past where every day was paradise for them. And I am here, in my moment, privileged to share theirs.

Kei looked closer at one distinctive female fin and couldn't believe her eyes. *Akenehi?*

Kei was completely naked and so did not have her orca whistle of Cetapiens in any pocket. It was back in her storage compartment, safely tucked deep in L-32. Silently walking to keep pace with the pod as they moved down the beach, she finally called out before she turned to return to her crumpled sandy garments and a careful time jump back to her team.

"Oh, it's good you made it, Akenehi! All is well, as it should be! All is finally well!"

*****

And, I'm relieved communication isn't a problem between us. And sorry, if...*everything*...has been any trouble for you...*all* of you...*any* of you." Kei time jumped as carefully as she possibly could, considering the last few hours, to pick up Fadwah and her thoughts and appear seamlessly back in her conversation, right at the time and location she had left.

"Through Fadwah, our connection is strengthened. She holds an entire universe safe within her, Orcasekai. *Orcasekai* is why we are here, now. We are all marked and will soon take our places on this beach to be a part of it." A stalk had formed out of the suit and indicated in Johnny and En's direction. "And it was no trouble."

The L's completed their exchange and L-23 pivoted 180 degrees, so that their head lamps faced, self-adjusting their illumination to Kei's comfort.

Johnny turned to where he had left Kei and saw two headlights glowing low. Realizing she was no longer alone, he pushed hard through the soft sand to get back to her. He tripped a couple of times and En took advantage, licking his face when he was down.

Mid-pounce, En happened to look around for Kei and only then noticed movement beside her. He ran, yapping that he was on his way, making slow time of his own, through the beach sand.

Kei rehearsed her summary, preparing for Johnny's inquiry. "So, I will learn that you could cross the barrier, Cetapiens during their 'bad puff', I couldn't get through, but you could...right? I voluntarily handed Fadwah over to you. And you picked this place to return her to me, and now we are all here to play our parts, pertaining to what Fadwah is protecting inside of her..."

En arrived first. He recognized the rider's scent as he approached. At that, the Dog Priori's demeanor changed from aggressive to excited and friendly.

"We have not met." Johnny sized up the dark figure, fascinated by the lit pinholes below the sphere swimming in subtle movement. He liked the way Kei's face was freckled with swaying specks of light.

"He says you *have*. And Me. And En, *obviously* En." Kei broke in. She displayed the whale in her hand and then handed it to Johnny.

"Ah, gross! Did you sneeze on this or what?"

"If you ever wish to join with your own L as its sole rider, learn some manners." She nodded meaningfully in the rider's direction.

"Sorry." Johnny involuntarily grimaced as he wrapped his fingers around the slimy whale.

Kei had readied her speech. Johnny now had Fadwah. So, he heard in exquisite stereo both Kei and then the rider's thoughts.

"In my future, I sought their help to cross the Cetapiens bad-puff, asked questions, entrusted them with Fadwah and now they are here and will report. Right?"

"Helmets. Visors down. Prepare for multiple perspectives."

"Right then. Ok, straight to business." Kei agreed as she massaged Johnny's chinstrap, stimulating its form to meld comfortably against the anterior and top of his skull.

Close enough to smell the brine on her, Johnny observed, "Your hair is wet. You could have waited, I could have done with a moonlight..."

She pushed the visor firmly down over his face "No playing, no interruptions."

"...swim." Johnny muffled through the shield.

"*Multiple* perspectives? Is this going to take long?" Kei asked the rider but tended to her trainee. She gently positioned his head with both hands, so his visor faced L-23, and indicated with a slight tweak to his neck that he should hold there. Reluctant to take her eyes off the hypnotic sway of the lights as they played against Johnny's face shield, Kei slowly lowered her own visor. Once it was down she was free of their distraction.

"It's a miracle *you* ever got your own ride with *those* manners." Johnny smirked behind his face shield. "You're *always* rushing! Unbelievable. Even *I* can perceive the *time* they traveled to get this to you..."

The rider's thoughts sounded over Johnny's voice, "For you, years will pass like minutes. For us, willing and able time travelers, we relived these decades of many, to integrate their long-cloaked perspectives at Kei's eloquent request."

"Minutes, Kei. Even *you* can do minutes. No need for me to even sit then. I'd rather stand anyway..." He checked his chinstrap and shifted his weight in the sand.

"Johnny, you have no clue..."

Without announcement, images reverse projected from the expanse of their visors onto their retinas, sounds swelled to their ears, breezes and temperature changes caressed their faces and necks and scents filled their noses.

CHAPTER 33

Universe: Sponge (Cetapiens) and Orcasekai

En was most fortunate. His Dog Priori olfactory sense was so keen, he fully discerned the rich chemical communication that leaked from his friend's helmets, most of which they were pitifully oblivious. He sniffed it all in, watching their every bodily movement for bonus information.

Both Kei and Johnny's helmets awoke together and remained in sync with each other. They were primed and ready to relay many experiences as lived by Orca, the People and Priori of Cetapiens. They were moments imperceptible to the outside multiverse, yet very much lived by its trapped occupants over the course of decades.

Kei addressed the rider while calibrations were bringing all senses to full function.

"Ah, swapped head gear, have we? Nice! Highly adaptive...extraordinarily evolved...superior intelligence. Amazing! What do you feed them?"

"Perspectives."

"Right."

Begin Perspectives: Part One: Cetapiens graft to Orcasekai. Amaranth catalyzed two tricky substrates marked as belonging to two distinctly differing universes: Cetapiens of the Sponge universe and the Metavoli-2 of the Vencello. Her intent was to save every endangered entity within those two substrates and combine them within a wonderful new universe.

She conceptualized Cetapiens as a distinct realm, compatible with universase action, of which she was authorized by nature to conduct. Cetapiens, however, did not self-adapt with other substrates of Orcasekai as expected. But it was not destroyed either. Rather, the Cetapiens sea, jungle, structures, and all inhabitants remained in their Sponge universe, but also in Orcasekai. During Orcasekai's existence, and almost to its very end, Cetapiens was in two universes at once. One of the consequences of Amaranth's catalysis was that the time travel puff, that kept Priori safe inside while still permitting time travel into and out of it, went bad. The Priori inside at that moment were trapped there.

They were completely taken by surprise. They had assumed the statistically insignificant possibility of a temporal prison spontaneously capturing them was equal to nil. They were concerned. They wanted out. But they were multiverse wizened. Their first response was to do nothing, expecting a self-correction would reestablish their freedom immediately.

All darkened and went quiet. Johnny took the pause as an opportunity to speak.

"Remind me to time travel to a university and observe a class or two on enzymes. I need a better grip on what exactly Amaranth does." Johnny nudged Kei. His elbow found her although his visor put him in a scene of Priori Templesekai elders in intense conversation.

"They won't have a class on that, but I'll join you. I could use a long break. Then we'll meet up with Amaranth and get up to speed on universases." Kei scanned the faces; a crowd of worried Priori through her visor, too. "Continue perspectives."

Perspectives. Resuming. Part Two: Cetapiens Orcas

Arva'Anati's Gemini transition to Cetapiens happened well before the puff went bad. Although hers happened through the same exceptional process as Alvar's, it was much easier than his. She was a cetacean after all. Akenehi helped her through it, just as she had helped Alvar, encouraging and affectionate, until their connection faded.

Arva'Anati surfaced for breath for the first time in the Cetapiens sea. Out of sheer habit she swam around once in a tight circle. The tank walls were gone at last. That once around was all it took. Magnificently, she arched her back and then straightened, diving straight down deep until the seafloor stopped her, adjusting her fins so she spun as she descended. She leveled out and scanned the seabed and the creatures that hid and swam, relishing new dimensions of freedom. She stretched and flexed to her hearts joy. She stayed down as long as she could too. Finally, she rose comfortably for air, spyhopped to the open sky and sun and submerged again. She called out to her mother and heard her answer.

"Swim now, find your new life, my beloved daughter, my fertile singer". Then her Vencello connection resumed its normal silence.

Arva'Anati's physical transition was complete.

Soo, the orca matriarch of the surrounding Cetapiens sea, and her young grandson, Yu were swimming close by. Soo had accepted Akenehi's request to care for her daughter. They heard Arva'Anati's strange but beautiful dialect through the briny distance and swam toward it.

Within minutes of greeting, the three bonded. Arva'Anati's name was specific in length and complexity to the clan of her birth, the 'singers'. So different from the orca names of Soo's family. In attempting it, Yu called her Avi. He tried repeatedly but could not manage to mimic the subtle details of her true name. He had sung as well as he was capable and was beginning to whine in frustration. Every note he made was a delicate, beautiful sound to her ears. She loved the shrill brightness coming from his sweet little body. Arva'Anati agreed that he could call her 'Avi' and she would always answer to it.

Soo was grateful for that and received Arva'Anati's permission for her entire clan to do the same. New name, new life. It sounded like beautiful music to Arva'Anati.

'Avi' instantly loved Yu very much. Heart wrenching memories of her own little ones, she had carried, born and lost during her captivity, surfaced at the sound of him attempting her name. Her maternal love received a new breath of life from this little orca.

Unlike Alvar absorbing a human language instantly through the multiverse, Avi learned much, but couldn't adapt to Soo's dialect as completely. Orca communication had a learned aspect, but it was more heavily influenced by acoustic neuroanatomy, which she retained genetically, than human language. It was not a serious problem however. Orcas were inherently extremely intelligent and acoustically inclined to solve such problems. They made quick progress.

Avi loved Yu more and more as he understood and accepted her so easily.

Avi tenderly asked how much longer would it be until Yu was taken away. Yu cried out at the idea. He begged his Grandmother to keep him. He had never thought of such a thing.

Soo did not understand why Avi could even conceive of such a horror, let alone suggest that the clan would allow it, but then she did. Captivity. She had heard it sung by Akenehi herself. Soo took these warnings of the suffering 'land stingrays' could inflict to matriarch heart. Akenehi had shared much with Soo about her daughter's misery, but nothing so tragic and cruel has having her children taken from her. Apparently, even in sleep-song, Arva'Anati had been able to spare her mother the worst of her suffering and so neither had Soo known. Soo was even more determined to help Avi now that she did.

The three swam together to meet up with the rest of Soo's family.

Avi was heartbroken to learn that Yu already had a mother, because she really wanted to keep him beside her, as her own. It wouldn't be too many years before Avi would give birth to her own precious little orca. Soo's mature sons were enamored with her gorgeous vocals. And when they heard her sad history, they were as protective toward her as one of their own family.

*****

"I know that orca. She's...magnificent." Johnny's interruption caused the repot to hold the image of Arva'Anati still to his eyes.

"She is as you described her. Well done." Kei gave Johnny the moments he needed. He had been the catalyst that had enabled Avi to become G after all. It was a bond like no other. "Whenever you're ready."

"Can I back this up, this perspective? I want to experience that again."

Kei prepared to speak her answer through her closed visor; she had no clue. She examined the image as Johnny saw them; three orcas, two adult females and a youngster, pulled along by his thought flow, as the vantage points smoothly slid from one to another. It never ceased to amuse her how visually oriented Johnny was, as opposed to her auditory preferences.

As Johnny thought his desire to relive Avi's introduction to her adopted family, and before his words had formed his sentence, the perspective executed the perfect image play back in multiple dimensions. For a few moments, he experimented with the controls, they were virtually his clearest formed thoughts as processed through his brain's language centers. He viewed the images from various angles, instantaneously without speaking directions.

"This is cool," Johnny breathed out at last, expected Kei to urge him to resume, but she was quiet. "Resume perspectives."

Avi's new life at Cetapiens was not even one sunrise in. The Priori puff had not yet gone bad. Soo had been jamming her orca brain with songs of the nuances of her clan and their long history within their beautiful ocean territory. The orca matriarchs of Soo's time kept the families relatively isolated from one another unless mating or ritual pod convergence was called. To initiate any purposeful mingling, a matriarch would make a special visit, accompanied by her eldest son.

Soo expected to call, or be summoned to, one such gathering soon. Avi was invited to swim along. She was to learn many rules of etiquette of all the neighboring clans.

Avi happily anticipated the long, straight swim. There was only refreshing brine, friendly orcas, tasty fish and exhilaration ahead of her. Her new clan's sea territory was so vast that it could take a several-days leisurely forage in a single direction before hearing the faint calls of a neighboring pod.

The Cetapiens sea was warmer than the cool water of her birth, her home in a distance time and climate, while she was still at Akenehi's side. However, Soo's territory let her dive at will to cooler temperatures, deep and bracing, eluding searing rays. She relished every movement of her Gemini restored orca body. She swam among the pod, often spontaneously pushing away, diving, surfacing, twisting, rolling, breaching high and hard just because she could. She tested her flukes against the very limit of ocean resistance. Even when she floated and began to sink, she tensed muscles throughout her physiology and concentrated on the pleasure the sensation produced. She was fully alive with prime orca health.

The exhilaration of hunting live, clever prey came right back to her, as did the skills of Akenehi and her matriarch, when applicable. New quarry, varieties and techniques of Soo's pod were just as stimulating.

The strange link between dead fish and conditional acceptance that had been the reality imposed by her human trainers was completely absent. Her fellow orcas efficiently worked out their few issues with one another with logic and compassion. They were fully honest. They did not confuse her with petty mood, short temperedness or stupidity. They were orcas. Being among them for only a few days healed her spirit of the damage humans had inflicted on it over decades.

Her joy was contagious. Soo's clan was even happier than their everyday utopian life had been without her. All of them mimicked her lilting vocalizations and were eager to adapt them to their own repertoires. They were at once more accepting and helpful than she could have hoped.

Yu sang that he anticipated every day with his new 'auntie' would be just as fun and interesting. Avi was ready for it too. By the end of her very first day at Cetapiens, she had made huge breaches toward synchronizing with the natural rhythms of that time.

"Beautiful. Such a place existed on my own home world." Johnny was adrift in a flood of endorphins.

"It is. Absolutely." Kei agreed. "Pause Perspectives? Would you like a repeat?"

"No. But…the clarity of the water, the sound of orca song through it. It was perfection, wasn't it?"

CHAPTER 34

Universe: Sponge (Cetapiens) and Orcasekai

Perspectives. Resume Part Two: Cetapiens Orca.

Within a few blissful days, Avi detected a rough orcaesque whistle wafting from a distant boat. Soo cautioned her back, but Avi was as completely fearless as she was content. Clearly humans were imitating orca whistle, but these sounded sloppily like her mother's, in enough of her unique clan's dialect to give her hope. She agreed with Soo's warning that humans were stupid, cruel and incompetent in many ways, but Avi had succeeded in training her human captors nevertheless. It was a skill that had come in finny. And within a few whistles, Soo accepted that their newest pod member wanted to give her a demonstration of how she might put human-stolen years to orca use. Avi went in close, spyhopping to observe the human whistler. The human came in close too. Too close.

Arva'Anati and Alvar made physical contact. They were Vencello cousins, Metavoli-2 products, and time travelers.

That intersection in Sponge space and time when and where Alvar's finger tips touched her dorsal fin created a fixed and clearly unique marker that distinguished that moment 'Priori Safe'. The influx of visits by time travelers over the infinity of the multiverse to that multiverse coordinate resulted in a protective reflex against the resulting temporal imbalance.

For the moments that were absorbed into that blip there was only herself, Alvar, Grandmother and the Admiral. The other humans and orcas were gone.

Fortunately, the potentially catastrophic paradox quickly self-corrected, all was seamlessly restored as it had been. The Vencello cousins had carelessly caused the Sponge world to gag, sort of, in reflex. They were lucky to have survived its vomit-recover cycle and

Avi knew it too.

When every orca reappeared, they did so in an excited state. The pod sang in overlapping whistles and frantic burps and buzzes of echolocation.

"An Alliance! Such agreements between orca pods, natural and necessary, yes. But with Land Stingrays? Unprecedented" And so on.

Soo heard Avi's insistence, in equally excited whistle and echo-click, that she had been else time, having a completely different, strange experience. *Alliance? I did not hear any of it.*

The matriarch listened patiently. When Avi had finished, Soo insisted that her clan had not disappeared. They had been together, right with her, and had not swum off in stealth. Indeed, they had witnessed Alvar approach and even touch her.

Soo suspected Avi had lost consciousness and dreamt. So, they would bring her up to speed in sleep song. The entire clan joined in, attempting to complete Avi's memory with multiple experiences.

A horrible din had erupted at the very moment of Land Stingray-Avi contact. Many unfamiliar orcas were heard calling through it. The least understandable of those songs was a vague warning of 'storms', to avoid them or be harmed. The clearest were Akenehi's, Avi's mother. Her calls were heart wrenching, as if she had lost, and was searching for, her entire beloved family.

At the same time, the Land Stingrays, in their boat, and Orcas, in the sea around it, had an extended epiphany, a clear, mutual understanding. It was as if they were no longer separated by their environs. An Alliance was, from that moment forward, in effect.

And then Avi gave Soo's family *her* experience.

They all heard it. There was no break in any memory. The waves of events had carried them all naturally.

Soo's memories, and those of the orcas that were present, converged again with Avi's immediately following the establishment of the Alliance between Orca and the People. The Alliance had happened and Avi had apparently missed it.

The recall of an orca was as reliable as the experience itself. Soo had only to sing it once to Avi and that would have been enough. Sleep song merely added their memories to hers. They did not argue that one was correct and the other wrong. They agreed that even though they did not understand, the two experiences were valid. Avi had been in two places at once. Although it went against their prior reason. Avi's presence and differing accounts opened their formidable minds ever wider.

*****

Not much could shake Avi's optimism. Captivity did.

Avi loathed it as those who had only ever known freedom of open ocean could not. She recognized its sinister persistence in subtleties of everyday life. For one, her body was a captive of brine. She could not swim onto dry land or time travel back out of it. For another, many of her thoughts were a captive of her past, especially the memories of her babies that were now probably as liberated in death as she was in the Cetapiens sea. They swam as little orca shadows, alongside her with hurried tiny flukes and their tinkling orca songs echoed 'mamma'. The vague orca warning of 'storms' could not be ignored. The anticipation of them was already keeping Soo's entire clan captive in its own way. They had postponed their swim to the neighboring pod due to uncertain weather.

Avi wasn't even sure that it was *weather* that was coming to them. But she was certain that what the others had enigmatically but undeniably heard was true, avoid it or else.

She had conquered some captivity. There was no doubt about it. Avi was ecstatic to be free of her tank. She was very fond of her new pod. Nevertheless, during her first days as a stranger, Avi longed to swim among her own, her matriarch, and especially her babies once again.

Avi was beginning to think it would never happen. But one day, as they had been warned, the first strange storm formed.

Concomitantly, the Priori puff went bad.

Avi spyhopped then turned her head so one eye was skyward. The alarming change of light refracting throughout the water was coming from above. She pushed her flukes to give herself a slow spin, then let herself sink a bit, switching sides so the other eye could have a full view. As she rotated she looked in every direction above. A dramatic patterning and coloration had manifested across the entire sky.

The other orcas were attracted by her reaction and her struggle to translate what she was seeing into orca song. All sounded normal. They did not *see* anything unusual either. Except for the storm, the sky remained to them as it had been. Avi was reminded, as if she could possibly forget, that she was different. This was another indication that she was of a different place and time.

Cetapiens had been grafted into Orcasekai even as it remained anchored in the Sponge.

Avi saw the blended two skies at once. They all saw was the Sponge universe's sky, blue by clear day and black by night. But only Avi was suddenly able to perceive the physical manifestations of the Orcasekai interface that no orca song could describe.

They all agreed perfectly on the obvious onset and duration of the *storm*. Once it had passed, Avi was the one orca that did not dread its return in the least. True, it raged, boomed, and unnerved the other orcas. But it also screeched and clicked. It condensed and then spread itself thinner in rhythmic cycles, like breathing and heartbeats. It *sang* to her. They noted a distant perimeter where the storm had appeared and eventually dissipated without advancing further. There was no ambiguity that the orcas had to work out regarding its spatial limitations.

The storm boundary revealed itself. Always at the same arcing altitude and distance at its thinnest, it scattered out to cover the entire range of Soo's territory, over the horizon and then down into the ocean. It domed across an expanse of sky over the tree line. At each climax, it condensed. The formation could be anywhere. Sky, over the tree line and out of their view or even in the sea.

When possible, they watched the cloud collapse to a single point and disappear beyond the jungle, as they spyhopped and viewed with one eye exposed to air. It was easily done. No raindrops ever fell from that cloud to obscure their view.

Any birds that flew overhead were unbothered by it, but if they got too close, they would splash through the surface, quite dead, bleeding from the inside out. Soo's pod had been sleep-song warned, and taken together that was all good enough for them.

If *that* was it, occurring at predictable intervals and never closing in on them, those storms would be easy enough for orca to avoid. They were heedful and urged Avi to do the same.

But Avi was what the other orcas of Cetapiens were not, a wonder-fluked Gemini. Inherent in that multiverse coolness was greatly expanded perception. She heard soft, complex echolocation that emanated from everywhere across the dual sky. Unfortunately, no other orca heard them. With her orca-G acoustic intelligence, she kept her ears on it without letting it become a distraction. While her reports of their environment through her senses were enigmatic, it reinforced to Soo's clan that Avi likely possessed a useful awareness.

During her brief physical contact with Alvar, who was also Gemini, their temporal blister made them one. What one remembered, so did the other. What one felt about what they remembered was also shared. That included insights of slavery, as Alvar understood it. In that short, limited glimpse, she was totally done with it. Avi would not suffer any form of captivity if she could help it. She was no longer a little orca. She would meet it, fight it, even if it killed her. She certainly didn't fear death.

When the second storm began to rumble across the distant perimeter, the entire pod spyhopped to observe its patterns, its behavior. The succession of thinning followed by condensation, in both thus far, were predictably rhythmic. The location of its center, each time the cloud progressed to a fuzzy smear, then solid, was difficult to predict. Even Soo, the most experienced predator among them, could not calculate its most vulnerable phase. Its song taunted her through the brine. Avi heard the challenge and accepted.

Alone, she sped away, exhaling in mighty plosive mists as she arced high through the surface for each new breath, altering course from one surface breath to the next, just enough to spot her quarry with one eye. When she was within echo-scan range, she took one last breath and stayed low, pummeling the sea with her flukes with all of her might as she homed in on it, at top speed.

Instead of two final fluke pumps followed by a leap and a chomp on her prey, as she planned, she swam full speed into the midst of her new pod. One just managed to twist out of her way to avoid their violent collision. In a punishing burst of echolocation, she spun around expecting her prey was close and would betray its location. Only the chatter of confused orcas, scattering in every direction, rang in her ears.

"Avi must have become confused in the excitement of the hunt."

"Avi must have swum in a circle."

"Avi charged that way but returned in the opposite direction."

Not believing what they sang could be correct, she rose to the surface and spyhopped. They sang true. With one eye she could see that she was much closer to the shore than she should have been. Her target had shrunk greatly, which betrayed its precise location to her. It was still out there.

Avi broke brine with her flukes, charging off at full speed again, calling out that they should swim as little as possible and be vigilant if she should suddenly reappear. This time she did not bother to look up. Relying solely on her keen ears, she made an orca-line directly at her prey.

She need not have warned her clan. They listened as in super stealth as her voice dimmed. After a drop then silence, she was back.

Again, they scattered to avoid collisions and again she screamed in frustration. Avi flung herself through the surface, crashed down, circled back up and spyhopped. It was out of sight now, but she still discerned its location. So, for a third time, she swam off in pursuit of it. The larger adult males followed. Avi did not hunt alone. Nevertheless, they looped right back again.

Instantly, a fourth hunt took formation. Emboldened by their safe, albeit frustrated, return, many of the other adults joined in too. They fanned out, planned strategy with each other as they neared their target. Again, they ended in consternation right back where they had begun.

The storms had imposed a puzzling confinement and immunity on the orca of Cetapiens.

Soo immediately calculated the disadvantage of their limited range apart from neighboring pods. She whined in fear. "How will my daughters find potential mates? Brothers are positively out of the question."

Now it wasn't only Avi that loathed captivity. They all did. They wanted OUT.

Over days, while Soo's pod puzzled over each storm, the systems came and went. Avi was especially goaded by each outburst. The orcas agreed that their best efforts to 'catch' it only stimulated its learning and gave them all some extra exercise. They were getting used to them too. Soo instructed her family to give up hunting them, hoping the storms would just go away for good on their own. But they persisted and so did Avi.

Even when there were no storms, the sky was weird. Avi couldn't compare her observations of it or its enigmatic clicking from one day to the next with those of another orca, because they never saw or heard it. Within several days, she noticed unmistakable, albeit minuscule, clear formations of normal blue sky had appeared, as if they had gradually broken through the strangeness. Those only grew as weeks passed. A non-linear but progressive increase in 'Sponge only' sky was consistently discernable. Avi suspected a 'count down', like one that the pod used to coordinate hunts, was under way resulting in a slow resolution to 'normal'.

Then, one storm sang, unlike any before it. As it raged, Avi heard orca screams emanating from it. It was no random sound effect from taunting weather. Not echoes and not from a neighboring pod, beyond the barrier. Even after decades, she remembered. They were unmistakably a distress call from Akenehi's clan. These emanated from the temporarily thinned, but most violent storm phase. She rose to the surface and spyhopped.

Soo rose close to her and exhaled a fine mist into the air. She asked in concerned tones, "What sings to Avi's orca senses?"

"My very own clan. Distress calls. They are in trouble." Avi beat several strong strokes before Soo chimed in. Avi was off at top speed.

Soo listened again and heard it too. She recognized the dialect, lovely, even in panic. Family was highly personal and that was Avi's clan. It was best to leave her to it. Soo gathered her family on high alert, following at a respectful distance, just in case their help was needed.

Avi made excellent time to the boundary of caution. She held a submerged position at the proximity just before the wall of fizzy brine, a thin barrier of Buzzpips, that threated to loop her right back to where she had come if she swam any closer. Had she not been desensitized from multiple failed encounters, she might have been driven back by the storms raging at such proximity.

All self-doubt was washed away by the beating of her orca heart. Fins and flukes adjusted only enough to prevent sinking. Underwater, she hung still, her jaw almost touching the closest of the Buzzpips. Their frantic vibration tickled the water and the tip of her skin. Its burning sensation as she slowly drifted into it reinforced the boundary's threat. She backed up, but only just. In slowest, careful echo scan she learned the wall was thin enough but as confining as her concrete tank had been. Enigmatically, memory of her contact with Alvar surfaced powerfully and she dared not touch it again.

But she didn't retreat either. She could hear them, her family. Their frightened calls to each other were as clear as they could be. They were her own clan and they were close. She sang out to them and waited for a response. She dared not even surface for breath.

"Do you need a break? Would you like to sit?" Kei asked Johnny, concerned that he had been standing all the while.

"I'm good. The sand feels great. I could stand for hours." Johnny voice was solemn. "How are you doing En? You alright buddy?"

En lay curled up near his feet.

"There is not much to smell under water, is there? Without a visor of his own to see what we do, he's lost interest."

En perked up at the sound of Johnny's voice and cocked his head to one side.

Johnny peeked out from under his visor and admired the sight of freckles of light dancing across En's beautifully marked fur in the dark. En looked straight into his eyes, ears raised in question. "You're fine. Keep sleeping, buddy."

En lowered his head, shifting to rest his long jaw between two front paws.

"Practicing your cetacean diving skills?"

"Huh? Why do you ask?" *Johnny examined the still scene of Arva'Anati, compliments of his visor. The orca hung immersed in clearest brine, so much more magnificent than he remembered in her tank. She fearlessly confronted yet another wall, this one of tiny dark specks.*

"You hadn't taken a breath for a while."

Johnny let out a single huff of a half chuckle, "Can never get too much practice there."

"Alright then, continue?"

"Continue Perspective."

CHAPTER 35

Universe: Sponge (Cetapiens) and Orcasekai

Perspectives. Resuming. Part Two: Cetapiens Orca.

Seasnàn was amazed that her clan was still alive. They were holding their breath as in deepest dive, caught up in the worst horrific fluid turbulence. None would have imagined such a force could surround them yet not rip them apart. The air was miraculously not forced from their lungs. She called out to her sisters to pool scans and help orient the family groups. None could gather a clue to where the surface might be, or even if there was a surface. Seasnàn's heart pounded a rallying rhythm against her eardrums. The clans screamed out to each other and kept their formation. But this was fresh steaming chaos. It took split second adjustments not to lose sight or sound of each other. They adjusted their positions to allow the youngest members to surf vortices. The young were crying out in primal fear. An orca would suffocate before they would drown. They were in agony, unable to open their blowholes. They were pelted and squeezed yet they fought orca-fiercely for life. The air was almost spent and the largest of them were growing faint.

As the Metavoli's transition from Sponge to Vencello to Orcasekai progressed, it dragged all Sponge orcas near its periphery with it. Seasnàn's clan and many other orca pods had gathered for evacuation just outside of the cone, doing their part to activate it, but not knowing what to expect once initiated. Now they were trapped in its slipstream as it settled in the periphery of the bad puff of Cetapiens. No orca could survive for long in that virtual hurricane. Orienting in the stream, Seasnàn tried to scan their position relative to *anything*, twitching her head smartly from side to side, up and down. There were so many clumps of free mitochondria, zippy and small that confounded her echolocation, but she could see their blur and hear them. Buzzpips rioting annoyed her to no end. It was almost impossible to communicate to each other over the racket, but the orcas vocalized lower than usual in their acoustic range and it worked.

Seasnàn called out again and again. Their returns were growing faint. She could visually make out white patches surrounded in black, identifying family. They were still in formation. She calculated a distance ahead of them. If she threw herself there, with all she had left, she might create a slipstream. The force of her last mighty lunge against the turbulence would injure if not kill her but her charges would be spared at least a few more moments of this. Her sister knew what she was about to do and blocked her. "Not yet!" She sang out, "We all still have some *orca* left in us. Dearest ones, sing for your very lives, your family, your matriarch, if not…our last song together!"

Seasnàn quickly selected a patch where the blots seemed to be collecting, ever denser. "Here! Let your voices and beating heart *blast* this!"

Akenehi's clan lead with screams, utilizing bone rattling, pure tones reserved for desperation when orcas curse their enemies to death and kill the most exhausting prey on the spot through their vocalizations alone.

*****

Sound is to an appropriately trained orca what a thumb is to a human craftsman. Certain prodigy orcas can do with their voices what humans could never even imagine sound could achieve.

Like her mother, Avi was an acoustic prodigy. She heard her family cry out as they fought the worst of it. Those trapped inside the storm were losing. Avi was determined to either get them out to safety or die trying. She cursed the storm to its death, a horrible one, a complete and utter eradication. In any universe, in all of them. The stereo effect of the bone shattering orca screams from her clan, inside, and from her, outside of it, blasted the Buzzpips clear between sources. A temporary escape route opened through which the trapped orcas could breach to the outside. Seasnàn and her family, were sucked through it and hurled out.

Once they were sent flying, they sensed a favorable external environment, each blowhole opened in reflex. They gasped in as much air as they could before the sensation of the first significant splash of ocean forced them closed again. Each landed clumsily with spectacular crashes through the surface of the brine. They were safe within the border of Soo's territory.

Seasnàn took several moments at the surface to breathe then count orca. Although relieved when her entire clan sounded off, she was alarmed that not a single member of the other pods had made it through. She quickly assessed the physical state of each of the youngest orcas, then going up in birth order to the adults. Everyone was pretty banged up, fins nicked, some chunks torn off too, superficial punctures and other minor injuries. Their prior identification marks, which Alvar would have surely recognized, were covered by multitudes of fresh injuries that would leave them all badly scarred. Scars were nothing to an orca except perhaps a source of entertaining song in the telling of each story behind it. It was their voices that made them fully orca. Everyone, even the very youngest, had survived, with voices and orca spirit heroically unfazed.

The receiving sea was warm, uncomfortably so. They dove down as far as they could for a little relief and came back to the surface.

One of her brothers complained in gorgeous orca dialect, "I hope this isn't what momma had in mind when she urged us to another world. I hate it."

Another brother called over him before he had finished, "Put your *whining* to useful song already."

The successive thunderous breaches of so many caught the attention of every orca within the boundary of the bad puff. Avi spyhopped at the first mighty splash, and watched as several orcas free fell in a tight cluster at a distance. She submerged and listened. They were close enough. With every ounce of ability, she pounded through the water as fast as she could toward the lilting dialect and orca commotion.

As she approached, she recognized the distinctive pleasing tones that matched her own. Then she became shy. She twisted her body and adjusted her fins and flukes to hang back. She hung and listened. She still remembered much of the family's style of communicating. It was coming back to her. She recognized some names, the comforting, assessment procedures, treatments being administered by the senior females. She had dreamt of joining her family again and now that she was there with them, she felt like an awkward stranger among them.

She called out and waited to hear what they would do. She hung near the surface for a moment, took the necessary breath, submerged, then swam slowly toward them. They had heard the call and gone silent, then came a flurry of happy chatter. The loudest called out, "Momma?" Avi hoped she sounded a lot like her mother. She called out her signature whistle then that of the clan: Arva'Anati, daughter of Akenehi. Within moments she was approached by her sister, Seasnàn, who had never stopped longing to swim with her again and was super orca thrilled to finally know her.

The sky remained a puzzle. Avi determined very soon out of the storm that the new arrivals could not perceive the differences she saw, nor hear its clicks any more than Soo's clan could. Avi did not wish to set herself apart from her reunited pod, so she did not sing of it. She only ever breached her tender subject when an orca sang out of affectionate curiosity, "How is your sky today?"

The storms, they all got. And hated.

Soo was not the least bit annoyed a new clan of orcas were sharing her territory. The solution to her progeny dilemma, if the trap persisted, seemed to have presented itself. And if they found they could swim to neighboring territories again soon, then all the better that such wonderful singers still might father her grandchildren.

Seasnàn considered that the pods that had not made it through with hers, might have survived nonetheless. The possibilities were encouraging.

Soo was concerned, as were they all, after a sweeping survey of the fish resulted in an elementary calculation that the current supply would not meet the increased orca demand. With the humans expecting a healthy haul of fish to feed their population, the orcas had a problem.

Fortunately, Seasnàn and her clan had brought knowledge of hunting in a severely depleted ocean with them. One was the experimental acoustic method to replicate fish that Akenehi had strived to master. So far, they had successfully produced eight edible fish from one. Perfect orca vocals, which many of Akenehi's clan happily possessed, came in handy. Now, Seasnàn announced, they required a Long Jaw's powerful echo-clicks. Unfortunately, Soo informed her, there wasn't one within the bad puff boundary.

Seasnàn and her family tried nonetheless with success. But they didn't achieve the eight results they expected. They got two. Without knowing how or why.

Had Avi known what Long Jaw echolocation sounded like from a distance, she might have recognized that much of the complex clicks from the sky were just that; Long Jaw scans from across Orcasekai. The molecule universe was awash in it.

But, the Orcas of Cetapiens did work out that the quality of the fish was best if they herded a bait ball, then replicated by surrounding them with singers, blasting them just so, *en masse*. Not all fish in the bait ball were replicated but not all were consumed or taken by net either.

It required a fine orca ear and vocal apparatus. All mature singers were needed. So, Seasnàn administered treatments to Soo's clan with ultrasound, per Akenehi's method. They improved. Eventually, all the adults could achieve fish duplication after lengthy songs. There were so many acoustic variables that the orcas could not control, they were never sure exactly why one trial worked and a seemingly identical one did not. Nor did they achieve the eight from one result ever again. They calculated that if they kept at it, the fish supply and demand would just about equal out.

Their calculated quota did not promise the easy life that Soo's pod was used to.

Gathering fish had always been easy for them. But now they had to be positioned in a precise formation and stay until sufficient replication occurred. They had always been hunters but only for a small enjoyable portion of their daily lives. They were singers, players and lovers mostly. Now singing was *work* too, time consuming and tedious by orca standards.

The upstroke was that they were all superior singers and connoisseurs of musical quality. Their own orca compositions quickly evolved beyond compare to any other clan in any time during Sponge history. The fabulous songs were entertaining enough to make the work tolerable. A counter stroke was that even a single note sang off-key caused short temperedness. A long extended acoustic cacophony could drive them all to distraction.

The storms were the worst. They were full of miserable notes. Those were especially unbearable until the orcas learned to sing masking tones that transformed them to a bearable harmony.

Right out of the storm, Akenehi's clan resented the Alliance with the land squid. They had not agreed to it. Those beasties had caused such destruction and despair from their own time. And then there were all the lonely years to which they had subjected their poor sister, Avi.

However, Avi was the first to insist that the People should be made tame through ample feeding.

Soo consoled them with her memories of the other orca territories. She sang of how pleasant it would be when the storms were gone for good and neighboring pods could be visited again. One day, Seasnàn and her clan would be free to swim off, if they wished to live separately.

*****

Decades passed and Avi had observed the dual sky every day. As years progressed, the cumulative changes from multicolor detail to uniform blue reminded her of a countdown. She had guessed right. Soon, the entire sky would be as it was before. The change to solid blue indicated self-healing. When it reached critical correction, the whole of Cetapiens would be drastically affected. As if they knew it too, and were afraid, the Buzzpips had become increasingly erratic and noisy. Avi hoped beyond reason it was an indication that their storms were somehow 'injured' and would soon die. It sounded increasingly like a death scream to her predator senses.

In any event, Avi and Seasnàn agreed that their mother had meant for them to swim to an orca ideal and they refused to believe that she would have mistaken the Cetapiens sea, domed by insane weather, as that. The sisters had found each other. The orca clans united and both were the better for it. Seasnàn fully credited Akenehi for that. Their beloved matriarch would never give up on them and neither would they.

Avi did not sing that she was G to any of her kind. She did not dream of the other her, Arva'Anati-G, else time in the multiverse. She was already 'different' enough.

The visors went blank for a moment. There were no interruptions or request for break from either Kei or Johnny. En had fallen asleep at L-32's rear wheel.

"Arva'Anati-G…"

"Arva'Anati-G."

"Perspectives, did Arva'Anati-G ever make it through to Cetapiens with the others?" *Johnny asked as he reached down and stroked the length of En's ear.*

En exhaled and kept right on sleeping.

Perspectives Continued. Part Three: The People of Cetapiens. Life within the Cetapiens bad puff did not come to a standstill….

"Apparently not while the puff was bad," Kei interjected, noting Johnny's behavior as a possible need for reassurance. "But we delivered her message to Akenehi. The rest of Akenehi's family made it through to Cetapiens. I didn't know that. I couldn't have known that. Until now."

Johnny nodded in agreement, visor down, to no one, "Resume Perspectives."

CHAPTER 36

Universe: Sponge (Cetapiens) and Orcasekai

Perspectives Continued. Part Three: The People of Cetapiens

Life within the Cetapiens bad puff did not come to a standstill for the People. The storms and the changes in the sky were quickly declared 'unrelated' by the Templesekai elders. That sufficed. They carried on as usual. They could not perceive the ultrasonic unpleasantness that the storm inflicted on the orcas. They did not experience the mass outbreak that struck many of their Priori visitors. Like Avi, the Priori perceived a strange and beautiful sky that popped and cracked. It kept them awake at night and distracted them during the day. Those stricken Priori had become dizzy and some even nauseous. The People were unaffected by much of it. They learned to tolerate the storms, administered medicines to afflicted Priori and soon life went back to everyday paradise. The weather was even more stable than ever. Crops did not fail. Each day was perfect for joining in the delightful orca cooperative hunts. Every encounter was exhilarating in its own way. During each, the People and the recovered Priori performed snappy music, of whistles and rhythms, which the cetaceans always seemed to enjoy immensely.

The hauls contained a perfectly titrated number of fish that kept the People tame as far as orcas were concerned. They were active, content and always striving for musical perfection.

The visors went blank again. Kei and Johnny stopped swaying and clapping in appreciation of the exhilarating Cetapiens performances to which they had just been treated.

The noise didn't rouse En. Their silence did.

En popped his head up and sampled the air through quivering nostrils.

Perspectives Continued. Part Four: The Acrituchi

En stood on his hind legs and leaned against Kei and Johnny in turns. The

Dog Priori inhaled olfactory data from each of the two helmets, sniffer going full throttle.

An 'injury' to the Acrituchi resulted when Amaranth wove Cetapiens into Orcasekai. It was as if she amputated a miniscule section of its multiverse vastness and reassembled it to pieces of itself that didn't quite match. It didn't 'hurt', at least not overtly, but its streaming emanations from Brough, the only sun of Orcasekai, did not align with the interior of Cetapiens. Of course, the Acrituchi immediately began to self-heal. It did not totally rebuild as a Cephalopod might with a severed arm. The injury site was the entire spherical boundary of the bad puff. That division between Sponge and Orcasekai was minor enough that pre-existing suitable emanations could 'find' each other. So, it proceeded like neurons vining out to reconnect rather than create a new bridge from O-O scratch.

The Acrituchi was so vast, it self-healed the botched graft job without even realizing it was happening.

The visors went blank, and Johnny took the opportunity to ask, "Can we hear some more music?"

L-23 and her rider complied, "Selection Ready."

"Let 'em sing."

Johnny was so engrossed in Cetapiens entertainment, the finest human performances the multiverse had to offer, that he did not notice when he dropped Fadwah.

En didn't miss a beat either. As soon as the whale hit the sand, En smoothly flicked the whale between his teeth and time traveled to one of his secret treasure troves. Guarded and suspicious at first, he made sure all the proper markers were intact, visual as well as olfactory.

He buried Fadwah and transitioned so smoothly back to Johnny and Kei that they never suspected he had left them for a split moment.

CHAPTER 37

Universe: Sponge (Cetapiens) and Orcasekai

Perspectives Continued. Part Five: The Priori (Masters of O-O) with Cetapiens Musical Accompaniment.

The trapped Priori witnessed the moment of Acrituchi injury and its relatively slow process of self-correction. Priori couldn't help but notice when, at a distance overhead, the clear blue sky of Cetapiens one moment was infused with Orcasekai the next. The effect was enigmatic translucence. The cross-section where the severed Acrituchi emanations were grafted from Sponge Cetapiens to Orcasekai, revealed a boundary to them. It veiled their utopia in an empyrean mantilla, impossibly patterned, dense with the myriad colors of the Priori visible spectrum. It was so brilliantly backlit that it's effect was visible during broad daylight. It capped well over the highest treetops and arching outward in every direction, horizon to horizon.

The moment it appeared, a Cetapiens-wide ruckus erupted like none other or since. Not only for the Priori, who could see it, but for the People too. They were deeply frightened and confused by their neighbor's sudden mass hysteria.

Those Priori, who were under roof or tree cover, heard the commotion outside. Many ran to the nearest clearing and some went to the beach for a wider view. The oblivious People were caught up in the uproar too. The long strand of Cetapiens beach was soon buzzing with chaos. Boats, urged to get back immediately to shore by the frightened and confused on board, were coming in from sea as fast as the rowers could return them. Along the vast spans of fluffy white sand, the People and Priori were making their way as fast as they could to help boats in. They hurried from group to group, to those just coming onto the beach. They compared accounts of how the sky looked to them now, exactly what they had been doing up until then, how they reacted when they first beheld the change, how those around them did and so on. The many details of that first traumatic day were being etched in their memories. It was a moment none of them would ever forget.

And then things got worse. The Priori began to experience a sort of seasickness. Many were staggering, some already sitting down, holding their heads, surrounded by concerned helpers. They didn't realize it, but they suffered a Priori version of brain fog too.

The People comforted and cared for their stricken friends. Strain their eyes as they might, they saw nothing but an azure sky. Aside from being anxious for those falling ill, they felt fine.

As far as Priori eyes could see, the enigmatic sky encapsulated them. With every passing moment that it didn't change back, panic gripped them.

A tsunami of Priori should have rushed in at that moment to share in the rare entertainment the sky provided. That didn't happen.

When Cetapiens was grafted to Orcasekai en masse, a virtual Priori blind spot resulted as well. It trapped Masters of O-O inside the puff. Regardless of perspective, inside or out, the boundary confounded Priori temporal navigation and therefore penetration. Those trapped inside were cut off from their multiverse marks. There was no warning. Those Priori within were thus rendered as time-linear and stationary as the orcas and People.

Those on the outside just couldn't perceive them. It was as if Cetapiens time had blended into the multiverse, dissipated. Because those outside the bad-puff of Cetapiens were blind to them, they could not assist.

The Priori had never been in one before, at least that they could recall, but they had experienced temporal self-correction. It only took a single failed attempted to home out to convince them the puff had gone bad.

By nightfall they were annoyed that the self-correction had not completed its cycle. They asked themselves and then each other, "What advantage was there to be a Master of O-O if constrained to a tiny range of dimensional coordinates, essentially frozen in space and time on a nano-dot of a single universe, pleasant or not?"

Not all Priori panicked or got sick. Pranaya didn't. She found a delightful and inexplicable comfort in the patterns overhead. She was amused at the uproar and the lack of understanding her Priori cousins exhibited.

Pranaya spent the first hours of that first day on one of her fine

Templesekai mats. They were crafted from freshly harvested Cetapiens botanicals, picked at their peak saturation with expressive Curl. She had an excellent cloak of her own natural ability and the sudden bad puff provided a welcome camouflage boost. But the mats were surprised too.

She got busy and came up with an elixir that treated the symptoms of a 'bad puff'. She administered it to her fellow Templesekai Priori elders. They recovered enough that they could function as community caretakers. They helped her make large batches of the beverage. The Priori elders and the People walked throughout Cetapiens providing relief.

Two, who were not Priori, saw what the Priori did, but what the rest of the People could not. One was Alvar. The other was the Admiral. Neither experienced any of the queasiness or loss of function that the Priori did.

Alvar feared the worst, and that it was all his fault. Specifically, that his time travel to them might have damaged space somehow. It hadn't. Then he considered the grim possibility that his wedding failure might have fractured it. It didn't. He withdrew into a hut until friendly faces came to fetch him out and ask what he saw, his thoughts and so on. There were no accusing gestures or questions. Alvar wanted to get away so he could observe from the open sky of the beach. When he learned from someone who was just returning from there, that Orcasekai elders were gathering near the sea, he took the opportunity to immediately excuse himself. He selected a smooth trail through the jungle and took off at a jogging pace that he was sure would get him there as soon as possible.

Meanwhile, on the beach, the Admiral walked steadily through the soft sand from one hut to the other, confirming that he saw the new sky too and was certain everything was going to be fine. He pointed out that he was not staggering, nor did he feel ill. That was a huge relief to everyone.

Alvar broke through the tree line and visually scanned the line of huts and the movement of People from one of them to another. He spotted the Admiral, so distinct even at a distance, surrounded and gesturing for quiet. Alvar made a beeline for him.

When the Admiral recognized it was Alvar, and he wasn't staggering, he had only one question in his mind. Did Alvar see the changes in the sky too? He wondered out loud and several of the children who were standing, sprang into action.

"I'll go ask him!" One little girl took off, pushing easily through the powder.

"Me too!" Off they went, following her, laughing and pulling any they could grab that were ahead of them. It was a race to get to Alvar first and yell back the answer to the Admiral.

"Alvar! Alvar! Look at the sky! What do you see? Are you scared?" Their tinkling little voices chimed over one another as they ran.

The approach of happy children, calling out his name really cheered him up. He imitated the Admiral's gestures as they got closer and didn't answer until they were all settled.

He looked down into the face at the little girl who had ran toward him first. Her eyes lit up at his attention. He answered her, "Yes, I see it."

They turned around and yelled, "He sees it! He sees it!" One quiet little voice piped up in disappointment, "It's only because he's so tall."

He didn't answer any more questions until he faced the throng that was still accumulating at the Admiral's hut. The walk had been awkward. All eyes were on *him*. The crowd was too quiet. Then he overheard the Admiral emphasizing repeatedly, "His walk is straight. He sees it. He's not sick. His walk is strong."

The crowd dispersed. They had news to spread regarding the sudden sky syndrome. "The Admiral and Alvar both saw the 'changes' and therefore should *not* have felt fine, but they did." Other news, "No one had died from it" and "Templesekai has already found a cure!" was spreading through the tsunami of communications. Things were already getting more interesting and far less threatening.

*****

The Cetapiens sky didn't change back all day. The Priori consistently responded well to the elixir Pranaya and other Templesekai physicians had titrated to treat their nausea and their nerves. They still saw the change, but they had decided they would stop rubbing it in, or alarming others as applied in each case.

As the afternoon progressed, the breeze quieted, and trees stopped rustling in the distance. As soon as everyone stopped talking, Priori noticed a soft clicking that accompanied the phenomenon. Again, only they could hear it. Each 'pop' was so complex and interesting, they didn't want to miss one. They encouraged hush, but it was hard to enforce. Priori started moving off in their own groups to listen.

Twilight came as usual, and the dome remained visible. With the setting sun, Priori could observe flashes of light too, tinted by the color patterns above.

Nighttime was met by a packed gathering on the beach where Priori remained to watch the most spectacular light show of their long lifetimes thus far. Silence was attempted. Torch-free darkness was enforced. It was easy to know which were Priori. They were still, faces turned upward and smiling, hands cupping their ears. When a spectacular blaze and pop erupted, they turned to each other to share their reactions and remark on the distinctive beauty of each.

The People would have appreciated torches, but relied on waning moonlight, which happily had risen in time for the all-night festivity. They shuffled through the dark crowds, many so close to shore, waves washed over their feet. They would have loved music, but they did without. Their kept their voices as lowered as much as the sound of surf would allow and still be heard. They eavesdropped intently on others and stopping to chime in, up and down the beach. The same conversations were flowing over and over. A few indicated, to those who had run out, where snacks of dried fish and fruit were to be had. But good luck trying to reach them in the hordes and in the dark. The People shared what they had between them. The crowds didn't thin. There was no way they were going to be able to sleep. It was too exciting to watch the Priori reactions and imagine. In Cetapiens tradition, they threw a party.

The Admiral and Alvar had stayed together all day. But as the cool of the evening set in, Alvar walked back to the village alone to where he had left his cloak and had returned wearing it. He found the Admiral and joined his group as they rehashed the events of the day. Instead of adjusting to allow him to join, the elder took Alvar away from the masses, toward the surf. He politely waved off any who tried to follow. Alvar was wrapped in the cloak that Amaranth had made for herself. He stayed clear of the water's reach and pulled it up higher over his shoulders, clear of the waves. They walked together, slowly, along firm wet sand.

The Admiral admired Alvar's cloak. He recognized it. *She* had worn it only moments before…

"How is your sickness?" The Admiral asked.

"I'm not feeling it, I've felt great all day, same as you, remember?"

"No, Amaranth and Grandmother, the separation. How are you healing?"

"I'm not. I don't think I ever will." But that wasn't exactly true. The moment he had put the cloak around him, his lovesickness diminished. The feeling that Amaranth had her arms around him replaced it.

"Amaranth made those herself. I was with her when she and Grandmother selected and cut those leaves. She took great care to weave those into the cloth. Have you looked closely and admired her skill? No? Well, next time you are in full daylight, really examine how she grafted the stems at certain points and left others raw and weeping..."

The Admiral's voice trailed away. In his mind's eye he saw her, bending in close and working delicately. "Yes, she was a master weaver." After a pause, "It made her sad to do it, to cut those leaves off. She loved them so. But she loved you more. And now they can sing her song, so you'll always know..."

"*Singing* leaves...hmm...I don't have *anything* like that where I'm from."

"Nor do I."

Alvar waited for him to expand on that. Up until that moment he had assumed *Cetapiens* was the Admiral's home. Before Alvar could ask, the Admiral's accent changed, and he added comfortably, "Love is chemistry. Love's molecules, in her, in that cloak, in you. You were compatible and, so you could see her, talk to her, walk with her. You even received her transfusion." He nodded toward the cloak. "But not compatible enough to father her children."

Alvar was stunned. The Admiral had never spoken to him like that. Used a word like 'molecules'. Amaranth might have. His mother did, and his teachers too, back *home*.

So Alvar decided to test him. "These lights, the pops, they remind me of little of fireworks." There was no gunpowder or anything explosive in either of the three realms of Cetapiens, Orcasekai, Eaglesekai or even Templesekai.

The Admiral didn't bite. He just snapped out of his reverie, and looked blankly at Alvar through the dim moonlight.

"They remind *me* of Grandmother's eyes, when she sang of Orcas."

Alvar looked up and slowly around to see if could make out any similarity. Nope. But now that he had brought it up, there were reminders of Amaranth in that sky cover. The flashes began to feel like the she was the entire world of Cetapiens and she was watching him. Each accompanying pop, like the clicks that had come up behind him on the first night she touched him in the jungle. The lights played across the sky and Alvar pulled the cloak even tighter. It was a wonderful effect, her chemistry preserved in the botanical host, coursing through his veins, as he looked up at her, watching him.

"How about a huge retina stimulated by photons." Alvar looked down at the Admiral's face and grinned.

The Admiral was looking up at him, watching closely. "A *master* weaver. She really knew what she was doing. And you are obviously feeling better." He changed the subject. "You were with Grandmother just before she died. Maybe she spoke to you. To be in someone's confidence as they are making that journey, it's very personal. A great honor. I should not ask…"

"You want to know. Alright…" Alvar knew they were very close and was ready to tell him everything. "Only two things. She said she was sorry. And that Amaranth lov…." The word broke off and stuck in his throat.

The Admiral easily finished his next thought, "And then she asked for me."

Alvar nodded the affirmative. He swallowed the emotion and asked, "Did she tell you anything you want to tell *me*?"

"She asked me to accept you, as my own son."

Alvar hopped and gingerly lifted one leg as he came down on a sharp shell. He had avoided it. But the Admiral continued without distraction, "Grandmother knew in my heart I already had. But I agreed, again." The Admiral wanted Alvar's reaction and waited for it.

"I'm honored. Thank you. But I must warn you, I don't know if I can be a man's son."

The Admiral added slowly, "It was an unusual request. We are all family here. But you were not born among witnesses that we know and trust. It's true, you are not a child. But you should have a family. Do you prefer another matriarch in my place?"

The Admiral stood still. Alvar stopped too and faced him. The family bit was true. He was smarting from the loss of Grandmother and Amaranth and not sure if he'd continue to be happy there without them. Arva'Anati was out there in the sea, but he dared not interact with her closely every again. "No, I didn't mean that. Of course, I accept. May I still call you Admiral? It suits you perfectly."

They did not embrace, but the Admiral offered him a celebration.

"No, I think with all of this," Alvar waved his arms in a sweeping gesture up across the brilliant show that was the night sky and toward the dark flowing throngs of revelers along the beach, "I think I'm partied out for a while."

"As you like. Oh, and she mumbled that Amaranth would find you again."

Alvar perked up. "Amaranth said so too. *She* did? Did she mention *when*? How?"

The Admiral looked at him with deep sadness. "No, we changed the subject and then...."

A warm foaming surf washed over their feet and they resumed walking for several slow, silent steps when Alvar blurted out, "Sorry, but, how much do you know? I mean, what exactly *is* Amaranth?"

The Admiral frowned, shook his head very slowly side to side, only once and sighed out heavily, "Complex?". He took one final breath, turning back around, toward where they had started and concluded their conversation. "Hmm. I don't think Grandmother exactly knew either."

CHAPTER 38

Universe: Sponge (Cetapiens) and Orcasekai

En scratched on Kei's leg.

"You're restless. Need some loving?" Kei reached down, grasping him under the jaw with the hand closest and peeked under her visor into his eyes but directed her observation to Johnny. "En is not going to hang around much longer. I don't want him to take off into the multiverse without us."

The scene transitioned. It was obvious from differences in the sky 'before' and 'after' that cued Kei and Johnny that decades were being omitted.

"We can get what is being skipped later, though, right?"

"Shhh."

Many Cetapiens years had passed since then. The shift back to 'normal' healthy azure that had begun as soon as the new sky appeared was almost completed. After decades, it was obvious to those with perception, that within a few short evenings, a moonless night sky would provide the backdrop for the last flash/pop.

What would happen after the last single correction was anyone's guess and there was a lot of quality speculation, both on land and in the sea.

On land, the People and their Priori visitors did what they always did. They celebrated the day, each other, and everything else. If the last sky pop brought the end of all with it, what better way to go? Across Cetapiens, the People and Priori gathered in entertainment plazas and boats. They adapted their favorite, most lavish performances to show their preferences for the most entertaining hypotheses. The night sounds of music and laughter wafted one into another, everywhere as optimistic as any other time in their lives.

The Priori had been trapped in the Cetapiens bad puff so long that they began to think in linear fashion, to expect one thing to follow another. They were surprised when the last tiny clouds didn't disappear gradually, in turns. Instead they popped and flashed en masse in one startling finale.

After that last bouquet of flash, the Priori looked around and at each other. Nothing noticeable followed it. One in each gathering time traveled away, just to make sure they could. When that one returned at the split moment of their departure and announced that they were free, they trusted it was true.

To the People, their Priori friends were as happy as ever. The calibration of time between the Sponge universe and Orcasekai had cured the Priori blind spot and so an influx of time travelers, into and out of Cetapiens, resumed as if nothing had happened.

The crowds dispersed, many helping organize and store the props and such before they too went off on jungle paths, safely managing their many small torches, holding hands, breaking away in small groups as they came across suitable huts with enough room to comfortably spend the night.

In the sea, Avi had calculated when the last click of her strange sky would sound. She summoned the clans to a superpod. At its dawning day, all orca, constrained to Cetapiens territory after all those years, gathered together. "After the sun sets, tonight is the night."

Like the Priori on land, they celebrated each other, the clans, their beloved sea and sky. Everything.

In one magnificent superpod, Akenehi's clan and Soo's, swam the distance of the entire Cetapiens shoreline with Avi leading their aquatic parade.

Superpods were always favorably anticipated, but this one was special. Seasnàn and the most senior orcas feared that even if the last flash had no effect on either of the clans, it might cause the death of Arva'Anati, their increasingly frail, beloved matriarch.

Until then, they expected to hear much from Avi. It was an ancient orca custom, common to both clans, to memorize a summary of their grandmother's life, at its very end.

As the sky darkened, Avi let out her matriarchal ritual call, "I am Arva'Anati, of the Singer clan."

The chatter of whistles and clicks grew silent.

The history of orca-kind as it had been sung to her, by her own grandmother, memories of youth at Akenehi's side, her capture by Land Squid and her unbearably long isolation from her beloved family. The loss of her precious little ones. Her Gemini transformation. One awakening in the Vencello, and the other beginning a new life in the sea of Cetapiens. Her love for all of them.

And then came the history of Soo and her clan.

Superpod ritual recitals were always memorable. Avi's was truly magnificent. But not enough to keep even appreciative orca fully awake for so long a performance.

Her grand aria was cut short by a miscalculated celestial finale. Avi described the surprising last flourish of color and pops, as only she could perceive them, to her audience of half-sleeping orca. They took her whistles for it, and remained as quiet as she, expecting more. Nothing happened. They kept their half-awake brains alert to her. Still, she did not sink, dead. She did not cry out in pain. It had been a long night and so, after a volley of sleepy orca 'I sang you so's', the superpod disbanded. Small dream-sharing groups drifted off together in every direction.

In other shades of the multiverse, the resolution of the Cetapiens sky heralded that Orcasekai had been successfully revived. The celebrated finale was only the beginning of an ignition of her Mighty O-Osis. What was born out of that flash began to stabilize into its own distinct colors, voice, and so on. Amaranth and those like her had executed their tasks flawlessly. Of course, Akenehi's markers and acoustic triggers were a famous success in helping bring it all about. She designated its collective song as the first in her Orca Priori Matriarchal Wellness repertoire.

Akenehi had perfected multiverse travel and saved her first universe. Now that Cetapiens had healed, she easily homed in on and penetrated the healthy puff. She popped her bubble right amid her beloved family at next dawn as they were agreeing on which direction to first explore their glorious expanded territory.

There is no human language or Dog Priori translation within these perspectives that could aptly describe the beautiful sound of that orca family reunion.

Eventually, when she attempted to sing of her Orcasekai triumph, as an orca, and of how she came to be with them again, she could only make sense of it as a birth announcement.

It worked. The clans were delighted and shared her joy completely. "Daughters! How wonderful!"

En yipped and the rider complied with his request. The orca chatter went immediately silent. The retinal images froze to the underwater vista of Akenehi, flanked by her daughters, Arva'Anati and Seasnàn. They lolled in affectionate formation with Yu and his niece in their slipstream.

L-23's rider announced:

"Perspectives Complete."

Their helmets kept their shape as Kei and Johnny removed them. Neither one of them had Fadwah. Johnny slapped madly at his pockets while Kei kicked gingerly through the surrounding sand in search of her.

"ENNNNNNN!"

EPILOGUE

"Come. Good boy, En."

En startled at the strangely altered scent of an old friend.

One deep sniff and he was at ease. This *was* where he had left Fadwah, buried her here with many treasures. He had returned to chew on her for a while, at his leisure.

Uniformly throughout his den, olfactory markers suggested to the Dog Priori that Orcasekai was *everywhere*.

"Don't be afraid. You recognize *me*. Here, you understand me *very* well. What do you think?"

"What...how is this...Orcasekai." En's first-ever words, whistles and clicks came staccato, slurred and uneven. En sniffed at the myriad scent coming in patterns that synchronized with pulses of light.

"Yes, I *am* Orcasekai. Good boy, En. You always were a fast learner."

En smiled and moistened his nose with his tongue.

"You like this, don't you? I knew you would. Me too."

"How...Orcasekai...scent?"

"We are calibrating, when complete you will understand. We have all the time of this universe. Continue, En."

First were the chemical communication of the plants, then the cephalopods. In increments they were the easiest for En to translate to his finest sense, smell.

Then came the acoustics. With every olfactory phrase, elements of familiar sounds filled their universe. Human language was the simplest of the acoustics and easiest for him to understand. Then came dolphin, then orca, then the virtually impossible click communication of Brough.

En's head ached a bit as his Dog Priori neurons branched out to each other and established wonderful new connections. Orcasekai waited for his cue to indicate that he was comfortable and ready to continue.

"What is Orcasekai?"

"Your friend, a molecule, an individual, a colony, a universe, progeny of the Vencello…"

En sniffed, watched and listened, reducing all to concepts of scent, which was his natural style of thinking. As a Dog Priori he received an excellent whiff of everything up to the progeny of…*what*? That last was concept, which offered little in the way of olfactory data. "Best friend, Orcasekai, clarify scent."

"Aw. Of course, dear En. Specify."

"What is 'The Vencello'?"

REFERENCES

Kroto, H. W.; Heath, J. R.; O'Brien, S. C.; Curl, R. F.; Smalley, R. E. (14 November 1985). "C60: Buckminsterfullerene". Nature. 318 (6042): 162–163.

Ruth Shady Solis, Jonathan Haas, Winifred Creamer. Dating Caral, a Preceramic Site in the Supe Valley on the Central Coast of Peru, Science 27 April 2001: Vol. 292. no. 5517, pp. 723-726.Image of light as both particle and wave

Sphere Eversion - In differential topology, sphere eversion is the process of turning a sphere inside out in a three-dimensional space. ... Remarkably, it is possible to smoothly and continuously turn a sphere inside out in this way (with possible self-intersections) without cutting or tearing it or creating any crease. (source: Wikipedia 11/16/17)

GLOSSARY OF FICTIONAL TERMS

Acoustic C-60 Sphere Eversion – The method Akenehi discovered and utilized as Priori to enter and exit C-60 molecule universes. She smoothly and continuously turned any Orca Priori acoustically manipulatable sphere (e.g. Carbon 60) inside out in this way without destroying the molecule/universe.

Acrituchi – An ancient multiverse survivor. Not a species as much as it was a vast multiverse sentient energy network that thrived through mutualism within universes on and compatible worlds of each. Through sheer size and multiverse adaptability, it was virtually immortal. It was analogous to a neural network of the multiverse. The Acrituchi was not the only one of its kind. It found its most efficient relationship with organic beings through direct sharing of its essence through its consumption at some point in the food chain. The Acrituchi and the energy with which it traveled were inseparable.

Curl –The finest discernable sentient pure energy beings at the deepest level of O-O. They exist as symbionts of the Acrituchi, are carried through universes along with it. Indications that Curl are present in a host are the chromatophoric responses and exhibitions of flashing lights and patterns, such those found in neural activity. Curl are especially apparent in virtually all Cephalopod Priori. The Curl consist of many types across too many universes to list, but so self-similar to each other, all enigmatic and strictly non-corporeal in their purest state, to be efficiently considered as one. For those Priori who never mastered human tongue twisters, multiverse chemistry, or color communication, they were known as the enigmatic Chromatophore Response Lovers or Curl, for short.

NOTE: The Sponge home world was one such system infested with life forms that survived by eating one another. Therefore, all of those were hosts to Curl. Plants, such as those in the Cetapiens jungle, fed directly off light in which the Curl existed. The Cetapiens jungle was infused with Acrituchi and therefore its Curl symbionts. On the planet of origin Curl entered a corporal form when a photon, which carried the Acrituchi, was captured by plant stoma.

G – A short cut designation at the end of a name that could be used to remind one that they had undergone Gemini (aka Metavoli-2) duplication. For example, Johnny-G

Gemini – A product of Metavoli-2. Rather than result in an original and a copy, the Metavoli reproduced sources through O-O. Therefore, *quantum* duplication occurred, and each product was as an original and immediately dispersed to a viable universe. A Gemini was one of two quantum O-O products identical in virtually every detail down to memory, personality, genetics and scars.

Marker – Markers are naturally used by universase and multiversase entities to enable alternate efficient pathways for Priori travelers. Often a prior used distinctive characteristic of anything that flags a known coordinate of multiverse, time, space, etc. Markers serve as an attractant and have various levels of difficulty in identification and use. A marker can be established through trial and error to a new target, but it involves substantial risk to the traveler.

Metavoli – An evolved sentient progeny of a universase that colonized in a self-similar manner to slime molds. As such, they alternated existing between phases of a mass of individuals that when desired or triggered joined together into a single complex being. The Metavoli manifested several types depending on how many copies of an original it could produce at once. A -2 indicated two, a -4 indicated four and so on. A Metavoli-2 was a progeny of the Vencello and began its existence within that universe. From its inception it had developed multiverse abilities that included but were not limited to reading, duplicating, and transferring organic substance and energy between universes through O-O. The Metavoli delivered their viable-adapted copies instantaneously into suitable universes. Through the Vencello's Metavoli-2, multiverse and time 'travel' for humans and cetaceans became possible.

Mighty O-Osis – A next generation phase in Metavoli reproduction, distinct from cellular mitosis and meiosis of its ancestral organisms.

Multiversase – Self-similar to universase but virtually unlimited and therefore can appear and effect anything, anywhere or any time, in as much of the multiverse, as desired. Rather than collect experiences in a single or small range of universe as in the case of a universase, a multiversase works across all universes to enable multiverse level events. Multiversase are closely associated with the Acrituchi.

O-O – The absolute Omni-dimensional-spatial-temporal essence of the multiverse; shared by all universes.

O-U-O – Unique particle-like universe stabilized and existing within a folded protective membrane of the multiverse O-O, a self-similar progeny of the Vencello Universe.

O-U-O song – The required unique harmonics determined individually for each Priori that resulted in enveloping themselves inside a protective resonating O-O membrane which prevented them from dissipating into the multiverse.

Priori – A designation of the broad range of self-similar types of sentient universes. They all were products of species who survived merge and stabilization from their original universe into their own realms. The Vencello Universe was a simple example of one.

Puff – An automatic, self-organizing multiverse response to temporal paradox or any other threat at Priori and universe level. Acting as a multiverse-sentient quantum computer, it sets an effected area boundary and enables O-O solutions to work within. It designates a safe zone where Priori and other time traveling beings can come and go without fear of paradox interference.

Bad Puff – A rare event where a puff stabilizes but traps Priori within the boundary. It does not diffuse, and the Priori cannot time travel within or escape from it.

Seed of Acrituchi – The Acrituchi's long cold and inactive universe of origin.

Sponge Universe (or Sponge for short) – The Vencello's universe of origin.

Universase – A multiverse enzyme-like being, hence the –ase ending. Rather than involving a molecular substrate, they were intentional weavers of *coordinates* in a self-similar mode resembling chemical catalysis but on specific *experiences* across the multiverse. Attracting markers were set and utilized, eventually weaving them together and therein increased from nil to near certainty the likelihood of Priori and universe survival.

Vencello Universe – An offshoot from the Sponge Universe. A product of a successful harmonic driven viable merge of multiple species (mainly sperm whale, orca and human) encapsulated in a carbon-60 molecule.

www.ingramcontent.com/pod-product-compliance
Lightning Source LLC
Chambersburg PA
CBHW070756280626
47162CB00016B/1068